SANGRE COVE

GINA CASTILLO

D1620470

CALUMET EDITIONS
Minneapolis

**CALUMET
EDITIONS**

Minneapolis

Second Edition December 2022

This is a work of fiction. All of the characters, names, incidents, organizations, and dialogue are either the products of the author's imagination or are used fictitiously.

10 9 8 7 6 5 4 3 2

ISBN: 978-1-959770-55-8

Cover and book design by Gary Lindberg

SANGRE COVE

GINA CASTILLO

To my husband and seven wonderful boys—
you are my muses.

CHAPTER 1

The aroma of old paper and lemon oil from freshly polished wood filled me with a comfortable warmth. When I was younger my love for fantastical stories brought me here to our small-town library, but today, it's a need. Not just checking off books on my college prep required reading list. Today, a search for something personal—or an explanation. The rich Texas history stored in this one-hundred-year-old building just might fill in the blanks that my father left out about my abilities and why others desire them.

My pen spun like a propeller under my waggling fingers, because I willed it to. I'd been so excited back in second grade when I first learned about my little trick. I ran home to show Dad. He wasn't fazed, save the slightest glimmer of pride just behind his eyes, but he told me it had to be *our little secret*. And that was the day the real overprotection started, not the regular freaky parent stuff. No, this was insanity at *DEFCON 5*. I barely talked him out of homeschooling us, my older sister Theresa and I, instead he opted for private school, which is where we went up until May, when my dad was murdered. My heritage lessons stopped, and the horrid taste of reality burned my tongue—in the form of public school.

While I studied the old dusty pages of *Sangre: Blood of the Tonkawa*, my left hand controlled the propeller trick. As for my right, it drummed a tribal beat in perfect time to the heavy beat of thunder. I peeked through the gap between my long brown curls to scan the room.

As the second beat roared along with our *unseasonable* weather change, my scan revealed a perfect smile flanked by the cutest dimples, not to mention the hottest tanned body. He rocked the line between boy-band cute and hot sweaty bodybuilder. And—he was watching me.

Joaquin, the chiseled Romanesque God, looking at me would be a distraction, and I have goals. Last time I checked, BOYFRIEND 101 wasn't one of the requirements for veterinarian school.

Crap! My hand dropped the pen. The drumming stopped, just in time for the light show to dance across the high windows above the library shelves. And the super-high industrial lighting buzzed and dimmed out for a few seconds.

Suddenly, I jumped at the hand that clutched my shoulder—an extremely strong and overly warm one. I knew him before I turned.

"Hey, Maria," he said.

"Teo," I grumped. Then through my teeth, I said, "What do you want?"

"I'm here to save you."

"Save me?"

"Yeah, save you," he flipped my book to check out the cover. "You know, from turning into one of those crystal-packing Goth girls like Scary Sally over there."

I looked toward where he motioned. A girl with black hair that fell past her waist and clothes the same color read a book similar to mine. She had elegance, not freak out your parents Goth. No, she had designer jeans, a black tank and this unique leather vest that fell way longer in the front than the back. And her boots were super cool, knee-high with a wedged heel. In this town, smack dab in the Bible belt, she was the spawn of Satan.

Teo was my friend Lexi's cousin's best friend and the resident "it" guy on campus. But right now, he was the bane of my book-topia. And he gave me the creeps, nothing I could characterize, merely a telepathic tug. Even the simplest request, I unconsciously followed like a Stepford Wife.

My nose curled as if a sulfur bomb exploded. The guy was hot, like *muy caliente* hot. With his black hair, olive complexion, chiseled features and muscles. But still, I couldn't believe I had to waste one of my best girly hair flips on him. And now, I was going to have to put on my own dazzling smile and continue to play nice. Keeping up with the social hierarchy of high school was exhausting. But I'd have to say, for a novice, I was pretty good at it.

As I talked, my eyes searched for Joaquin—the dimpled guy from earlier, aka BOYFRIEND 101. As my eyes found him, he smiled and gave a little chuckle—at me, not with me, I'm sure. And he walked out of the library. My eyes lost a bit of their sparkle, but Teo didn't miss a beat. He jabbered on about football as only a Texan could. Tired of the load of bull he was shoveling, I decided to cut it short.

"OK, Teo. Cut the crap. What do you want? This isn't exactly your scene," I said.

He was definitely style over substance. I think the only book I ever saw in his hand was the football play book, and let's face it—not a real book. I would save that snide little piece of information for the next time I saw it rolled up in his hands, stuffed into his back pocket, or if he pissed me off.

Before he could answer, Lexi bounced up with her cousin Jim in tow. "Hey, girly. Do you want to go to our land with the guys?"

"Yeah. We dropped the paddle boats in the lake, and we need a couple of girls to help us with the leg work," Jim added.

"Seriously, guys. Sounds fun, but I've got some work to do here. Maybe some other time."

Lexi's lip came out, and I knew it was over, but she knew I wouldn't give in with that act alone. In my mind, I was fighting the good fight, but on the outside, I just shook my head.

"Come on, Maria," Teo added. "Don't make me beg, 'cause I will. I'll embarrass you right here in your sanctuary. Nobody knows me here. Now you, on the other hand, you have your own nameplate. I know these things," Teo had me.

"I've got a report to finish."

"This book doesn't look like something I studied junior year. So, why bother?"

"Extra credit. Raising my GPA. Prep for college."

"My GPA is fine without extra credit. Unless you count my perfect spiral as extra credit."

"You know, Mr. Football, cut it out, or I'll embarrass you one Friday night," I scowled.

"Not really possible," he shrugged at me.

Teo was such a bonehead. Wrap that around the fact that he was the quarterback of a winning team in a small Texas town. They lived for that shit down here in the south. Any infraction, short of murder, wouldn't even be questioned—it'd be revered.

With an overexaggerated sigh and a slam of my library book, which drew a dirty look from the librarian, I stood. Confidence gave me height, but genetics had me a little over five feet tall. On my way to return my book, I gave Teo a nudge with my shoulder. He grabbed it to feign an injury like my hundred pounds could have done any kind of damage. Jim and Lexi laughed. My head snapped around with a spiteful look.

Lexi and I may not have been friends for long, but she had this charismatic way of talking me into crap. Like I was some easygoing follower, which was the farthest thing from the truth. That was up until my junior year—you know, this August—when I started public school and met Lexi. My kryptonite.

When I banged the book into place, thunder roared, and I smiled. Electricity ran through my fingertips, and I ran my thumb across the ends of each finger, soothing the sensation. It felt good—like power.

* * *

The closer I got to the water, the slower my steps became. My heartbeat quickened. I loved the water, either sitting on a blanket beside it or with my feet in the shallow end of a pool. But deep murky lake water with fish and whatever else swam around in these back wood country waters gave me goose-bumps. Despite all my athletic activities, I never learned to swim. Not ready to reveal this factoid to my new friends, I decided to join them. Or it would be impossible to sit at our lunch table if some of the gang found out. They'd have commentary for weeks.

We strode along a short wooden dock where two paddle boats floated, tied to a cleat. When Teo took my hand to help me into the boat, I squeezed it tight. He stepped in and leaned forward to untie the boat. The rock of the boat made me grab for a handhold.

My feet slipped into the straps of the pedals. We backed away from the dock, and Teo shifted a lever. With a chug, we moved forward, across the lake. Jim and Lexi paddled over to us, and Jim called us *losers* and *slowpokes*. A couple of ducks swam around the lake, but they flew to the opposite end whenever Jim or Teo came close. I envied them. Why did I let Lexi talk me into this?

The view of lush trees and green open spaces sprinkled with wildflowers far away led to a secret place my father took me to "practice." We'd walk out into the field, and I'd raise my hands toward the sun calling upon Mother Earth. The openness made my chest lighten and my breath come naturally.

The lake is centered between the tree line and Jim's house. It made an irregular oval shape and took up about half an acre of land—maybe more. The sun shone, and the birds fluttered and sang. I pressed the back of my hand softly against my nose to relieve the burning sensation from the bright sun. The smell of the water, flowers and fresh-cut grass made this moment near perfect. Lexi's laugh bounced off the trees and surrounded me. When Teo relaxed, he was more like a boy I wouldn't mind hanging out with, but there was still something about him. He asked the usual questions—what I liked and where I came from.

"How do you like *real* school, Maria?" he asked.

"Real school? I've already been invited to take some summer classes at The University of Texas as a junior. How's that for *real* school?" I said.

"OK, I'll give you that," Teo held up his hands, admitting defeat. "Well, one thing's for sure."

"What's that?"

"Catholic prep school has the right idea about those uniforms," Teo flashed that creeptastic smile that made my skin want to slough off, like the molting epidermis of a snake. Lexi owed me big time for this.

Lexi decided to make things interesting. "Y'all want to race?"

My competitiveness bubbled up, and I smiled. A heavy aura of darkness filled the space between us. A jagged row of tall trees that lined the far shore blurred with clipped visions of wavy darkness. My legs peddled faster as we raced to the far bank. Our boat pulled past theirs, enough for Jim to bump the rear corner. The boat wobbled. My fists clutched the side handlebars with such force my knuckles changed from white to purple. Then he bumped us again with more force. We wobbled from side to side. Panic struck me, and as Teo tried to compensate, we flipped.

My body sunk low under the water. I fought to pull myself to the surface. Even though the water was warm from the sun, it still took away my breath. As I grabbed for the boat, my hands met the bottom, slick with pond slime, and found no place to grip. They slid off. Again, I tried to heave myself up onto the bottom, but I slipped off. This time, I went deep underwater. I flailed. It sort of worked. I climbed back up to the surface, and as my head emerged under the boat, something banged my forehead, metal and unforgiving.

The shock of pain stilled my body. I sank deeper and deeper. My mind told me to move my arms and legs, but my body ignored the command. Enveloped in darkness, white stars dotted my vision. It occurred to me—I might drown. Death would come way too soon. This would send me to join my dad, but my mother—this would shatter her.

A jerk of my collar pulled me upward. The water around me grew brighter, and then the sun blinded me as the air touched my face. My mouth gaped wide open as I tried to fill my lungs with air, but with every breath, a cough shoved the oxygen back out. My vision flashed back, blotchy and broken. My rescuer swam toward the bank, in smooth, sinuous strokes.

My body ached, too weak to move. It felt lifeless and limp as it moved through the air. Then the rocky ground poked my back and shoulders. Someone's scream helped me break through the darkness. I squinted as Lexi's form grew small in the distance. Again, my vision melted away, and the sky split apart and came back together. A growl rumbled from near the water, and Jim moved out of the water toward the bank. The muck and dark water followed him and morphed into something alive—something animal-like swam around his torso. He dipped underwater again. Out of focus, too dizzy and weak to watch, I passed out.

CHAPTER 2

"Maria! Maria! Are you OK?"

My eyes opened to Teo on one knee beside me. Then my eyes rolled out of focus. My head fell to the side. I watched Jim emerge from the water and run toward me. He kicked a hairy-looking tree limb out of the way. His body appeared normal, except for a crimson streak on one shoulder and a couple of small tears in his T-shirt.

Then screams from Lexi turned me away. She ran back to me with two women and a man at her side. The man went straight for Jim and started to yell things I couldn't understand. The ladies came over to me. They both gripped towels and started to check me over with a seasoned mother's flair. They made sure I could move all my limbs and didn't have any cuts or bruises.

Lexi's face hovered inches from mine. She shook as mascara ran down her perfectly made face. I pulled myself up on my elbows and gazed at the water. "Where's the animal?"

"What animal?" Lexi's eyes searched the tree line.

"The one that bit Jim," I pointed.

I looked over at Jim and his dad. They pulled the boats out of the water. Jim hadn't been hurt, far less bitten. He did have a scrape on his shoulder, but he said he caught his shoulder on the tree limb and scratched himself. My fingers shook as I struggled to remove the hairs stuck to my face. I clasped my hand on my forehead.

"You must have hit your head hard," Jim said with a laugh.

I rubbed the top of my head. The small, raised bump sent knives across my scalp. I crossed my arms and sucked in several quick breaths to catch the air my body required. Lexi draped a towel around my arms and rubbed it up and down against my skin.

Teo stood up and pulled me to my feet. He supported me with his arm around my shoulders. For the first time, my skin didn't try to creep away from his contact. A screech in the distance fractured the silence. My eyes went to the sky, and my head moved back and forth in search of the sound. Everyone stopped. Lexi asked what was wrong. I told her, "An eagle flew over." They looked up and then back at me like I had a third eye. Jim laughed.

When I steadied myself enough to move, we started toward the front porch of a huge, white farmhouse. They positioned a set of wicker furniture on either side of the door. A woman Lexi called Aunt Tammy checked the bump on my head. Teo stayed back by the porch steps and leaned against a post. Lexi wilted in a chair and clutched her hands in her lap. Her leg bounced, and guilt washed over her face.

A few short minutes later, the other woman came back with a handful of dry clothes. Lexi called the first woman Aunt Tammy, so this must be her mother. From previous conversations, I knew Lexi lived on Jim's family's property. The ladies helped me inside to change, and Teo left to find Jim and his father.

I closed the bathroom door and changed, still numb, almost as numb as the day my Dad was murdered. Maybe when you're close to death, that's what happens.

Lexi apologized so many times on the way to my house, it literally made my head hurt. At my front door, I turned and waved good-bye.

I didn't head to the living room, not with my hair all wet and different clothes on. A trace of my earlier panic lingered, too, and I didn't want Mom to read my face and ask questions. So, I blew her off, in no mood for a Spanish Inquisition. I clutched my wet clothes close to my chest and went upstairs to jump in the shower. I scrubbed all the muddy lake water off my skin and out of my hair—trying to scrub the incident away.

As the water flowed over my face and down my back, my mind replayed the events of my father's death. Then, I was startled by a knock.

"What kept you?" Mom yelled from behind the door. Her speech slurred.

"I told you. I went out with a friend." I said, my voice heavy with agitation.

"Well, I got the job, and I'll start work in the morning."

"That's good, right?" I asked.

"Yes, of course. I just wanted to tell you and you didn't come home."

"Are you serious? I need my bed." This disappointment in her voice was comical. Mom hadn't been hands-on since my father's murder—unless you consider her "hands on" a wine bottle being hands on. She definitely didn't want to 'talk.'

As the water flowed over my face and down my back, my mind replayed the events of my father's death.

The words from this point on rambled together. I remembered something that mimicked those of the parents from the Charlie Brown movies, jumbled honking sounds that didn't make any sense. Now, in my mind, the day starts to fade, and it's a little fuzzy. They said, "We are sorry for your loss." Loss. The finality of the word caught my breath. "We have everyone on this case, and we are going to find this man and bring him to justice."

Who? Why did I need justice? I pushed out one word. "What?"

"Your father has been shot," he said.

My knees buckled, and the world started to spin.

Everything from that moment forward swirled like an out of control tornado. It fades from a sunny bright day to a blurred vision with fuzzy edges, and then it's foggy. My body recoiled with the tightness of a hangman's noose. The descent of each step out of the school jolted through my body, the car seat stiff against my back, the click from the seat belt and the vibration of the engine were enhanced. The school's main driveway and its backlit announcement board all smeared together into a colorful blob. My head fell back against the headrest. I tried to stop the world around me from spinning out of control, but nausea swept over me. My fingers fumbled at the switch to open the window and summoned a cool Texas breeze present at the end of May.

Even when I closed my eyes, it didn't prove as helpful as I hoped. The car stopped, the door opened, and a hand helped me out. I caught a glimpse of tan skin, dark hair, and a scent of cologne, almost an antidote to the nausea.

Next, I arrived close to my mother on the living room couch. I shivered. Mom clutched a tissue. Tears welled up in my eyes. Words rambled together. My eyes wouldn't stay focused on any one spot, and my heart pounded.

Two men stood there in military stance. My mind refused to recall his name or the name of the younger guy with him. I remembered some sort of introduction at the school, but I couldn't pull their names. Mom reached over to squeeze my hand.

She stood up and made her way to the door. I followed, mechanically, like someone programmed the steps in my brain. We got into the car, the man with the suit drove, the smell of leather and gun oil surrounded me. I looked out the window as we passed the suburban houses, which eventually gave way to the bigger buildings of town. We turned down the curved entrance toward the most massive of the structures. A young man opened our door. My mom took my hand and led me inside like a five-year-old. Isopropyl alcohol filled the air, the coldness stinging my face. People in smocks and scrubs ran by with trays full of tubes and needles.

Mom stopped for a moment at the front desk, then turned and pulled me along with her. We waited in front of six silver doors. I gazed into the broken and distorted reflection of myself. One of the policemen leaned forward and pushed the button on the wall. The double doors opened with a thud, and we stepped inside. With a lurch, we began to ascend, then with a second bump, we stopped. A loud clank and the doors opened to a white, sterile hallway where the fluorescent lights buzzed. At the circular nurse's station, one woman in pink scrubs stood and took us to a curtained hospital room.

The next sight bared the unimaginable: tubes, electrodes, machines and beeps, all this covered up the awful silence at their center. My dad lay still, eyes closed and no smile. He always smiled. His face looked like a wax figure. I ran to his side and held firm onto his hand.

With a face full of salty wetness, I begged God for a miracle. Recalling some of our lessons on healing, I began to chant—only loud enough for me and him to hear. His hand tightened around my hand in return.

The suited man told us he sent someone to pick up my sister from college in Austin. He handed my mother his business card and said to call for anything, such as a ride or information. I didn't need any of those things; I needed my dad to wake up.

We waited, as each tick of the clock hammered at my chest, as the seconds morphed into hours before Theresa arrived.

She ran into the waiting room and hugged Mom, but I don't remember anything before that. She staggered to my father's bedside. She kissed his cheek and took his hand. Tears spilled from her chin. Father Chris from our church arrived and gave my dad his last rites. My eyes shifted back and forth between my mother and father—someone needed to put a stop to this. We needed a nurse.

Nurses and doctors swarmed the room. Relief washed over me until they started to remove the tubes. They unhooked electrodes and pushed buttons on machines, I moved forward, but Mom stopped me.

I screamed, "No! He squeezed my hand!" She held me tighter. They stressed the impossibility of movement. I needed to try the chant one more time.

"Mom, you have to tell them I wouldn't lie. He squeezed my hand," I shrieked.

The nurses continued to pull things loose. Thud, thud, thud, whoosh… The machines were silent. I crumbled to the floor; cold, hard and the smell of bleach stung my nose. I watched as my father's chest sunk its last few times, before it didn't rise again. His eyes were shut, and it gave the illusion of a peaceful sleep. Then I crumpled with my face on the floor, making a scene, as nurses and doctors stepped around me and headed out of the room.

Later, I realized we waited for Theresa and Father Chris before taking him off life support. It was final.

How do you live without your dad?

With the tears down the drain and the few that lingered on my face absorbed into the towel, I dressed for bed. Then I went into my room and curled up tight in my bed. The calmness helped me remember my moment in the library with Joaquin. He sat in front of me in study hall and politely introduced himself on my first day, pronouncing his name with an ever-so-slight Spanish accent. But when the bell rang, it was all business, unlike the throng of cackling football players in the back of the room. So, when he made his way across the commons area of our lunchroom, said *hello* and gently slide his fingertips across the small of my back, I caught my breath. I could only nod my head because the words wouldn't come. Then today at the library, he had caught me doing my little propeller trick. Somehow it didn't worry me. It made me smile—a small, but sweet moment of my week.

And then there was Teo's introduction. Without a strand of subtlety, he threw his arm around my neck, talking to everyone around me like we were together or something. I guess, in his overconfident jockish mind, he knew I had been *filled in* about him because he was big news and all. I used my finger and thumb to remove his hand like it was some filthy bug and simply asked, "And you are?" Several people in our group snickered, and I saw Lexi capture her own laugh by covering her mouth with her hand and turning away. It wasn't easy to keep a straight face, but I managed.

Staying true to form, he clutched his chest and over-exaggerated his surprise that no one had told me about him in an entire school day. My snarled lips and flared nostrils didn't deter him from his over the top introduction. You know, he was the big-wig football player, senior, hunk, by his own actual words, and best buddy to all cool guys or more likely *wannabe cool guys*. His wide-open trap from my reaction, or rather lack of reaction, makes me smile—not a Joaquin kind of smile, but a smile.

I turned over on my side. As I closed my eyes, the suffocating feeling of water squeezed around me. Sharp animal claws raked over my shirt. My fear of drowning returned full force. Sleep evaded me.

Quiet settled over the house. Even though the dark reminded me too much of a dank lake, I shut my light off. In the dark, silence surrounded me like a cold, wet blanket. Since Dad's death, a shroud seemed to cover the house and all its inhabitants in sadness. I stared, unseeing, into the darkness, missing the way my life used to be—the not knowing chipped at my stone veneer. Questions filled my mind late at night.

This is the worst part, the silence.

CHAPTER 3

Today, Mom rushed around like a bee after nectar as she dressed for her first day of work. She would be helping teach a Kindergarten class.

We made our way out the door together; I waved and backed out of the driveway. She pulled out right behind me, and we were off—to another day of pretending that we were normal, and everything was fine.

* * *

"Hello," a voice said from behind me—Joaquin. He was beautiful, in a very masculine way. With his chiseled dark features and bulging muscles, past what was common among high school boys. I couldn't help but smile as he quickened his steps to open the door for a girl that wouldn't even look at him. She just nodded and hid behind her long mousy hair.

My jaw worked without sound for a moment until I blurted out, "Hey, how are you?" I tried to calm my jitters, but my voice sounded distorted and cracked. He smiled and kept pace through the cafeteria with his food in hand.

"I'm good. Did you find a good book?" He asked.

I shook my head. His brothers called him over to them. He said, "Gotta go," as he waved and walked away from me. My body trembled. A rush of blood tingled through me. This sensation never happened to me before; well, not before the first time he spoke to me in class.

No use in standing around like a statue, I scanned the cafeteria for my group of friends. "Maria, over here," called Becky. She carried a tray of food. I'd brought my lunch and followed her back to the table.

Lexi laughed out loud. "You want to make Teo jealous?"

"Huh?" I said.

"Your heroic rescuer," Cindy said in a sarcastic tone. "Who cares about Joaquin, the muscle-bound freak? Especially when Teo is after you."

Lexi reddened. News of what happened at the lake got around fast.

Teo rocked his creepy, *I'm awesome*, grin. His eyes were full of a steely confidence that he would get exactly what he desired. And if a chill didn't dance up and down my spine every time he came near me, I would probably fall in line with all the girls who followed him like he was the leader of some cult. Basically, he is hot.

Cindy radiated beauty with all the stereotypical mean girl crap that went along with being beautiful. But she didn't exude confidence. She was worried someone would knock her off the top rung of the high school social ladder. For some reason, she loved to tick me off. It took all my restraint not to knock her off that first rung.

Xavier, the guy Lexi used every trick stashed in her pocketbook to show her interest, asked, "Did you guys hear the news?"

Everyone stopped and looked at him. He explained that there'd been another animal attack last night. There were reports of a wolf or maybe a small bear.

"For real? A bear?" I asked.

"Oh yeah, last year six kids went out camping near the county line. It ended in a bloody mess. The kids were torn apart, identified by dental records."

I gasped and clasped my hand over my mouth, "Seriously?"

Xavier's lips parted in a huge grin and then a guffaw. "No! How gullible are you? We don't have bears around here. C'mon. But there was some kind of animal attack."

We finished our lunch and crowded out into the hallway, heading for our classes. A tingle of excitement rushed in my stomach. Not that creepy strange tingle I got when Teo came around, but a sweet, excited tingle of electricity. When I looked up, Joaquin stood outside the cafeteria doorway. He waited for me. I bounced over to him.

"Hey, how are you?" I said.

He laughed. "Do you mind if I walk with you to the next class?"

I took a deep breath. "OK. No, I don't mind!"

Way to be discreet, I said to myself. I couldn't even spit out a coherent sentence. My palms began to sweat a little. I rubbed them together.

We stepped out into the hall, and everything around us fell away. We were all that remained. My eyes set on him, and nothing around could draw my attention. Everything about him screamed meticulous, even the respectful way he fell in beside me as we traveled through the halls. He carried himself with a grace—almost a humility—unlike Jim and Teo's preening football star friends.

"Tell me something about you," he said.

"What would you like to hear?" I asked.

"Anything? It's odd. You're different than your friends." He said it in a calm and serious voice. Except for occasionally playing around with his brothers, he was slow to speak and sauntered like he owned the hallway.

"Well, I'm new—sort of. I'm from Cove, but I went to private school. I live with my mom. Nothing special."

"I doubt that," he tapped my notebook with his pen and winked.

"Oh," I said, surprised. "Here we go. Study hall." I thumbed the room behind me.

"So, are you going to give me any answers?"

"I've got tons of answers. Do you have the right questions?"

He laughed.

"I can give you some of my answers after school. If you're lucky, they'll match your questions."

"Sounds like a plan. It'll give me time to solidify my questions."

I hugged my books against my chest and tapped my pen against my books. Then I stopped, knowing he had caught my little pen trick. My face flushed feverishly, and I couldn't have been more overwhelmed if I'd run a marathon. The heat made its way to my cheeks. I'd always been controlled, sarcastic and light. Now, my words failed me. All these new emotions bubbled to the surface, giving me a fun rush. I bounced once and almost skipped into my classroom. He followed.

I started my science homework. Most people sneered at the mention of anatomy class, but I loved to learn about the human body. Thanks to Dad's guidance, I already put a lot of work into my future, an expectation at my previous school, too. If you learn to make grown-up decisions early, those decisions help you to map out your future. I plan to attend The University of Texas. Getting straight A's. Getting into top veterinarian schools. Only I had one problem, the human body I wanted to study was sitting in front of me.

I'd planned on my dad being there for all of it, too. He still had more to teach me.

I could control my grades, though. School was my passion. But now this guy could be a wrecking ball to the carefully built house of cards.

To destroy is always the first step in any creation.

The quote by E. E. Cummings was scrawled across the cover of my spiral notebook. Something deep inside possessed me as I traced this particular quote. The words haunted me—what would the destruction of my family create?

Toward the end of class, Becky, probably my second closest friend, leaned up and whispered in my ear. "For what it's worth, Joaquin's too hot. You shouldn't pay a lick of attention to Cindy. Micael and Enrique got their girlfriends, and now it looks like Joaquin is interested in you. She's super jealous, as usual."

Cindy, a girl in our group, determined to be the "bestest prom queen ever." She threw her punches and danced back to the ropes, but her solid blow being the day she announced the details of my father's murder to the cafeteria. Pure evil, this girl. But a solid part of the clique.

After class, Joaquin waved goodbye, and Becky and I talked and laughed the rest of the way to my locker. I'd always been a person who talked to everyone, no matter the social group. But I felt more like a girl these days than I ever had. I wore dresses every day to class for the last ten years, but here, in jeans and boots, I considered myself more feminine than any other time in my life.

After school, I hurried out front to the covered sidewalk, and an irritating pinch gripped me with a lurch deep inside. Lexi at my side, and sure enough, Jim and Teo watched her leave the school. After yesterday's debacle at the lake, I hoped they wouldn't want anything more to do with me.

Lexi and I didn't talk long out front before we took off toward my car.

"What's going on with you and Joaquin?"

"What do you mean?"

"Cut the crap, Maria. Your eyes do this funny sparkle thing every time you look at him. I thought that was just some BS they fed you in chick flicks."

"Stop it. He's hot. We talk. End of."

"I call bullshit. And speaking of…"

As we stepped into the road and headed toward my Jeep, I caught a clear sight of my new crush. A big black Ford SUV with dark, tinted windows parked about three spaces from me. Joaquin and his four brothers stood beside the vehicle, this time with two girls. One with silky straight black hair, which hung to her waist, and a tanned olive complexion. The other girl stood taller with long black hair, and each spiral curl was uniform to the next, almost like a girl from *Seventeen* magazine. The sting of jealousy ran from head to toe, but he wasn't my boyfriend. I held no claim over him. No reason, nor right, to be jealous.

Lexi leaned into me, "Those are Micael's and Enrique's girlfriends. They are super beautiful, but no worries—Joaquin's not taken."

I nudged her with my shoulder, "Cut it out. I wasn't thinking about that."

"The heck you weren't. You got that crazy look in your eyes, and I didn't want you going all Black Widow on those poor girls."

"Shut up. I didn't look all crazy. And I'm not a fighter—most of the time."

We laughed—loud.

But when I got to the car, I caught a glimpse of Joaquin out of the corner of my eye as he headed in my direction. Or I hoped he was headed in my direction. I stopped at my Jeep and threw my things in the back as usual, with keys in hand and sunglasses on. The flutter hit me and tossed my stomach. Joaquin stopped and leaned against the hood. With his elbow bent, his biceps flexed into a rock-hard mass pulling his sleeves taught and making my throat tighten. With the sun shining, the bronze in his skin almost sparkled. And his teeth had the slightest overlap making his smile impossible to look away from—perfect in a less obvious way.

"How's school going? Are you going to stay?" One side of his mouth lifted in a boyish grin.

I tried to remain calm. Even though things here weren't too bad, this place was forced on me and made me feel completely out of control. "Even if I hate it, I'm stuck here. No more private school for me."

Thanks to the murderous bastards who killed my father, I was forced into all this newness—alone. My dad was the kind of guy everyone could talk to about anything, from weather to my secret problems. He gave the best advice. Even when I was off the charts wrong, he could lift me up while chastising me. He offered direction without a push either way.

Lexi strolled around to the other side of the Jeep to put her stuff on the seat. My body's early warning system cued the presence of Jim and Teo—the energy bristled around them set off the second Joaquin left his brothers and started to talk to me. Jim asked Lexi what we were doing. He grabbed her by the arm. She stuck her tongue out at him and pulled her arm away.

"Is everything OK?" Joaquin stood up straight and moved closer to me. "There were whispers of some kind of boating accident…"

"Rumors. Yeah, it's all peachy." I forced a smile. I wanted to talk, but I needed to start a chant. A calming chant. The wind swirled and tossed my hair.

Jim skulked around behind me. As soon as my stomach cramps worsened, it was clear. Jerk on board.

Joaquin stood with his jaw clenched so tight a spot of blood oozed from the corner of his mouth, but he remained unobtrusive. Maybe a bit extreme for a teenage boy rivalry. The tension might have dissolved if I'd said goodbye and let him return to his brothers, but Teo came around the other side of the Jeep and slid between Joaquin and me—and grabbed my hand. His hand rough and hot, like he had some claim on me, which ticked me off.

Joaquin's brothers watched his every move and now started to drift toward us. The tension around them crushed me like a vise clamp. I tried to pull away from Teo, but he secured my arm.

Teo pushed Joaquin in the chest. "You can go. Now."

Quietly, I started to chant. The wind kicked up, and my hair tossed around my face.

Joaquin stepped forward and returned Teo's push. Teo lost his balance, and it jerked his hand free from mine. He steadied himself and swept me behind his back with great force, and I fell on my butt, losing my train of thought. I heard an animalistic growl. Joaquin took his stance, and before I could blink, he punched Teo in the jaw, knocking him to the ground. I jumped to my feet and flew in between them, pushing Joaquin with both hands.

"Go, just go!" I shouted. "Please, before the teachers come out and you're in trouble."

Joaquin threw up his hands in surrender and backed away from us. When I turned, Teo and Jim were already headed for his truck and away from my Jeep. I threw open my door and climbed inside. It happened fast; a few students noticed—but no time for them to congregate.

Lexi looked worried and hopped into her seat. "Oh. My. God. That was freaking insane; we need to go." We both caught our breath, and I started driving.

"I know, right!"

"Are you pissed at Joaquin?"

"No. They seem to have some issues, other than me."

"Yeah, but they never even talked before. This seems like something that's been ongoing. Have they given you any inkling?"

"No, but here's Teo. Maybe he'll clue us in."

When I drove up to Lexi's driveway, the boys had already arrived. I parked at an angle to Jim's truck. Teo slumped on the tailgate with a bag of ice clutched to his jaw. When he spotted me, he dropped the bag of ice and spit blood out into the dirt and hopped down. My eyes bulged—one hit from Joaquin caused some serious damage. Without thinking, I placed the palm of my hand over the injury and closed my eyes. He jerked away from the heat. I drew my hand back and balled my fist.

"Are you OK?" I asked.

He grabbed one of the belt loops on my pants and pulled me over to him. "More important, are you?"

"Seriously, cut it." I shifted my hips, trying to wiggle free. I slapped his hand to release his grip on me. He gave me his attempt at a hurt look. I guess I gave mixed signals.

"I'm fine."

He led us back to the tailgate and patted the spot beside him. Jim and Lexi fought their way over to the house, already deep in some kind of an argument, they left us alone. My stomach did a couple of flips, and he moved closer to me. He put his arm around me softer than the other times. He leaned over and kissed me on the cheek like we'd been together for months.

"Thanks for the rescue. I could have taken him—but then Coach would have been pissed."

At this moment, I was surprised to see him acte like he cared about anything other than himself. He saved me at the lake, but athletics was his thing—adrenaline and physical stuff. His eyes shifted from their usual blackness to a warm mahogany brown.

"Hey, want to check out what I wanted to show you before you went for a swim yesterday?"

I punched his arm. You've got to give it to him, he possessed some of that bad-boy charm, but I didn't want to laugh at something that came nowhere near being funny.

He pointed out the wide flowing creek that ran behind the house—the area sprawled open, even beyond the huge lake. The jagged line of pecan trees made a curved line parallel to the highway above us. Birds emerged from the trees from time to time and swooped down over the water. Through the crack in the tree line, I could see the distant creek bank. My eyes lingered on the breathtaking view as he spoke to me.

"Bee House Creek." He stressed the importance of the sacred land of the Apache and Tonkawa Indians. "The two tribes didn't like one another and were, like, at war all the time. The Apaches were on the Bee House Creek, and the Tonkawa lived on the Cowhouse Creek. The two tribes worked the land during the day, but at night, they fought by the light of the moon." He grinned and added, "Since you haven't spent much time in your own town, I figured I'd fill you in. Nice of me, huh?"

By the tone of his voice, I could tell he tried to make fun of himself, but at the same time, pointing it out in case I didn't notice. His attitude came off half annoying, half endearing. He allowed his intimidating manner to melt away, just as the appearance of a black and blue mark that spread from his ear to his chin—all this damage inflicted by one hit.

"Well… Want to hear a story?" he said, bumping my shoulder with his.

I rolled my eyes, "Yeah, sure."

"You've heard about the animal attacks, right?"

"Yeah, I've heard," I said, remembering Xavier's joke at lunch.

"OK. The attacks started at the end of last school year. Everyone freaked out. They imposed a strict curfew—and what I am hearing from the sheriff is things might tighten up. The worst one came around the time when Jim's brother went missing. He and I were great friends. Anyway, some kids were out camping. Rumor has it, they were experienced campers, and their knowledge exceeded most old-timers about animals, hunting and fishing. Well, sometime during the night, they split up. One of the guy's faces got clawed to the point that they identified him by the license in his wallet. Even his jaw went missing. Now the other guy, he could be identified—one problem, they gathered the rest of him from around the area. They never found one of his arms."

My heart jumped, and my stomach flipped—this sounds like some good Halloween tale. "You're kidding, right? The kids at lunch called me gullible."

"I wish." He fidgeted with the ice from his jaw, then asked, "Hey, how about letting me take you to dinner?"

"You spit blood at me, tell a gory story and then ask me to dinner. You know how to win a girl over."

"C'mon. You loved it. Please?"

He put the ice pack to his jaw and jumped a little and squinted his eyes. This guy tried to gain an edge—he worked it. It freaked me out, and I kind of didn't want to be alone. I shrugged. With a tug at my sleeve, we jumped off the tailgate and stepped toward the house to meet up with Jim and Lexi.

* * *

We ended up at Poppa Gino's Italian Restaurant. By this time, Lexi and Jim made some sort of peace and we all shuffled in the restaurant's front doors, Teo's arm around me. I stiffened but didn't pull away because I didn't know if he'd get upset.

We went inside, and the hostess gave us paper menus for the wait. I feigned interest in it to pry myself away from clingy Teo. They printed a legend about the Cowhouse Creek and the Tonkawa Indians. It told about how they settled here many years ago and that the Apaches almost wiped them out. The Tonkawa were intensely spiritual and believed in the Great Spirit and Mother Nature. The Apache believed in war.

Teo poked the paper. "See, I told you."

"You made it seem like a mutual fight, not a slaughter."

"Whatever. Tomato, tomahto."

"Are you ready?" Lexi asked.

I folded the paper and slid it into my purse. I stood up, and the hostess showed us to our table. We ate, talked and for the first time, the guys set me at ease. They laughed, told jokes, and Lexi laughed. She seemed more relaxed. We finished dinner and went back to the house for my Jeep.

The driveway had no lighting, and the hair on my arms stood on end. Lexi gave me a sideways hug in the backseat and then headed off to the house with Jim. And I found myself alone, at night, with Teo.

I slid out of the truck and picked my way over the uneven yard with my arms crossed over my chest. The headlights cut off. The light faded to almost absolute darkness, except for the house lights that bounced off the Jeep's bumper. The gravel crunched as Teo moved closer and put his arms around me. The wind tossed strands of my hair against my cheek. His body emitted warmth and roughness, but he smelled irresistible. The smell of grass and wood, real outdoor musk, piqued my senses. I wouldn't unfold my arms, though, because years of admonitions about boys caused guilt for being out here alone with him at all. Quickly, I wiggled loose and hurried around to the driver's side. I turned to tell him goodnight, keeping my head low, and my arms crossed. Then, I rubbed my hands up and down my arms.

He put his hands on my Jeep, one on each side of me.

"Tonight was fun," he said in my ear.

He leaned in close and pressed his body against me. The wind picked up, my throat tightened, and my heart sped. The oxygen between us was sucked out, and my lungs could not draw in enough air, suffocation mere seconds away. He leaned in and pressed his lips against mine, hard, and then he put his arm around my waist. The drowning sensation flowed over me again, flailing in the black water.

I shoved him away. Bent at the waist, I grabbed my stomach and tried to fill my lungs with air.

He put his hand on my back. "Are you OK?"

"Yeah, I think I may have eaten something bad. I better go," I said.

"Did I do something?" he asked.

"Maybe the food made me sick. I'm serious. I need to go," I said.

I jumped into my Jeep and took off down the road. My tires throwing up gravel. By the time I hit the main road, I could breathe again. As the air hit me in the face, I could breathe, which kept the nausea at bay. I made it to my house, went inside and I dropped my stuff at the door. I wandered upstairs, pulled up my email account and wrote a long letter to my sister. I could tell her everything. A serious sister code existed between us. With her away at college, we didn't visit a great deal... since Dad.

Today, I needed her—filling Theresa in on all about my first few days of school and how I made friends. My conscience tugged at me, urging to free myself of the whole near-drowning thing and maybe glean some greatly needed sisterly advice. If the water incident came up in conversation, she would understand the severity of the situation since neither of us ever learned to swim. So, I passed over it. Not wanting her to worry and call Mom, I hurried on to happier things; told her I met Lexi, Jim and Teo at school—and Teo was loads more into me than I was into him. Next, I told her about Joaquin. The mention of him made me smile. I tried to describe the spark going through me with him around—the good kind of stomach tingle and twist you suffer when you're wholly interested in a new guy.

The email took up about a page by the time I finished. I closed the email with *Love, Maria*, and then pushed send.

I didn't have to wait long. Five minutes later, my phone began to ring in my pocket.

"Dish," she sang those four little letters. The words seemed to gush past my lips like water that overflowed a dam. All the information about my days at the new school and the accident. My voice cracked—she wanted answers. Still not prepared to give her every detail, I tried to explain the heart of the problem. I enjoyed Lexi, but a friendship seemed to be a package deal with her, and she let those guys push her around, and me along with her.

Theresa was forceful in telling me I needed to be careful, a stern reminder that those boys didn't go to our church or school; therefore, they may not have the same values.

"What else?" she said and waited. Always, or ever since we were little girls, these magic words caused the information to spill from my lips.

Finally, I told her Jim knocked me out of the boat, and I hit my head. Then I told her it must have been pretty hard since I hallucinated about animals in the water. Trying to lighten up the situation, I told her the animal attack fell more on the wishful side. Then I begged her not to tell mom. Mom managed to drag herself out of bed one day at a time, and she didn't need this.

"Well, carry your pepper spray, OK?"

"I'm not going to be alone with them."

"Carry it anyway. Promise."

The line fell silent for a while, and then she asked me about Joaquin. My face lit up at the sound of his name. Not loads to tell, we hadn't even engaged in a full conversation, but I tingled all over when we spoke in the hall. She told me to focus on my schoolwork—and less on Joaquin. We laughed.

"And hey! Be careful," she said. "You met all these guys like two weeks ago—not even. And Dad talked to us about the boys in town."

"Yeah…"

I wanted to say more, but she would worry about me. She'd mentioned our father. I couldn't believe it.

"Thanks. Theresa." I heard the front door open downstairs. "I gotta go. Mom's home."

Downstairs, Mom looked a little tired and a little stressed. As a result, I said goodnight, grabbed my purse and went back upstairs.

At the restaurant, I'd slipped the paper menu into my purse. My curiosity piqued about the history—Teo seemed engrossed in it. First, I searched online for the two creeks. According to the map, the Cowhouse seemed more like a river than a creek, with a wide mouth around Pidcoke and thinned as it moved closer to Austin. Bee House Creek ran thin all the way connecting to the Cowhouse, closer to Lampasas. I couldn't believe I called this town home for my entire life but learned about it on the Internet.

Next, I looked up the Apache Indians in the area. Teo said *tomato, tomahto*, but I wanted the facts. The article said they were warriors and fighters—warring and fighting over this extraordinary land my house was built on and the rest of my town. They migrated to the area, but the Tonkawa claimed it years earlier. The Apaches did what they did best and took it by force.

Last, I followed a link for the Tonkawa Indians. The first thing that popped up was "The People of the Wolf."

CHAPTER 4

The days passed swiftly. I took Theresa's warning seriously and tried to ignore Teo. He crossed the line with that kiss. I made small talk with the usual crowd after school, and then Lexi and I would split off to my Jeep and head out for the day. She must have sensed my aversion to Jim and Teo because now she insisted that I drop her off at the end of her driveway. I didn't argue.

At home, things were quiet. I went to school and cooked supper in the evenings. Cooking reminded me of happier days when Mom, Theresa and I would work in the kitchen together, as well as the times I secretly mixed concoctions with my father. We, the girls, would spend every evening in the kitchen preparing things for my dad to come home to. One of us would set the table, and the others prepared the meal. Now cooking was a chore.

Not wanting to spend more time than necessary, I decided to make tacos. The meat in the fridge was turkey—I figured it would be bland. As a result, I added a second spice packet. Proud of myself until we started to eat and there wasn't enough milk to soothe our scorched tongues—but at least we laughed a little.

Friday arrived. In Texas, that meant nothing less than Friday Night Lights. The ritualistic pep rally, home football game and party in the nearest pasture—this would be my fate. With Lexi being the "it" girl on campus, there was no way I could separate myself from all the so-called fun. I braced myself after the last bell and then headed toward the gym. Lexi and Becky found me quickly, and we pushed our way through the crowd to a line of bleacher space piled with the boys' backpacks to save the seats for us. We were the farthest inside at the end and in the front row. Not my favorite place to be, out in front of everybody, I wanted to blend.

The gym was packed with teachers, parents and students. At my old school, we entered assemblies respectfully, like adults. Here the students entered like the hormonal teenagers we all are. The boom from the metal gymnasium doors slamming shut made me jump. A hush moved across the gym. Being new at the school, I had no idea what to expect; my Catholic school didn't have a renowned athletics program. The whoosh of bodies running past caressed my right side. The whole football team charged onto the court from behind the bleacher seats like a herd of elephants. The crowd erupted in cheers, and I recognized Jim, Thomas and Teo. Thomas made the third in their little trio, he was quiet and stayed back most of the time, but he always sulked in the background—lurking. His girlfriend, Crystal, came off as kind of a loner super athlete. She hadn't said more than "hello" to me.

Teo caught my gaze and gave me a quick smile—almost devilish. I flashed a halfhearted grin back to him, trying to ignore the pinch in my stomach. No other way to describe it, but *eerie*. I hated this negativity about people Lexi admired, but I couldn't shake this sixth sense.

We followed the cheerleaders in their chants. It was a little fun if you allowed yourself to let go and enjoy it. The boys exited the same way they came, but instead of the smile, Teo stopped.

"Will you meet me out front?" he asked.

I nodded yes. After the other night, it made spikes run up and down my spine imagining what he might want to say now. He gave me another devilish grin and jogged off behind his team. Lexi and Becky looked at me. I pulled my shoulders up with both palms in the air.

"What does he want? And I thought you guys were kind of at a weird place?" Lexi asked.

"We are. So, I have no freaking idea what he wants."

"I'll come with you."

"You better."

In front of the school, I scanned the sheltered sidewalk. I didn't see him; he must still be with the team, but I timed my exit perfectly. Joaquin stood at his SUV. He stared back at me with his little sideways smile. He gave me a little dip of his head, meaning, *Hello, I see you looking at me.*

Lexi leaned into me, "He's the guy I want to talk to. He's ever so yummy."

I smacked her on the arm, "He is yummy." We laughed.

The nauseating tingle plopped into the pit of my stomach, and then everything went black. Two hands covered my eyes.

"Guess who?" he said.

I did not have to guess. I responded in my sappiest voice, "Ugh. The stench suggests Jim?"

"Come on! Give me a break."

"Showers would be nice. A little Axe would do wonders. Seriously, just spray it in the air and walk under the mist. It's a fabulous invention."

"Hey, Maria," Teo said. "We wondered if y'all would want to go with us to the after-party?"

I was stumped. To everyone else, he came off as a decent guy with tons of friends, and he couldn't be all bad, but the same spark of electricity that flew through me when Joaquin spoke to me was absent. I didn't even want to be alone with Teo.

I looked down and started to twist one of my rings. "What kind of party? Is it in the gym?"

"In the gym? No way, Maria. This isn't second grade. It's a real party," Jim teased. Lexi thumped him in the stomach.

"I don't think I'm up for a party. But thanks."

"Everybody will be there. You can go home if you don't like it," Teo said.

Then I watched Lexi deflate a bit and sighed.

"Augh. Give me a break."

"Please," Lexi mouthed to me.

"Maybe…I guess. Lexi and I will meet you there." Everyone laughed.

"Well, we have to be at the field house hours before the game. Can y'all meet us at the field house afterward, and we will go from there," he asked.

Jim said, "I can ride with Teo, and Lexi can pick up Maria in my truck. Then, we can all ride together."

There it was. The train sped toward me with the horn blasting, but I froze, unable to step out of the way. My feet planted on either side of the rails, shocked and speechless. "Together," fumbled out of my mouth.

Teo lit up. "Sounds like a plan. Is it good for you girls?"

Lexi looked at Jim. "You trust me with your precious truck?"

"Sure," Jim said. He grabbed Lexi around the neck. "You wouldn't give me any reason not to trust you, right?" He laughed with a fiendish tinge and rubbed the top of her head with his knuckles. She punched him and straightened her hair. It sent chills up my spine.

Lexi said, "We are most definitely in! Right, Maria?" She jumped at the chance to drive Jim's truck.

I hesitated, then gave a barely audible, "Can't think of a reason to say no."

Teo smiled the sincerest smile I'd ever seen on his face. He seemed eager to be friends with me. "Well, all right. If I weren't so ready for this game, I would wish it was over already."

I slumped, trapped in this space like a scared animal. "Well, I need to hit the road," I said.

Lexi and I headed for my Jeep. Loads of emotions rolled up inside me. I could not describe one of them. They were all twisted and inter-twined, making it impossible to separate them. Did the party scare me? Or the boy? Or both? I tossed my things in the back in a fluid motion that seemed involuntary. I hadn't even taken out my keys or sunglasses. Leaning over the side of my Jeep, I dug through my purse to find them. Finally, I located them when my body tingled from a light brush across the exposed skin of my back. It couldn't be. Even this wonderful spark couldn't remedy the horrid lurch deep down in my stomach.

I turned to face him, staring at his adorable half-smile. Leaning to look past him, I observed his brothers allowing the girls to enter the vehicle first. Then, the boys jumped into the car after them. Micael started the engine while they waited for Joaquin. I turned my eyes back to his magnificent face, a deep dimple in his chin and faint ones on both sides of his mouth sunk with his bright smile.

"Hi."

"I wanted to come over and apologize," he said. "My behavior the other day was unacceptable."

"Maybe. But I'm not the person who deserves the apology." I lowered my voice. "I'm not saying I'm Teo's biggest fan, but you messed up his face." I laughed, and he joined in.

He looked down at the ground and kicked a rock across the parking lot. Then he smiled and leaned against my Jeep.

"Are you going to the game?"

"Yeah, Lexi and I," I said.

"How about after?" he asked.

"We're going to a party with Jim, Teo and Thomas." I reminded myself it's not a complete lie, not for me anyway. It didn't matter what Teo wanted.

"Oh, okay." This smile didn't quite make it to his eyes, but he looked at me a little suspiciously. I also noticed his fists clenched, making his knuckles turn white.

"Is everything OK?"

His body shook, and he looked a little flushed.

"Oh yeah, I'm fine. Something from the other day flashed in my mind," he said.

"It was pretty intense," I said.

He touched my forearm; a tingle surged all the way to my chest. "Hey, maybe we can sit together during the game and say more than 'hi' to each other." I ducked my head, hoping he would not see the flush of my cheeks or hear my heart pounding against my ribs.

"Sounds like a plan," I said.

"Bye… See ya soon," he said.

All smiles, tenderness swept over me. It left me in the grips of elation. He jogged back to his brothers' car and hopped in with a wave. I pressed my palms to my cheeks, trying to cool down the fever. Lexi buckled herself in my Jeep and looked at me with the biggest, most mischievous smile on her face.

She started right in. "I can't believe you have two dates in one night. I haven't been invited on two dates the entire time I have been in high school." She rolled her eyes. "Thanks to Jim."

"Well, believe me, it's a first for me, too." I looked over at her and made a face. Then, I went back over things for a second. "Wait, it's not a date. We're going to talk, and the thing with Teo… What the heck? He doesn't give up."

"I know, right!" she said.

"I hope he doesn't consider this a date."

She put her feet on the dash, and we both started to laugh. The wind blew and she lifted her head, letting it blow her hair back.

"I am sure he does."

"No. I'm sure it's because Jim wants to keep tabs on you." I poked her side. "Lexi, after the other night, please don't leave me alone with him. Promise me."

"Wait, what happened?"

"He's pretty forward. It's intense and makes me nervous. Please, promise."

"He kind of gives me the creeps, too. I promise," she said.

"He gives me a funny feeling. Like, funny 'odd' not funny 'ha ha.'"

She didn't respond, her head ducked, and her eyes were on the ground in front of her.

"Are all the guys at school like him? At my old school, all the boys were longtime friends, and they never overwhelmed me or made me—afraid. Or at least they weren't this pushy."

"I guess it's some kind of testosterone football player thing. Xavier isn't like them. He's warm and sweet." She shrugged. "Did you date the guys from your other school?"

"My dad kept me on a short leash. I met them at the movies and stuff, but he always drove me there and picked me up, sometimes he even popped up in the back row."

Lexi grinned. "Seriously? I guess my family isn't so protective, after all. Well, other than Jim. And we are about to have it out."

"He is kind of forceful with you. Why don't you say anything?"

"It's a guilt thing. I guess it goes back to the whole—I am grateful to have them. If I say anything negative, guilt washes over me. It makes me appear ungrateful."

I understood why Lexi allowed the loads of crap he piled on her. She loved them even though they lacked boundaries. You had to admire her unconditional love.

The dread started to fade the farther we drove. My stomach didn't calm down until I drove into her driveway. I waved goodbye, and by the time I pulled into my driveway, I was almost in a good mood. Mom was already home—she'd mentioned something about short Fridays for a while. I pulled all my junk out of the back and headed for the front door.

As soon as I entered the kitchen, Mom looked stressed but composed herself when she saw me. "Hi, honey? How are you?" I could see in her eye's things were wrong.

"Hi, Mom. Is everything... is something wrong?"

"Oh, no, honey. Nothing to concern yourself with," she said.

She pushed the sides of her mouth up into what almost looked like a smile and wiped her nose with a handkerchief. "Any plans for tonight?"

"Yeah, but I can stay home if you want—"

"No. Absolutely not. What plans do you have?"

"Lexi and I are going to the game, then some kids planned a bonfire afterward. I'm riding with Lexi, and I'm not sure where we're going."

"Sounds like fun! Please be safe and don't stay out too late."

"I won't. I'll call if the plans change," I said. "Are you sure I shouldn't just—"

"Oh, go enjoy yourself. That's the most important thing, right?"

"Hey! I have an idea. Do you want to go to the game?"

I went over and kissed her on the cheek. Mom patted my cheek, smiled and mouthed, "No thanks," and something about the look in her eyes made my stomach wrench. I trudged up the stairs and grabbed my purse on the way to my room. If I decided to stay home with her, she would insist on me going, but it killed me to look back and watch her stare into space. "Be home before midnight," she yelled after me, halfheartedly, as if she'd realized at this moment, she should seem more concerned.

The weather would cool off during the game—it would be in the nineties until the sun slipped behind the trees. Then, the night would drift downward. I decided on a white chiffon blouse with a small sleeve and grabbed a three-quarter-sleeve sweater from the back of my closet for when the setting sun dropped the temperature. I riffled through my bag to make sure nothing would be left behind. Remembering my promise to Theresa, I dug out my pepper spray from my top dresser drawer and put it in my purse—just in case.

At my full-length mirror, I checked myself out. I put some lip gloss on and plopped the tube into my purse. A little pep talk released some of the fear that seeped its way back into my body and mind— Lexi would have my back. She promised.

The doorbell rang. I ran my fingers through my hair one last time and hurried downstairs.

"Bye, Mom! Love you!"

"Midnight," she said.

"Yeah, yeah," I said and laughed out loud for her to catch the joke.

Without saying a word to Lexi, we headed toward the street where she parked Jim's behemoth, midnight blue Dodge Ram. This chrome-accented monster complete with a roll bar, floodlights, a dual exhaust and huge knobby off-road tires made it impossible to step into the truck. I grabbed the *oh shit* handle to hoist myself up. The truck screamed to hit the trails and throw up some mud, yet it didn't have a speck of dirt on it.

"I can't believe he let me drive his truck. This is his baby." She giggled and hauled herself up into the driver's seat.

"Well, we better be good," I said.

We burst into laughter. I shoved my sunglasses onto my face and tossed my purse in the back seat.

Traffic was thick. It took about fifteen minutes to make it across town to the football field.

"You ever been to a game before?" Lexi asked.

"Not since I was little."

Memories of watching some of the games with my dad flooded my mind. He loved football. The memory drew a knot up in my chest. We would talk about the game all the way home, and in the morning, I would sit next to him at breakfast and read the recap in the newspaper, me and him—our thing.

She must have sensed the shift in my mood because, in nothing flat, Lexi produced laughter. Ready to cheer on our team, all the fear faded, and I almost become as giddy as at the pep rally. Her positive outlook was contagious. We got out of the truck and headed toward the open gate, gave the attendants our tickets, then made our way toward the concession stand. We both asked for a Coke and danced up the stairs, heels clanking and clattering toward the student section of the aluminum bleachers. The students started to cheer and stomped their feet along with the cheers, rattling the metal like thunder. We identified our group and set out toward them. I made sure I positioned myself at the open end, awaiting Joaquin's arrival.

During the anthem, I spotted them. He and his family stood with their hands over their hearts. When the anthem and prayer were complete, Joaquin found me almost effortlessly and pointed them all toward our section. The four brothers and their girlfriends filed in front of us. Joaquin took his place in the empty seat next to me. Elated, I shrugged my shoulders and wiggled in my spot, edging a little closer to him.

"Hola."

"¿Cómo estás?"

"Muy bien. Que pasa?"

"Just watching some football." I shrugged my shoulders and held my hands palm up. We laughed, and I reached out to touch his rock-hard biceps, but I withdrew my hand, surprised by my forward behavior.

Suddenly, an odd *somebody's looking at me* sensation runs up and down my spine. On the sideline, Teo pierced me with his stare. Joaquin snickered. Looking down, not quite embarrassed, but a little freaked out. I heard a low growl, maybe from one of Joaquin's brothers, and Teo shoved his helmet on his head, slapped the top and headed onto the field. He was the starting quarterback tonight.

We watched the game, making small talk in between plays. The conversations were easy. I couldn't hold anything back. It flowed, and I even mentioned that my dad passed away. His eyes jumped to mine, and he frowned.

"We were sorry to hear about your father—we go to church together, and my dad joined the Knights of Columbus with him."

"You seemed familiar, but I couldn't place you."

He smiled with a sweetness as I said I recognized him. This must be part of the reason he made me feel so comfortable. He introduced me to all his brothers: Micael, Enrique, Alejandro and Gabriel. Their girlfriends are Marisol and Alyssa.

The conversation ran smoothly, but before I realized it, the game ended. As everyone screamed and cheered, I let out a long sigh. Time flew, and I craved more. I tried to recall saying even two words to anyone else. But my eyes hadn't left his the entire two and a half hours. My mind spun over the fact that he would leave me, and it made me ache.

I began to rub my palms together and fidget with my rings. The game ended, and everyone gathered their things—the final score was twenty-one to six, us. Joaquin and I remained in our spot until the bleachers cleared out. I mulled over how to say goodbye, but that's when he tapped me on the leg.

He said, "We'll catch you later." His family at the bottom of the bleachers turned toward me, smiled and then waved goodbye. The easy part was over—now, time for the hard part.

Cindy bounded over before Joaquin could make it down to his family and grabbed his arm like she owned him. She told him we were all going out to the party and she even gave him directions. He told her they might show up later. Then looked around her and smiled at me.

"Yes, come!" I said in a shaky voice.

Lexi joined me, and we worked ourselves up for the party to come. I told her multiple times she would ride with me. "Yes, yes, I remember, Maria," she said as if the reminder annoyed her. Then, we strolled under the bleachers toward the field house. It would take time for the boys to talk to the coach and shower. And from the stench I'd caught of the player's locker room, I wanted them to take plenty of time with that shower.

"Hey, Lexi, you swear? I don't want to be alone with him."

"I've got it!" she said.

"Where is this party, anyway? Cindy gave Joaquin directions I didn't recognize," I told her.

"Oh, it's at this place called the Ozone. It's nothing more than a country road. We build a bonfire in the middle of a field." She rolled her eyes and twirled her finger in the air. "Fun, fun! We hang out, tell stories, roast marshmallows and listen to music. Nothing major."

"It sounds harmless enough," I said.

At that moment, the boys broke through the metal double doors of the field house with a bang. They laughed, pushed and gave each other high fives. Jim threw a heavy arm around Lexi, knocking her off balance. Teo fell into his rhythm and threw his arm around my waist, pulling me close to him. My body contorted into a sideways C. Thanks to his aggressive public display of affection, everyone would assume we were a thing. As I imagined the flying rumors, an irritation simmered.

Jim said, "Y'all ready?"

The guys pulled us toward the parking lot like we were on some kind of repulsive double date. Surely, Lexi was mortified. She broke free from Jim's clutches and smacked him a couple of times on the chest with her open hand. I tried to wiggle away from Teo's grip again, to no avail. His strength amazed me. At this point, the group outing seemed like a foregone conclusion. We made it to the vehicles. Lexi parked next to Teo's bright yellow Camaro. He went to the passenger side and opened the door for me.

I yelled, "Lexi, ride with us." I shot her a look and jerked my head, motioning for her to come.

Jim said, "Nope. She's riding with me. See you there." He shot Lexi a look. She looked at me with her eyes wide and mouthed, *Sorry*.

"It'll be fine," Teo promised. "I don't bite."

CHAPTER 5

I slid into the stiff black leather seat and tried to grow comfortable. Immediately, my stomach wretched. Overcome by fear, I remained motionless with my hands clamped together in between my knees, occasionally rubbing my palms together to remove the sweat. Comfort wasn't an option after the incident at the lake. Even though Teo pulled me from the water, I associated him with the black water, panic and pain—maybe some PTSD symptoms lingered, I couldn't quite put my finger on it. He tried to be nice, though. I couldn't decide if my awkwardness was a part of reality or the paranoia in my head. While he drove, I sat motionless, gazing forward, trying to catch a glimpse of him from the corner of my eye—prey scrutinizing its unworthy predator. He glanced to the side from time to time, watching my chest as it rose and fell.

He said, "Do you want to stop and pick up a drink? I have sodas in the trunk, but you might want a cup and some ice. I'm not sure what you like to drink."

I rubbed my palms on the leg of my jeans and exhaled. "Thanks, I would like that." I still didn't look at him and kept spinning my rings.

He pulled into the convenience store, cut the engine and turned sideways to look at me. "What flavor do you like?"

"A Coke. Let me give you some money." Still, without looking at him, I grabbed for my purse. He put his hand on top of mine, stopping me. It sent a sensation like crawling bugs across my skin.

He smiled. "No way, I've got it. You're my guest."

I gave him a shaky smile, "Thanks."

His left hand rested on the steering wheel when I noticed something red on his wrist. My curiosity got the better of me, and I poked at his watchband to urge a better look. It caught him off guard. At first glance, I pictured an injury from the game, but it wasn't—his wrist was tattooed. A bloodred V inked in an ornate script that made one bar of the letter look like a dagger and the other like a snake and at the bottom where they met, it flowed out into a *fleur-de-lis*. The entire tattoo stretched about two inches down his wrist. Teo jerked his hand away and resituated his watch.

"Bad tattoo," he explained. "And I don't want anyone to see it until I save enough money to have it fixed."

"Well, at least tell me what it's supposed to be."

"It's a V. For Valdez, you know, my last name."

He jumped out of the car. I waited, filled with embarrassment as he behaved like a true southern gentleman—what was my problem? He may not be the guy of my dreams, but he tried to be friendly. I would try harder. When he returned to the car with my drink, I shook off my paralysis and started a conversation by congratulating him on the game. This made things a little more comfortable. He talked about football, losing me completely. But my stomach settled into a dull roar. My palms began to dry, and I could breathe more easily.

At the Ozone, things were in full swing. A bonfire blazed in the middle of a pasture. Teo disappeared to the back of the car and popped the trunk. I stood by the door, looking toward the fire.

Teo said, "Can I have an extra hand?" He peeked around the side of the trunk lid holding up a blanket. I smiled and made my way toward the back of the car.

"Sure, sorry about that," I said.

He handed me a multicolored blanket and a bag of marshmallows. I held them in one hand and my cup in the other. I left my purse and sweater in the car—the temperature stayed in the eighties, and who needed a purse in a field? He grabbed the cooler, shoved a flashlight in his back pocket, and we stepped over large rocks on our way toward the fire. Glad our hands were full, even though comfort crept up on me, I needed distance.

As we got closer, they'd arranged four makeshift benches squared around the fire. They were made of two cinder blocks and a two-by-six board, a country kid's seating. He set the cooler at the end of one of the benches. Groups of people gathered in knots around the bonfire toward the nearby tree. Several passionate couples disappeared into the surrounding darkness. The sick heave of my stomach grew worse.

Beyond the fire's illumination and the silver gleam of the full moon, the night sunk into a black hole. The sky glittered with brilliant summer stars. The wind rattled the distant tree branches, and a bank of clouds rolled over the stars on the horizon. The moon's glow softened and expanded as the high, thin clouds moved closer. I started to second guess leaving my sweater in the truck. But in front of the fire—a perfectly choreographed dance of yellow, red, orange and blue—leaped above the blackened barrel. The air was filled with the aroma of cedar smoke and fresh air. Someone started the music, and the boom of the bass made conversation difficult. People leaned in intimately close, speaking into each other's ears or migrating in the opposite direction of the stereo.

Teo took a seat on the bench and patted the spot next to him. I stepped over to the bench, hugging the blanket against my chest and slammed down on the wood with a thud. He laughed and put his arm around my back, slipped his thumb into my back pocket and tugged me closer. It turned out better than I expected. Or at least I didn't want to jump out of my skin. I wondered if the crushing nausea would return with Jim's arrival, or had I loosened up and started to realize that my eyes played tricks on me that day at the lake. That wasn't reality.

He reached over with his free hand and arranged the blanket where we could both sit on the clean blanket. It's not cold enough to pull it over my shoulders, but it was nice to have something besides the dirty wood to sit on. Teo leaned close to me and asked me about my classes. Since he was a senior, we didn't have any of the same classes, but he'd suffered through some of the classes I'm in now during his junior year. We talked about the dinner a few nights earlier, and by the tone of the conversation, he counted it as our *first date*. It took me by surprise, and I wanted to correct him, but something told me it would be pointless.

Suddenly, I realized Lexi hadn't arrived. I scanned all the people around the fire, even the kids who made out under the trees.

I leaned over, close to Teo's ear, and asked him, "Where is Lexi? I'm worried."

He looked surprised and studied the people gathered around the fire. "That's weird. We stopped, and they still haven't made it?" He looked toward the makeshift parking lot. He pointed out Jim's truck and said, "No, there's Jim's truck." He made another sweep of the area around the bonfire and gave a little shrug. "Maybe they went for a hike? Do you want to go check?" He stood up and grabbed the flashlight stuffed in his back pocket. My entire body tensed—no way did I want to be out in the dense, dark area by myself with him, especially when he seemed a little too eager to go.

"No, that's okay. We can wait a little while longer," I said.

A few minutes later, I heard a scream that made me jump to my feet and whirl around, looking into the darkness. Then out of the trees bounced Lexi, slugging Jim with a closed fist on his arms and back. He doubled over in laughter, amused at whatever prank he pulled. Lexi fumed.

"What's going on?" I shouted. "Are you okay?"

"Jim and his stupid scary stories—that's what's wrong! You jerk!" Then she kicked up some dirt at him. I stuffed back the laughter that welled up inside me.

Jim continued to laugh hysterically. "What's a bonfire without a scary story?"

"I hate you," Lexi said.

"Oh, come here and give your big cousin a hug." He threw his arms out in an exaggerated stance and tried to hug her. She punched him once more and pushed his hands away.

"No way. Get off me." She couldn't help herself. The harder she tried to hold it back, the more the sides of her mouth turned up, and the more her voice cracked with laughter.

Lexi flopped down beside me and almost fell backward off the bench. I reached out to help steady her. She tried to act mad, but as soon as our eyes met, we both exploded into laughter and tears.

"We were about to send out a search party," I said.

Teo laughed. "When it gets a little darker, I'll take you out."

I said, "Gee, thanks!" I rolled my eyes and scooted away a couple of inches.

We all began to talk, and the evening turned fun. Maybe the newness wore off, and I started to enjoy everyone, or maybe all the happiness around me diluted the weird gut wrench. We roasted the marshmallows, laughed, and I refilled my drink cup. Someone brought Hershey's chocolate and graham crackers. I grabbed some, and Teo pulled the marshmallow away from the fire and held it out for me to squash between the crackers and chocolate. The chocolate and marshmallow oozed over the sides, a guilty temptation. I held it out for Teo. He chomped off half in one bite. I inhaled the sweet scent of chocolate, and then I took a crumbly bite.

Lexi tried to eat the rest, but a piece of the graham cracker fell in her lap, and marshmallow stuck to her face. We threw our heads back and laughed at the mess. Teo picked a piece of graham cracker from my lip and used his little finger to wipe off the chocolate. Then he threw the cracker in his mouth. I ducked my head. It grossed me out. He tucked his finger under my chin and lifted my head, trying to gauge my reaction. I pushed my hair behind my ear and gave him a little forced smile. He stared at me, making me wipe my face for any stray crumbs or chocolate.

Lexi scooted over next to Xavier. They interlocked arms, melting into each other, and Lexi tossed her hair a lot, being extra flirty, and I hoped Xavier picked up on the signals. Teo possessed that look in his eyes that said, *I want to get you alone*. His mouth was poised, ready to ask me to take a hike with him. The Coke simmered in the pit of my stomach like when my Dad used soda to clean off the acid from the car battery. He tapped me on the arm, I turned toward him, and we began to talk about the football game. I could see the motor inside his head spinning.

"Would you like to take that walk?" he asked.

"No, thanks," I said.

"Come on, Lexi, tell her it will be fun," he said.

"Yeah, sure, tons of fun," Lexi's eyes never left Xavier's face. Remaining swept up in her attempt to gain a boyfriend, she screwed her girlfriend.

He stood, took my hands and pulled me to my feet. *Relax,* I told myself. *You're a big girl, Maria. You can take care of yourself.*

He caught my elbow to steady and guide me. I shivered. He stopped and looked at me.

"Would you like your sweater?" he asked.

"Please," I said with a nod.

We headed to the car, and he got my sweater. He wrapped it over my shoulders as I threaded my arms in the sleeves. He slipped his hand into the curve of my back and led me toward the darkness.

"Wait," I said.

I hurried back to his car and rifled through my purse. I grabbed my pepper spray and slid it into my front jeans pocket. I stood up and threw a mint in my mouth to keep him from realizing what I'd done.

I stumbled over a broken oak branch. He caught me and pulled the flashlight from his back pocket. He tilted the light toward the ground to guide our path. The ground sank in spots, and after months of near drought, there were loose rocks all over the cracked earth. After we traveled pretty far, the music was a light echo. The vibration of the drumbeat faded in the background. The gurgle of water caught my attention. Teo brought the beam of light up to expose an old rickety bridge. Then, he dropped the beam back to the ground in front of us to guide our feet.

"What? Does a troll live under there?" I said with an uncomfortable chuckle.

He laughed as we creaked our way onto the bridge, and I leaned my stomach against the rail. I listen to the crackle of the bridge, a bullfrog's croak and the buzz of cicadas in the trees. He pointed and said, "Look."

I tried to focus my eyes in the direction of his pointed finger. A group of firefly's buzzed past with their bodies aglow. "Beautiful…"

I said quietly. *One of the best things I have seen in my life.* The wind blew away the clouds, and you could see every star in the sky. The atmosphere shifted, and now the moon shined a harvest gold with silvered contours.

"How 'bout that story?" he asked.

"Another one of your gore-filled stories? No, thanks," I bumped him with my shoulder.

He leaned his back against the rail, making it easier for him to look at me. Then, he leaned in close to my ear. His steamy breath tickled my sensitive skin sending my body into an ultrafeminine frenzy. "Let's keep walking. We can take a short trip into the woods to look at those fascinating fireflies and the stars. I'll be a good boy." He used his finger to cross his heart and then put the palms of his hands together. "I promise."

I looked around. Things seemed calm enough. My stomach had settled for the moment. And he at least played at being a nice guy. What could it hurt?

"Oh, all right, but you'd better be good," I said.

I slapped him on the arm and stood on the opposite side of the path, placing us several feet apart. As we slipped down the path, he slid closer to me and held my waist to guide me into the wooded area. I stumbled a little on the rocks and held my hands out in front of me for balance. The trees started to close in, their tips entwined, shielding the light from the moon and stars, making it impossible to see even the outlines of trees beyond the flashlight's paltry beam.

He stopped, turned off the light and stuffed it in his back pocket. One of those sharp pains stabbed my stomach. I stumbled backward until my back pressed against the pebbly bark of a pecan tree. My hands went straight back, clutched the rough ripples of the trunk, and for a moment, a twinge of safety flushed over me as I braced myself against it.

Stupid Maria, I said to myself. What did I believe would happen? He wouldn't be forward enough to make an advance, would he? I reached for my pocket and pulled out my pepper spray—he struck my hand and the canister fell to the ground. I couldn't even see the direction it flew.

"Oops," he said.

Despite the darkness surrounding me, my eyes darted back and forth, trying to catch a glimpse of him rustling closer. My heart thumped against my chest; my breath wheezed between my lips. Something warm and wet pressed against my face. My skin went from hot to cold, like a fever. Teo's sickly sweet breath was on my face. When did he get so close to me? I edged to the side to escape his nearness. The comfort of the tree turned claustrophobic. His arms caged me between him and the rough bark. Hard and rough, his lips closed over mine. I moved my face from side to side, trying to keep his lips from finding mine.

Once I wrestled my mouth free from his, I yelled, "Stop!" He continued to hold my hands in one of his. His other rough hand moved over my shoulder and slipped into my shirt. I barked and spat, "Stop it!"

"Yum. I like a girl with a little fight in her," he growled.

I struggled harder to unbind my hands. He slung me to the ground. With my palms as a guide, I tried to slide across the rough ground. He fell on top of me, turning me onto my back. His body pressed between my legs. His hand went under my shirt again. This time I heard the rip of material, and a button bounced off my arm, making its way to the ground.

I found my voice and screamed, "Stop it!"

He covered my mouth. My screams continued, but they were muffled. He leaned in close to my ear and said with spit spraying from his mouth, "Shut up and be still."

My struggles made me weaker. One hand pinned my arms to the ground. His weight compressed my ribs until I couldn't take a full breath. My legs cramped from the struggle. I pulled one hand loose and cast around for my pepper spray, a rock, a stick, anything. He moved his hands down my stomach and popped my top button open. I tried to flip him off me by kicking my feet and lifting my hips off the ground, but his strength proved too excessive.

A rustle and crack of a branch came from the darkness. I took in a deep breath and yelled, "Help!"

My eyes began to adjust—the flat darkness gave way to faint shapes. My fingers found a rock.

The sound caught Teo's attention, and he turned away from me, straining into the shadows. I pulled my other hand free and grabbed the rock. I scratched his face with my nails and the rock's sharpest edge. He fell to the side, clutching his face. I did a crab crawl backward and away from his grip.

"Crap! The he… What the heck are you *doing*?" I yelled at him. As I pushed on my hands and knees, I slid my hands across the ground. Under my breath, I said, "Find things that are lost." My pepper spray jumped into my hand. My arms straighten out in front of me, I mashed the button down while I swept it back and forth. I heard him coughing and spitting. A sensation of heat and the sting of the spray diffused in the air.

The low growl and rustling of leaves got louder. Goosebumps crawled up and down my arms, but without his body pressed against my ribs, I could breathe. Pepper tickled my lungs. Then, I heard a second low animalistic hum, and my eyes landed on something moving out of the trees behind him—a man. I blinked away the tears blurring my eyes and recognized Joaquin. I stretched my neck and blinked again. My eyes played tricks on me.

Teo began to shake and snarl. It started with his feet. They turned into large paws.

Next, the tremors moved up his flanks. He tore his shirt off. Dark hair covered his skin. He transformed.

His face stretched into a long muzzle, hovering inches from my foot. Within moments a fully formed wolf stood before me. Red eyes glowing like the taillights of my jeep, and his teeth were stained dark with dried blood and bits of flesh. I froze for what seemed to be hours, trying to push myself out of what I now hoped to be a horrifying dream. But I never woke.

Joaquin stepped between us with a powerful stance. He crouched down protectively, touching the ground with one hand. It could have been an imitation of the football crouch we'd seen Teo take on the field earlier. With his free hand, he pushed me backward and said, "Go."

As involuntary as breathing, my body scooted back a few feet, rolled over and scurried in a bear crawl. And then, I pushed myself up to a sprint. I ran toward the light of the bonfire as a growl and thumps vibrated under my feet. Still only half-convinced that I dreamt the whole Teo's a wolf thing, the sting of the pepper spray on my hand told me otherwise.

As the light grew brighter and the breeze cooled my chest, it reminded me about my torn shirt. I clutched my blouse together with one hand and continued running. Alejandro and Gabriel, Joaquin's younger brothers, fell into my view. They stood with their hands in their pockets on the opposite side of the bonfire. I ran straight for them, somehow sure they would keep me safe. Gabriel caught and hugged me close to him. He looked down and noticed the tear in my shirt. I slipped my hands down in an attempt to button my jeans, but my hands shook, making it take longer than usual.

Alejandro asks, "Are you okay? You're shaking."

"Teo's a total creep."

They tensed and stood up a little straighter.

"Joaquin showed up, though," I said.

This made Alejandro's fist unclench. I looked back for the first time at the dark wooded area, then back at them. They exchanged a look, but neither of them made a move toward the woods.

They calmed, once I said Joaquin. I guess they considered the situation controlled. We stood a little uncomfortable about the unspoken words. Alejandro broke the tension by asking how long I'd been at the party. Gabriel pulled my sweater together over my torn blouse and started to button a couple of the top buttons. I finished with shaky hands.

I could see Lexi and Xavier cuddled up on the other side of the crackling fire. They hadn't even noticed me running past—too involved with one another. The need to go over to her flooded me—like a moth to a flame. The boys followed me, one right in front and one behind, like bodyguards.

Lexi looked at me, wincing—my hair a mess and scratches down my neck. A piece of my torn shirt flapped through my sweater. She gawked at me, her mouth agape.

"Where were you?" I demanded.

"Wh-what?"

"You left me alone with him all evening after you promised me! I have let this crap go on too long. I asked one favor. One. You promised!"

Lexi's bottom lip started to quiver. She stood and reached out, trying to hug me. I batted her hands away.

"I'm sorry," she cried. "You seemed to be having a good time."

"It looked like I was having a good time? Are you serious?"

Tears began to flow down Lexi's face, and she shook, the realization of what happened and horror flashed in her eyes. She lifted her hands toward me but stopped at the sight of my glare. Standing here, watching the tears flow from her eyes, the gravity of the situation hits me, and an enormous lump formed in my throat, making me swallow hard to rid the tears threatening to emerge.

At that exact moment, Joaquin came up behind us from out of the trees. He tapped me on the shoulder with a gentle hand. I jumped at his touch, but I turned and fell into his arms. The safe place I wanted to be all night long. My skin is soothed by the warmth and safety of his chest. He squeezed me against his chest, and he gave me a security that I hadn't enjoyed since I left his company at the game. My arms were around his waist, and I clasped my hands together, locking him in my embrace.

Alejandro asked, "What's up, bro?"

He leaned his chin on my head and said, "Oh, I had to squash a bug." They all laughed like they shared some inside joke.

Something slammed behind us with a thunderous boom. Everyone turned to look. Teo returned, shut his cooler and grabbed it off the bench with the blanket.

"Later, y'all!" he said with a fake kind of cheerful, but his voice trembled with rage. He kind of swayed from side to side with a deep scratch across his cheek. He headed straight for me. Joaquin tucked me behind his back and stepped forward.

Teo growled through his teeth, "Let's go, Maria."

"She isn't quite ready to leave. Are you, Maria?" Joaquin gave my hip a squeeze.

My face remained pressed against his back. I shook my head and said, "I'll find my own way home."

"Fine!" he said.

He slammed everything around, stumbling as he headed for his car. He kicked my drink cup out of his way. My only worries were being ostracized by our clique, boys like him could spin a story. After the near-drowning incident made its way all over school, I could visualize how this whole thing would twist and turn in the high school rumor mill. This freak acted like someone did something to him when he tried to rape me.

Joaquin turned and slid his hand down to the small of my back. He leaned down, close to my ear and said, "You don't have to worry, Maria. We'll drive you home and make sure you're safe."

At that moment, I could breathe with less of a struggle. The shakes didn't stop, but I managed them. Tonight could have resulted in a hospital visit, or even a police intervention, because of my bad choices. When I looked deep into his eyes, we were connected. I trusted him with a faith from deep within my core. I threw my arms around his neck and gave him an appreciative hug. His strong arms enveloped me, and I swore his lips grazed the top of my head.

"Thank you," I whispered into his ear. It seemed time for me to let go, so I edged my arms from around his neck.

He whispered in my ear, "Tell me the truth, are you all right?"

I gave a weak nod.

Alejandro's brown eyes lit up. "Sweet, can I drive home?"

"Doubtful. I promised her we would make sure she got home safe," Joaquin said.

Alejandro kicked a rock. "Awe, man."

"Maria, are you ready to go, or did you want to stay a little longer?"

"That's enough *fun* for one night," I said. "How about you?"

"Don't worry about us. We don't ever go to these stupid parties anyway," Alejandro said.

Joaquin elbowed him in the ribs and shot him a little glare. A tickle moved up my arms at the idea he came for one reason, to see me. Joaquin held his hand out to let me go first, but he kept his palm against my back. After all of this, I didn't mind his touch—he arrived at exactly the right time to save me. He wouldn't do anything to hurt me. Something deep within me confirmed it.

His brothers followed us. At the parking area, my purse lies upside down against the SUV. The entire guts of my bag splayed across the dirt. Joaquin picked up the contents and opened the passenger side door. I climbed into my seat, and he handed me my purse. Alejandro and Gabriel got in the back of the SUV; Joaquin got into the driver's seat. It smelled familiar, and it soothed me, my hands steadying. We drove toward town and then headed to highway 116. I gave him directions, but his blinker was flipped before I called the turns. Once we were at my house, he parked in the street out front. He came around and accompanied me to my front porch. He waited as I dug my keys out of my purse. We didn't speak. Even though Joaquin gave me protection, I'd been through the worse situation of my life, and this proximity gave my stomach a tug. My emotions were mixed.

I looked down at the doorknob. My hands shook as I tried to put the key in the door. He reached out and steadied my hand. I whispered, "He's a werewolf?"

I raised my eyes, checking his reflection in the window of the door. He nodded.

"He's an Apache," he explained.

My back still turned to him, and my hand on the door, "And you are...?" I asked.

"Tonkawa," he said.

My mind flew back to my internet search. The answers to the rest of the questions flew by like I flipped through pages from an internet search. What and who he could become was clear, but it didn't change the fact that my instincts were finite. I should have listened. Even my sister warned me. She said to trust the things taught to me by our father. I didn't need to ask him any more questions, but I wanted him to say it. I turned this time to look at him, face-to-face. Staring into his eyes, I searched his soul for a place of truth.

"Are you a—werewolf?" I asked.

"Not really," he said. His eyes never left mine, and the intensity became deeper and stronger between us.

"Shapeshifter?" I said.

"Yes," he answered.

The words burned deep into my soul, and my head started to spin, causing me to wilt. He caught me and put both arms around my waist. My arms flew around his neck. We were face-to-face, millimeters apart. Stepping close, the warmth from his cheek radiated to mine.

Stepping back, I apologized and thanked him for everything. The gratefulness intensified to a point I could never express. My mind displayed a nasty picture of what would've happened if Joaquin showed up a few minutes later. Thankful that the pain in my ass Cindy had invited him. I needed to trust myself. My father, a good judge of character, gave me the tools to use—I needed to summon the courage to use them.

He whispered goodnight and brushed the back of his hand across my cheek, turned and headed for the car. His touch gave me chills, the good kind.

I tiptoed upstairs, flipped the switch on my computer and shot off a quick email to my sister. I told her about the game and Joaquin but downplayed the incident with Teo. I didn't want her to say, "I told you." I fell back in my chair, pulled my knees in tight to my chest and chewed on my thumbnail. I needed some answers, but nothing except this impersonal machine had answers. Clicking the top of the page and opening the Google search page, I started typing. I put in everything from Apache, to Tonkawa, to shapeshifter—and got nothing. Each search pulled up legends and folklore that increased the questions in my mind.

No way. It couldn't be that obvious. My body shook, and I tried to muster up the courage to type the words that scrolled through my mind. I slid in close; my fingers hovered over the keyboard for a moment. I pulled them back and slid them through my hair, then back to the keys as I typed, *Cove Folklore*. The bar at the top spins, and it took a minute before five pages of links appeared on the glowing screen. My head shot up. Sitting in my room, I swore the needled gaze of staring eyes fell on my neck, but it must be paranoia.

Some of the page summaries mentioned werewolves, Apache slaughters, annihilation of the Tonkawa and—shaman. My hands shook. Then without closing any of the links, I closed the browser and shut down my computer. The screen fell dark.

I fell across my bed and stared at the ceiling. My head thumped and spun, made worse by staring at the fan for too long. After laying there for a few minutes, I took a deep breath, pulled myself up, and got dressed for bed. Leaning on the bathroom counter with my hands palm down, I stared for a minute in the mirror at the scratches going from my neck to my chest, tracing the lines with the tip of my finger. The touch stung and made me grimace, and I dug under the sink for some of my best ointment. As I rubbed the cream along the streak, a heat rose from the wound. It started to fade a bit, and I let out a breath.

Luck, and Joaquin, kept me from irreversible harm tonight. In many wonderful ways, Joaquin's presence made me happy. But I couldn't rely on him to save me every time I found myself in a bad situation. I would have to be more careful in the future.

I would not put myself in that situation ever again. I cuddled up in bed, covered myself up and fell asleep.

CHAPTER 6

Saturday morning, my mom stayed in her chair at the small round table under the kitchen window, reading the newspaper and drinking coffee. She dropped the newspaper a smidge to greet me with her usual, "Good morning, sunshine."

After a night filled with flashbacks of Teo's attack, her tone helped my mood. I rolled my eyes.

Neither of us could contain ourselves, and we laughed. This is the part of my mother I missed—the teasing, fun and happy mom.

I plopped a bowl on the counter and filled it with Pops and milk. Slinging open the drawer, a spoon met my hand, and a slight calm crept over me. My abilities brought that serenity to me. The torn clothes were in a plastic bag under my bed, and I'd drawn my bathrobe tight to my collarbone to hide the scratches. Healing small cuts and bruises had become easy for me, but, for some reason, these weren't completely gone.

Mom folded the paper to frame an article and pushed it across the table. The headline read, *Woman Found in Trunk of Wrecked Car*. My eyes bugged. "No way," I glanced at her.

"Read it," she said. "This place is going to the dogs. A little more every week."

The article read that District Attorney Alberto De Luna and Cove Chief of Police received an anonymous phone call leading them to the accident on Lutheran Church Road. The small silver Nissan rolled over at least twice. It threw the driver, an unidentified male, fifty feet from the vehicle. The passenger, a female, was found huddled with her arms around her knees outside the car. When the police opened the trunk, they found the other woman, immobilized and silenced with duct tape.

I dropped the paper and looked at my mom. She sipped her coffee and peered at me over the cup. "This town isn't what it used to be. I've considered moving."

"No," I said. "That isn't normal for here." I pointed my finger down toward the paper. "I am not leaving because of some freaky thing."

She raised her eyebrows but didn't catch my eyes. "Look at what happened to your father," she said. Her expression stayed stoic as she sipped from her cup like any other morning and like we were having a normal conversation. Her cool demeanor made me wonder about the contents of that coffee cup.

Mr. De Luna was the one who collected me from school the day of my father's death. A flash of someone lifting me, then a memory of him close to me. I am almost certain, I saw Joaquin. Joaquin De Luna, of course.

* * *

My mom acted moody all weekend, assuring I would avoid her when possible. The memory of Friday night made me shudder. I broke out my ugliest, favorite, most comfortable sleep pants and pink tank top. Snuggled down under the covers, I willed myself to dream of anything but Teo.

My dreams appeared more vivid—green and tan stalks of grass waving in the wind. An immense field sprawled out before me, filled with brilliant bluebonnets and Indian paintbrushes. The pecan and cottonwood trees lined the field's parameter. They seemed to define the edge of the whole world. Then, as the wind pinned the tall grass close to the ground, my eye caught an animal.

No fear. The adrenaline coursed through my veins. The animal began to glide up close to me. His flanks undulated with the dense, long fur of a wolf, and a gold eye flashed between the stalks of grass.

The most massive animal stood in front of me—and rubbed against my side. A peace came over me and reminded me of how my father's safety kept me in my special place. We lay down on the earth and I rested my head on his rib cage. He warmed and comforted me. I talked to him and it seemed like he talked back. The thump of his heartbeat, the heat radiated from every pore and the sensation of safety…love.

* * *

The beep of my alarm jolted me into Monday. No time to lie in bed and replay the dream all day. I struggled awake, disoriented as if the field were real and my room a dream.

I loaded my things into my Jeep, and as I arrived at the school, I realized I didn't remember anything of the drive. I scanned the parking lot for Lexi—no luck. She must have already gone into the building. I grabbed my things and went straight for my class.

A twinge of unease hit me, and then I spotted Teo.

"Hey," he yelled.

I shook him off. "Get away from me." Before he could catch up with me, I power walked my way to first period. How could he have even tried to talk to me? He must be delusional—or on crack.

Lexi ran toward me, waving and calling my name. "Hey, Maria! I'm glad I caught you."

Bags hung under my eyes, and my face was swollen from the weekend's debacle. My hair in a ponytail, I'd skipped my makeup, and my shirt didn't cover all the marks on my neck. Lexi reached out to tug at my collar, and I jerked back like she'd contracted some contagious disease. She yanked my arm, and we moved in the opposite direction, back toward the parking lot.

"We need to talk," she said.

Instincts forced me to pull my arm away, but I stayed with her, scowling. We headed straight for my Jeep. My stomach clenched. Confrontation made my stomach turn over. Deep down, it pained me to acknowledge that partial blame over the weekend's fiasco belongs to me, too, but I couldn't forgive her. My mind reeled over all the things I still wanted to say to her, but none of them seemed right—all the words were stuck in my throat. We got into my Jeep without a word, and the tension built to an explosion. My hands twisted around the steering wheel, and I hurled accusations.

"You promised. I trusted you to be my friend, be there for me. And you encourage him to take me out for a walk. In the dark."

I could not even look at her until I heard her say, "I'm sorrier than you can imagine."

In a slow, deliberate movement, I turned to face her. Tears streaked her face, and black mascara ran down her cheeks to the crease of her neck. The whole weekend I busied myself with being angry, without giving any consideration to her heavy guilt over her role in Teo's attack. She wanted to apologize and to beg for my forgiveness.

"Maria. I'm sorry. Those are two simple words, but I mean it with my whole heart." She wiped her cheeks with both hands. "It's a lame excuse, but I got caught up—self-absorbed. Engrossed in my conversation with Xavier, I assumed everyone had a great time, too." She tried to steady her voice, but the strain of holding back tears made it shake. Pain flickered in her eyes. "I didn't even notice you were gone. A friend shouldn't do that, but you have to believe I never imagined he'd go that far—to try to…" She covered her face, and I patted her knee. I shouldn't console her. I was the one almost raped, but she acted too horrified to even say the word.

"Rape me," I said.

"I would never have left you alone if I had any idea he would hurt you. It's hard to believe someone in my circle of friends would be so vile." She closed her eyes and balled up her fists.

I cringed at the word *friend*; his name should never be synonymous with that word. He was evil.

"He's a pig." She tried to interrupt, but I held up my hand. "But, I guess you couldn't have known he would go that far." I hurt with a true physical pain and an inner emotional pain. "I was mad at myself, but I tried to put *all* the blame on you—that's not fair."

"Oh, yes, it is—I promised."

"Yes, you did. But I went with him out of your sight. I should have trusted my instincts. He is the only one to blame."

"He's dead to me. You realize that, right?"

I shrugged and wiped a tear falling from my chin.

"No. For real. Jim's been told, without a doubt, Teo is a piece of trash and not to bring him around me. But Jim won't stay away from him." She wiped her eyes. "He's being such a douche. Jim is almost spellbound by him. I hate it."

If truth be told, this made me pause for a moment. I chewed over it, taken aback. Something about Teo made people defy their better judgment—some kind of appeal. He presented a good-looking, all-American guy facade, but something evil lived right under the surface. The outer appearance made you second guess yourself instead of trusting your instincts.

"Look, I will accept your apology under one condition," I said. "We don't bring it up again. I don't want to be reminded of that night. It's over."

After tons of persuasion, she concedes.

I bumped her with my shoulder, and we hugged. She wanted it as far from her mind as I did. We got out of the jeep and headed back to school.

"Are you and Xavier official?" Asking her about Xavier helped me avoid any more questions about what happened.

The smile that swept across her face sent a quiet serenity through me. "Yes, well, I hope we are." She scrunched her face in confusion. "He's great. He came over again on Saturday. Do you mind if I ride home from school with him—if he asks me?"

"Not at all! I can't believe you even asked if I would mind. You better go with him, or I'll kick your butt," I said. Inside, jealousy peeked its head. I wanted time with Joaquin, but the only time I spent with him was the few minutes on Friday night. For a quick moment, I fantasized about spending time with him on a Saturday—watching movies, eating popcorn.

"Thanks, you're the best!" She grabbed my arm and kissed my cheek. I pretended to swoon and fan myself. She landed a playful slap on my arm. "You're silly." We burst out in laughter.

Once inside, we took a detour to the bathroom, cleaned our faces and applied fresh makeup. In true Lexi form, she emerged fresh and beautiful like she hadn't shed a tear in her life. As for me, my reflection revealed a very swollen face.

We jogged to our classes and promised to meet out front after school. Since our records were spotless, no one said much about us being tardy.

* * *

Bent at my locker, a tender caress of a finger slid across my back. A light fingertip was running from one shoulder blade to the other, but it sent shudders up and down my spine. Without a word or a glance, I sensed who stood behind me. I was elated, and I spotted an addiction in the making.

Joaquin said, "Hi."

"Hello." My voice cracked. I ducked my head, letting the loose tendrils of hair fall over my face and hoped no one would see my blood rush to my cheeks.

The bell rang. We had five minutes before we were counted tardy for our last class. "May I walk with you?"

I nodded yes and crossed past him. He held the middle of my back. Telegraphing to everyone around that we were together. We strolled in silence, enjoying being next to one another, and then I stopped at my next classroom. He slid his hand across my back and skimmed his fingertips down my arm until he squeezed my hand. We exchanged glances but no words.

He leaned in to whisper, "I'll see you soon." His lips grazed my ear and sent a literal shock through me—I smiled.

I breezed through my test in last period. The rest of the class left me stuck to my own thoughts—the teachers didn't even trust us to do homework from other classes without somehow trying to cheat. School policy. With all the free time, I replayed the past weekend. The low points were at the forefront of my mind. Then I traveled further back, about a year, to a memory of a time with my father, a time when I messed things up.

I'd gotten mad at him because he told me I couldn't spend the night with my friends. I didn't have many, and when they invited me to a party, I was desperate to go. Everybody would be there. When he left my room, I packed my backpack and sneaked out of my bedroom window onto the patio roof. I swung my legs off the roof and dropped to the ground.

In the pitch dark, I jogged down the road to town. I made it inside the city limits, like two steps past the sign, when the reality struck, I wouldn't make it on foot. I decided to try to hitch a ride. I stuck out my thumb, and a car pulled to the side. I approached in the red light of its taillights. A seedy-looking man opened the passenger door, letting a foul-smelling gray smoke billow out the door. I backed away. He grinned at me and told me to come into the car. At that moment, a car screeched up behind him. I shielded my eyes from the blinding high beams.

Someone bounded toward me, and I backed away. A hand gripped my arm and slammed the guy's door shut. My father dragged me back to the car.

At the house, he pointed to my room, way too angry to even speak to me. I dropped on my bed, rubbed my palms together and waited for his wrath—something that I'd never seen. But tonight, I noticed it in his eyes.

There came an unexpected tap on my door, and my father entered. He pondered in a chair next to my desk with his head down and his elbows on his knees, and then he looked up with tears flooding his eyes—not from anger, but sadness. He told me to consider my actions. He wouldn't be here to bail me out every time. He told me to trust my instincts, something that most people didn't possess, and I needed to tap into those inner impulses. He told me to trust them and trust myself.

The bell pulled me out of my foggy dream-like memory. Those words were long forgotten until this week. But his advice to trust me and my instincts would be heeded.

* * *

When Lexi and I emerged from the building, Joaquin leaned against my Jeep with his ankles crossed and his hands in his pockets. I said goodbye to Lexi, and we split up. I picked up my pace to meet him. He took out one hand and touched me on the arm, sending me right to the edge of an emotional mountain.

"Hey!" I said.

"I see Lexi has made a new friend," he said.

"Yeah," I glanced back at her as she headed to Xavier's car and couldn't help but smile. "She seems happy, and I'm happy for her."

"That's nice for her." He slid his hand down my forearm. "But what about you? Did you talk to her? You seemed pretty mad at her this weekend."

"Yeah. We rumbled. Kidding, we talked, and we're good."

Taking my hand, he smiled at me, his thumb lightly brushing over my knuckles. He smelled of cologne and fresh-cut wood. Heat rose to my cheeks, and I pushed my hair behind my ear, meanwhile wondering, *When did this happen? When did I become that girl?* You've come across the type, the swooning girl who flirts like it's her job. He curled his finger and placed it under my chin, raising my gaze to meet his. I looked over to the black SUV that held his family. They pulled on their seatbelts. My knees bounced, and I chewed the inside of my mouth as I tried to figure out a way to offer him a ride. Mostly, he rode with his family and wouldn't want to go with me. Pulling in a large gulp of air to build up all the courage I could hold, I asked anyway.

"Are you going home with your brothers?"

"Yeah," he said.

"Well, that's too bad," I said, pushing a rock around with the toe of my tennis shoe.

"What do you mean?"

I leaned in and pulled on one of his belt loops. "Well, I wanted you to ride with me."

"That's what you want, huh?" he said.

"Yep," I said. I ran my finger up his stomach and left my hand flat against his rock-hard chest. Every pulse of his heart bumped against my palm, strong and warm. "It would have been nice."

He straightened up and took a deep breath. "Can you wait a minute?"

Without my answer, he left for his car. A thrill of excitement ran through me, and I let out the rush of breath that I'd been holding.

For a quick moment, I lost sight of him. And when I looked up, Teo stood in front of me.

Right there, with an open-collared shirt that showed no trace of Friday's fight. The gash totally healed. He reached out for my shoulder.

"Take your filthy freaking hands off me." I slapped his hand away and backed up. "What the hell do you want?"

"Didn't you hear me call you earlier?"

"What if I did?"

He reached for me again, and I took a step back against the Jeep.

"Well, what're your plans now that Lexi is riding with Xavier?" He waited for an answer. Standing next to him brought hot acid into my mouth. But past his head, I could see Joaquin in a half jog on his way back.

"Not that it's your business, but Joaquin will ride with me," I said.

Joaquin wedged himself into the space between Teo and me, and I settled my hand on his side. With all the animosity boiling behind their eyes, an eruption was sure to follow. The need to keep these two separate overwhelmed me.

"Teo," he said.

"Joaquin," Teo growled through his teeth. "I guess another time."

"Another time," Joaquin said. He stood tall, with one arm against the Jeep, barring Teo's way to me. After Teo backed to a safe distance, Joaquin turned to face me as if nothing transpired.

"Do you need to go straight home?" he asked.

I shook my head. He shook off his anger within seconds, but his antagonism with Teo seemed so habitual that perhaps it didn't rattle him. I shrugged it off, too, not wanting to spoil the afternoon. We got in the Jeep and headed around the path toward the intersection. When we hit the four-way stop, he pointed left toward Highway 116.

"Man, of few words—I get it," I said.

He balled his fist, held it to his mouth and tried to hold back his laughter. "Sorry, well, I would like to take you to a little place I like to

62

go, and—meditate. It'll take a little while to make it there and back. Do you need to call someone? Or… do you even want to go? I guess I should have asked that first."

"I'd love to! It'd be a good idea for me to call my mom."

I reached in the back, still looking forward, and dug through my purse. He grabbed the wheel and held it straight down the road. "Oops," I said. He let go and let me take control. I pulled over to the side of the road, found my mom in my call list and pushed send. I told her not to keep dinner. I would be out late. I pushed end and tossed it back into my purse before she could change her mind and decide to be a mom for a change.

"Where to?" I asked.

"Keep straight," he said.

We drove out of Cove, then turned at the T in the road and headed toward Highway 64. I loved this drive. Warm air rippled in the high grass, sending an almost hypnotic wave across the dry landscape. Where farmland broke the grass, the fields were filled with hay, corn and cotton, or pastures with sheep, cows, horses or even a few alpacas. A place you go to forget—forget about the loss and pain. We crossed several small bridges over the county's winding creeks. To the horizon, there were more plots of land separated by barbed wire. Some entrances were more elaborate than others, ranging from rickety wooden gates to metal gates with brick end posts to ones with stone walls on each side, supporting a rustic Lone Star iron gate.

Joaquin pointed left. He told me we were going to the State Park. All these places right in my backyard, yet I had experienced none of them. Joaquin helped me unroll the top of my Jeep so we could lock it up. I didn't want to have to carry anything with me. While we hiked, I spun my key ring around my finger, not wanting to stuff it into my jeans pocket. Joaquin held out his hand and slipped them into his pocket. We connected with this odd communication that seemed to transcend words, and I smiled.

He held his hand out waist-high with his fingers spread. "Do you mind?"

I took his hand in mine and swung it back and forth like a happy toddler. I leaned into his shoulder and gave him a little nudge. My stomach fluttered. The wind blew, but since the sun was out, it wasn't too cold— perfectly pleasant. Leaning against his arm caused my skin to burn, but it still gave me goosebumps. The summer heat hadn't been too harsh; there were still a few scattered wildflowers. The tall grass bent in the wind. The trees rustled, and leaves fell. A bird sang in the distance, and a couple of big dragonflies buzzed the grass. And, in the moving grass, I could see a hopping bunny.

"I hope you don't mind walking," he said.

To my surprise, I'd dressed right. After the incident with Teo, I went for comfort and concealment. My neck, unlike Teo's, wasn't completely healed. The acute need to impress my new classmates wore off, too. It didn't bother me a bit going to school in my tennis shoes.

"I like walking, but not by myself. I don't like to be alone," I said.

I caught myself giving up a great deal too quickly. I stopped short after my last statement to mull over what I wanted to divulge and what I didn't.

"Well, maybe we could have a conversation and learn a thing or two about one another."

My guard slipped around him. He made me feel safe.

"Hey, I do have one question for you," I said.

"What's that?" he asked.

"Is your dad Alberto De Luna?"

"Yeah, that's my dad." A smile crossed his face. "You must have read the news. He's prosecuting the big case, the one with the lady in the trunk. She's lucky."

He combed his fingers through his hair and looked over at me. "Can you believe her own daughter did that to her?"

"I read the news. Talk about a lucky car crash," I said. He gave me a sideways smile. "Somebody said there were animals on the road. Wolves, maybe."

I looked at him, wanting some answers. I'd grown up hearing about coyotes, raccoons, even wild boars, but never wolves. If the attacks on the people of town were at his hands, I needed to be aware of it. In my heart, the answer rang clear, but my mind struggled to comprehend the whole shape-shifting thing.

"Do you believe in fate?" he asked.

"I do. All things happen for a reason."

He smiled and squeezed my hand. His smile told me that my answer was the desired response.

Ahead of us, a tall, round structure made of native stone stood; a staircase encircled it. As we got close, he let go of my hand, letting me clamber up the steps. He trailed behind me like he wanted to be able to catch me if I fell.

The view amazed me; I stood for a moment and took in all the nature. The wind blew my hair and filled my lungs with fresh warm air. It took my breath. Déjà vu hit me. My memory jolted, and I realized the whole panoramic view came from my dream. From this height, it amazed the eyes. The trees knit together around the perimeter of the field. The dark green pecan trees, Texas burr oak and peaked cottonwood trees lined the outer perimeter of the park. The high grass swayed with each gentle breeze, like an inland ocean. Even though it was hot this August, the summer rain preserved a few bluebonnets—my favorites. I took a deep breath, the scent of mesquite and cedar in the air.

As we stood taking in the view, I heard a familiar cry in the wind. This time I caught a good glimpse of the bird—an enormous eagle. My eyes swept the lot in search of Joaquin, wanting him to see it, too.

"Beautiful, isn't she?" he asked.

"I didn't imagine it?"

He laughed, "No. You're more in tune to nature than most other people. You're sensitive to it—not self-involved. You see the beauty in our world."

We stood for a long moment staring up into the beautiful light blue sky until we lost sight of the soaring raptor in the blazing Texas sun. I cupped my hand above my eyes and tried to find her again—but she left.

"How about a picnic?" Joaquin asked.

The view caught my attention, and I didn't even notice he held a wicker picnic basket. He bounced the basket with his knee once.

"Where did that come from?" I smirked.

"I found it," he said.

I tilted my head to the side. "Seriously?"

"My family brought it out here for us. See—" He tapped on the monogrammed D above the buckle.

"Did you have this planned? You knew I'd come?"

"Not planned—hoped." He smiled.

He reached out, took my hand and pulled me close. I wanted to be close, but it caught me off guard.

"How did they bring this out here?" I asked.

"I can't give away all my secrets," he teased.

We made our way down the stairs and found a shaded spot under a beautiful pecan tree. He spread out the blanket, set the basket in the middle and motioned for me to sit first. Then he laid down and kind of leaned over on one elbow. He opened the basket with his free arm. He pulled out a container of fruit, some forks, a whipped cream dip and two white cups with straws. He handed me one. I took a long draw from the straw and found sweet tea. Most of the ice had melted, but it was still refreshing. As the wind blew through the leaves, little beams of light danced across the blanket around us.

We shared the food; then we took turns feeding each other. I got a smudge of cream on the side of my mouth, and he leaned in and wiped it off. I took some on my finger and touched it to the tip of his nose. I laughed. We fit together—perfect bookends. I loved this atmosphere of elation and hoped that somehow we could stretch this moment into the evening, into tomorrow, into the rest of the year.

We talked, too. filling in all the gaps, small and large—almost all of them. He told me about his family. I told him about my older sister at college, whom I never saw anymore. I found out about his love for soccer. He was like the Teo equivalent to the soccer team. He clued me in on more of our town's history.

Then it happened, he asked me *the* question.

He tapped my leg, "So, how long have you been able to do that little trick of yours?"

"What do you mean?" Making sure not to make eye contact.

"I think we are kind of past pretending." He leaned in close, "You know I can turn into a wolf, but you don't want to talk about spinning a pen and causing a little thunder. Give me a break."

"You saw that, huh?"

"Yeah, I saw that."

"I don't know. I can just do things. My dad helped me out, but now I have nobody to talk to about it." My head bowed, and my hair covered my face, "Sometimes, I feel like a freak."

He pushed my hair back, "You're no freak. You—You are amazing."

Warmth spread across me, and I wanted nothing more than to be right here—right now. I pressed my palm to his chest and felt the warmth and steady beat. My other hand came to my chest. They strummed in perfect time. I pulled my hand back and rubbed them together, then put a rock in my hand and held it tight. I opened my hand, twirled my finger from my other hand over the crushed rock and formed a mini-tornado. Opening both hands, it fell to the ground.

"Ta-da. Impressive don't ya think?"

"I do. Intrigued, too," he said.

He checked his watch and asked if I needed to go back home. Not ready, but it was time. We packed everything back into the basket, folded the blanket into a perfect square, and started back toward the Jeep. He held out his hand and waited for me to take it. I threaded my fingers between his and leaned in a little closer, touching our shoulders together while we moved. All too quickly, we were back at the Jeep and on our way home.

"Take the left, there before the Cowhouse Bridge." He lives on Cowhouse Creek; the legend rang true. I made the connections from all the stories I heard and read.

His driveway crunched with dirt, and trees canopied the path. We drove through a tunnel of shade and then broke through into a clearing to see the huge *hacienda* with a fountain out front. An intricate fountain of ceramic tiles was situated in the center of a circular driveway. The road circled around the fountain and then came back together. On the other side of the fountain stood a massive Spanish style home: a one-story ranch with high ceilings and a red clay roof. Its fence, half brick and half ornate rustic iron, sheltered a type of courtyard with a couple of trees and bright green grass under the shade. The house included two long wings sprouting from a spacious central area. To the far-left rests a large building in the same style as the main house, four garage doors with black metal handles and hinges. There were iron stairs on the side of the garage leading to a second-floor door. The garage was connected to the house by a covered breezeway.

As I marveled, he jumped out of the Jeep. He grabbed the basket from the backseat and sauntered around to my side to open the door. I slid out of my seat and rubbed my hands on my pant legs. My stomach twisted in knots. He slid in close to me, closer than usual. Warmth radiated from him, and his heartbeat pulsated against me in the narrow space between us. It made my own heart rate speed, and a fierce bolt of electricity shot through me. He took a strand of hair from my face and pushed it back with a light touch down the side of my face. As his lip grazed my ear, he whispered, "May I?"

"Sure."

He kissed me on the cheek in the exact place his finger caressed as he pushed my hair away. His lip lingered for an extended moment longer than a usual kiss on the cheek, and it sent chills through my entire body. The electricity from his gentle touch coursed through me, trembling under the skin where his lips touched me and traveling down to my toes. He pulled himself back. "Tomorrow?" he asked.

"I can't wait," I said with a slight crack in my voice.

That statement resonated truer than he could have ever imagined. I stepped back into my Jeep. My eyes lingered on him as he crossed in front of my Jeep and headed to his front door. He grabbed the handle and turned to look back at me. With a wave out the open top, I headed for the highway.

I found myself stopped in the driveway of my home before I wanted this to be over. I got all my things together, and I entered the house. I must have beamed because Mom asked if my day was pleasant.

"More than pleasant. It was a great day," I told her. School wasn't what I expected and then headed upstairs for the night.

I laid across my bed and asked myself, *Am I falling for someone who shouldn't exist—a myth?* He seemed too good to be true.

CHAPTER 7

Nothing held my attention, aside from Joaquin. Absorbed with my new infatuation, I'd forgotten about the incident monopolizing the news. My mom left the paper folded on the counter. I guess she wanted me to pay attention to it because the crime happened too close to our house. I noticed a picture of Mr. De Luna in front of the courthouse lectern. *Wolves in Our County* reads the headline.

The police took a statement from the passenger of the car, who confirmed that she witnessed five large animals in the road before the crash. During additional questioning, she revealed they were wolves. The wolves stood across the entire path, causing the driver to swerve, lose control and turn over. Indeed, the woman in the trunk turned out to be the mother of the passenger. The crime seemed to be foiled by the animals.

"Common sense pokes some holes in the story," they quoted Mr. De Luna as saying. "We will be releasing more information as new facts are uncovered." I throw the paper back on the counter and head for the door.

* * *

The afternoon classes passed faster than the morning ones. I stuffed my backpack in my locker and when I looked up, Joaquin leaned against the next locker with his thumbs in his front pockets. "Do you mind?" he asked.

"Only if you left without me," I said.

69

As we headed out to my Jeep, his palm fell to the middle of my back like it was made to fit there.

"What is on the agenda for today?" I asked.

"Anything you like. We can go for another hike or hang out. What's your preference?"

"Well, that's a tough one. I shouldn't stay out late two days in a row. Would you like to visit my house for a while?" I asked.

"Sounds like a plan. Let's go," he said.

"Do you need to tell your family?" I scanned across the lot but didn't see the huge SUV.

"They're gone," he said.

As we sped around the lot, I caught a vicious stare from the football boys out front. With Joaquin at my side, it made me laugh. I couldn't have cared less.

We made it to my house and found an empty driveway. Mom stayed late at her school for some kind of training, and with being out of education for so long, she works late a lot.

"Is your mom home?" He asked.

"Not yet, but it's fine."

"Maybe we should sit out front until she gets home. That's not the first impression I want to make when I meet your Mom."

"She won't mind," I repeated.

"My family wouldn't approve. Disrespect isn't tolerated. We can sit out here and talk until she arrives," he said.

I shrugged and asked him if he minded waiting while I dropped off my stuff inside. I dumped my stuff right inside the door, ran to the fridge and grabbed a couple cans of soda. Outside, he'd settled into one of the porch chairs and admired my Jeep. I came back and took a seat by him in the other chair and placed the drinks on the table between us.

Words flowed easily. I asked about his Dad's case. He told me they were done with the investigation; they needed to decide on the charges. We talked about the class we shared, and he told me he took it to help with his application for college, too. He wanted to go to The University of Texas. I looked at him, surprised to find another major goal in common. The rest of the conversation flowed.

"Would you mind coming over to meet my parents? I'd love to have you over one weekend. We cook out on Saturday afternoon and they are dying to meet you," he said.

"You told them about me already?"

"Four brothers with two girlfriends. They get told."

"I'll have to ask my mom. Oh, look, here she comes." Her car passed in front of the house and pulled into the garage.

Like being attached to a spring, Joaquin bounced to his feet as my mom moved toward him on the porch. The first light I'd seen in her eyes for months shines when I smile.

"Did you forget your key?" she asked.

Joaquin said, "No, ma'am, my parents wouldn't appreciate me going into your home before I met you. It wouldn't make an appropriate first impression if you were startled by some stranger in your house." He held out his hand. "I would like to introduce myself. My name is Joaquin De Luna." It made me smile to hear him pronounce his name with his slight accent—it sounded romantic as the words rolled from his tongue.

She took his hand. "How polite, Joaquin. It's not often you meet a young person with such respect and manners. Would you like to come in?" The most upbeat thing she's said in months as if a teenage boy on her porch awoke her from the dark place she'd retreated to when my father died.

"Yes, ma'am, but I can't stay too long. I need to get home for dinner." He stepped to the side, letting both of us head into the house ahead of him.

I stepped up onto the first step of our staircase, giving him a tiny grin as if to say, *Are those manners for real?* "Would you like to come up?" I asked.

He shook his head. "I would rather sit down here if you don't mind."

A little deflated, I stepped back down off the first step and started toward the living room. "OK, this way." We slouched out on the sofa, and I turned on *The Nature Channel*.

A light went off in my mom's head. "De Luna? Are you related to Alberto De Luna?"

71

Mom entered the kitchen. Joaquin leaned over the back of the couch and said, "Yes, ma'am."

"He's a kind man. Give him our best."

He placed his hand over the top of my hand and squeezed, giving me a silent clue that our time together expired. I popped up.

"Mom, I need to take Joaquin home. I stole him from his brothers for the day."

"OK, honey, be careful," she said, wiping her hands off on the dishtowel. "Nice to meet you, Joaquin. It's nice to see Maria has some new friends. It's been a tough year."

I shot her my *be quiet* stare and shook my head. He told her it was nice to meet her, too. She stopped speaking and returned to her work.

He held his arm out, letting me lead the way to the door. We went outside and got onto the highway. Too soon, I turned into his driveway. All the while daydreaming about how this evening would end—maybe with a kiss. To some people, I'd received a simple kiss on the cheek, but to me, it represented loads more.

At his front door, I stopped the engine and removed my key. He jumped out and strolled around to my side of the Jeep. My heart was about to jump into my throat. As before, he pushed my hair back out of my face. His fingertips grazed my forehead, my temple and my cheek. This time my face was heated and flushed. His fingers continued to trace along my jaw and down to lift my chin. He leaned in. Warm breath brushed my skin, and his lips met my cheek. They lingered even longer than the first time—all I wanted was to turn my head and meet his lips with mine. My knees bounced a little, but his arm came around my waist to steady me. He pulled back with a serious look on his face. Our eyes fixed on each other.

"Goodnight," he whispered.

Breathless, I smiled back—I drank in every moment.

"Be careful going home. I hate you being out after dark." He ran the back of his hand across my cheek. "Can I pick you up and drive you to school tomorrow?"

"Sure. I'd love that."

"I guess I'll see you in the morning," he said.

As he walked to his door, I fumbled to insert the key back into the ignition. He turned, and I waved as I headed down the drive. It gave the impression of something important. I'd done the same thing before—we made it a ritual, a language for being together. I stopped at the end of the drive and put my head on the wheel to allow myself time to pull myself together before I drove home.

"You can't stay out this late," Mom said.

"I won't," I said. "Also, Joaquin's picking me up tomorrow."

"Well, OK then," she said, then took a long swig of her wine. Some of the darkness left her eyes. He put both of us at ease.

* * *

The next morning, Joaquin made it right on time. Mom gave a puzzled look at the doorbell.

"Joaquin," I said.

"Oh, yeah. I forgot," she flapped her hands at me. Wine's not really conducive for conversation. "Be safe."

"I will, Momma," I said and kissed her cheek as I ran for the door.

He wrapped his arm around me, and I snuggled close on our way to the street, taken aback by the view. Expecting the black SUV full of his family, instead, a black convertible Mustang sat next to the curb. He moved around to the passenger side and opened my door; I slid into the leather seat. It seemed to close in around me like a warm winter glove. I wiggled a little, like cuddling up in my bed. With that stroll of his, he made his way around the car. Starting the engine, we headed to school.

"Please tell me you at least have an ugly pair of pajamas or something," I said.

He grinned. "Sure. Who doesn't?"

"What's up with the animal attacks?"

"It's not the first. It made news because of the wolves causing that wreck. People want to make them related," he said.

"Are they related?"

"No," he said, and I sighed in relief.

He reached over with his hand out. "May I?" I gave him my hand, and a warmth traveled over my entire body.

I said, "You don't have to ask anymore. Take charge and just grab ahold."

In a few quick minutes, we drove into the school parking lot. He parked, and before I could blink, he opened my car door. He led me into the building with his hand. Out of the corner of my eye, I caught sight of Teo glaring at me. The *wind* accelerated, and a trash barrel slid in his path. I lifted my chin and passed right by him, but not before I noticed a long deep scratch on his face. Did another girl claw her way out of a relationship with him? Joaquin's hand gave me safety, a similar sensation to the presence my father brought.

During social studies class, the teacher announced a new assignment. We would be building a family tree—and part of the assignment would be to find out where we'd gotten some of our dominant features, like eye color, hair color, face shape—that kind of thing. As she started to hand out the instructions, Joaquin raised his hand and murmured something to Mrs. Hayes. A deep look of concern flashed across her face, and she patted his arm.

I heard her say, "It's your choice. This is more about the research process than the information you obtain." He looked over at me and gave me a smile.

He must have asked about his missing ancestry. I cannot imagine how hard that would be to explain to the outside world. From my research, I'd learned of his family's slaughter. Records revealed less than fifty people were left from his tribe. Today, they lived in secret, and advertising his lineage for the likes of Teo could be detrimental. Another connection between us; most of my family passed on, too, and the few on my mother's side fell out of touch. It made our little family seem smaller and fragile.

The papers made it back to our desk, and I read over the outline. We needed some marriage certificates, birth certificates and pictures. Each item past our immediate family would gain us extra credit. The research made this an important assignment—the deeper you dug, the better your grade.

"Looks like we have some work to do," I said to him, smiling.

* * *

After school, Joaquin and I decided to go home and dive into our assignment. I didn't spend a great deal of time with my grandparents or the rest of my extended family, making this project tough but interesting.

As we pulled out of the parking lot, though, I heard from Teo one more time. A car horn sounded behind us, and Teo and Jim drove up beside me and waved down from the behemoth truck. They smiled like we were best friends or something. It made me sick to my stomach, watching Jim still being friends with Teo.

Joaquin squealed the tires out of the lot and headed toward my house, away from Jim and Teo. "You all right, sweetheart?" he asked.

A little stunned by being called *sweetheart*, I said, "He invited me to that party, right?" He nodded, and I continued. "I don't like to recall my stupid decision, but sometimes my mind wonders…Did Teo plan to try and do that to me?"

Joaquin ducked his head and began to fidget with the steering wheel. "Something about the idea of you at that party bothered me. That's why—part of why, I decided to show up."

"When you came up, I'd gotten loose from him. I'm not sure what you got a glimpse of, but things went bad. He isn't—He's no gentleman, I'll put it that way," I said.

Sweat formed on my upper lip, and a flushness crept up my neck as visions of that horrid night flashed in my memory. Unable to look at Joaquin, I turned to face the window and let my hair fall over my face. My voice cracked as I said, "How stupid am I?"

Joaquin's hand touched my arm, and I jumped. He recoiled. After a moment, he slid his hand over and took mine. I let him, but I couldn't look at him while I spoke. The horror splashed across my face, and the tears that filled my eyes revealed more than any of the words coming from my mouth.

"He said he wanted to go for a walk—a walk, right." I shook my head, having a hard time believing I had been that naive. "I went. Next, the flashlight was off, it was pitch dark, and I'm trapped against a tree. I tried to fight him off. Honestly." Tears fell, and my shoulders began to heave in a heavy sob. I took frequent breaths to push the choppy sentences out. "He kissed me." I cringed, saying the words. "His hands were—everywhere. We struggled and fell to the ground, and he climbed on top of me. I tried to fight him off—I tried." I glanced in his direction to collect his reaction. Rage crossed his face, causing me to look back toward the window. "Are—are you mad at me?"

He rubbed his thumb across the top of my hand and gave it a squeeze, "No. No way. You didn't do anything wrong. It should have never happened." He ran his hand through his hair and sighed. "I'm a little mad at myself for not getting there sooner. And words cannot describe my revulsion toward him."

I tried to look at him, but pain struck me. "Honest. I wish you would have gone with us. But it is what it is." I shook my head and wiped my face with the palm of my hand. Joaquin opened the center console and gave me a small package of tissues. I wiped my face and began again. "Anyway, I carried along pepper spray, and I used it. Then I searched for a rock and used it and my nails to fend him off." I took a deep breath. "Then you appeared, and I ran. Did Gabriel tell you about my shirt? I'm glad I brought my sweater."

"He told me," he said. Comfort came to me as he squeezed my hand, pulled it to his lips and then set our hands on my knee. His hand jumped, and he moved it back to the console. I took his hand and pulled it back to my knee. A smile crossed his face, and he spread his hand on my knee, telling me with his touch that all that was over. He would keep me safe. I wanted to believe it.

* * *

At my house, he jumped out of the car, did a little turn and opened my door. The out of character gesture helped my mood. I laughed out loud. He held his hand out, and I took it, happy to see some of his seriousness fade away.

We went inside and pulled out our assignment. We filled in the easy parts first—our immediate family. Then, things got a little tricky. Anything else would require help, and I wasn't getting that these days. I waited there with my head in my hands, looking at all the blank spaces, then I looked up. Joaquin filled out more than half of his paper with no aide. He even wrote most of the birthdates.

"Our family is really close," he said.

"I haven't even met much of mine," I shrugged. "Well, I've got some names, but most of them passed away before I was born. I have one aunt on my mom's side, but she and my mom fell out of touch, and they don't speak."

"Well, do you have a Bible with one of those family trees? Or do you have a lockbox where your mom keeps important papers?"

"Oh, yeah," I said.

Quickly, I ran upstairs to my mother's bedroom and the trunk placed at the end of her bed. I looked around the room for something to help me turn the lock. Then, I pointed my finger at the lock and made a turning motion. With a click, the lock popped open, and I smiled. My tricks came in handy from time to time. The trunk held an old, round hat box that she took out during the weeks after my father's death. I opened it up and hit the jackpot—a treasure trunk filled with yellowed papers, marriage certificates, birth certificate, and some black and white photos.

One, in particular, caught my eye tattered on the edges with yellowed paper. I flipped it over; nothing was written on the back. But it did have a fancy calligraphy "R." I assumed they were my father's family. Then, I remembered Teo's wrist. My head shook, no way it was related. The man is in a dark suit with a hat. His hair is slicked back on the side and seems long and was pulled into a sleek low ponytail. His facial features are sharp; his expression is stern. The woman looks a lot like Theresa and me. Long hair pulled into a puffy bun with some curls hanging. Her dress is white with layers of lace ruffles at the collar and long lace sleeves. She has a hint of a smile, and her eyes are warm. They must be my great or great-great-grandparents. I dropped it back into the box and headed back to Joaquin.

Downstairs in the living room, I dug through the papers. I found some wedding pictures and held them up for Joaquin to see. I found a picture of mom and dad from high school. I covered my mouth to stifle a laugh—Dad's hair grown long and pulled back into a neat slick ponytail—awfully Steven Seagal. And Mom's hair hung super long, straight to her waist with what looks like a hint of a thin feather on one side. Frozen in laughter as they relaxed on a small wooden dock next to a river.

I dug out one of the documents and found a marriage certificate delicate from age, yellow and brittle. My eyebrows pulled together, and I rubbed my forehead, the name on their certificate said Rios.

"What are you doing?" The voice startled me.

Mom stomped over and snatched the papers from my hands and threw them into the box and shut the lid.

"We need to fill out a family tree for class." I held up my assignment sheet.

Mom stepped over to the bookshelf, pulled out a thick Bible and plopped it down on the table with a huge thud. "Use this! No more snooping—got it?"

"Yes, ma'am," I said.

After that little display, Joaquin decided to hit the road. At the door, he rubbed my back and acted unfazed by my mother's psychotic behavior, but I was mortified.

"I'm totally sorry," I said. He held his finger up to my lips.

"Can I pick you up tomorrow?" he asked, backing away from me.

"Seriously, you don't have to ask anymore. I'll be waiting," I said.

We made it out the front door to the porch. I bounced around a bit, and he caught my hand. He pulled my hand behind his back and tugged until I pressed up against him, touching his warm chest against mine. With his free hand, he ran his fingers down the side of my face, pushing my hair back. He placed a soft, warm kiss on my cheek, then turned his face to the right, then pressed our cheeks against each other for a long moment. Warmth spread through my entire body. I wrapped my free hand around his neck and ran my fingers through his short, silky hair and grabbed a handful. Wishing I could force him to stay pressed against me. He pulled his head back, and like magnets, our lips touched. His lips moved soft and warm against mine. My hand pulled his head closer. As close as we were, it wasn't enough. Heart thumping against my ribs, my breaths become shallow.

My excitement must have made him happy because the biggest smile I'd ever seen appeared on his face. His cheeks were tinged a rose color. I couldn't believe it. I'd made Joaquin De Luna blush.

CHAPTER 8

That air of euphoria fled as soon as I took a step back through our front door, and my mother beckoned me to the kitchen. Argh! My head jerked downward, followed by a sensation like a punch in the stomach. Mom stood facing the window over the sink—an opened wine bottle in one hand and a half-empty wine glass in the other. She took a swig.

Typical of my mother. If she's pissed—she drinks. If she's sad—she drinks. If she's upset—she drinks. On the rare happy occasion—she drinks. I rolled my eyes with a huff, not needing any of her crap.

"Maria, I'm sorry I embarrassed you in front of your friend. I don't mean to be harsh, but some of my things have to remain private. There'll come a time when I let you see everything in that box but now isn't the time. Can you understand?"

"Yes, ma'am," the politeness is from habit, "—but it's for school."

"You should have asked." She turned to look at me, but she drained her glass before she spoke again. "You and your father talked many times over the years, right?" My head pops up, surprised she knows about our personal conversations, "Don't look so shocked. Do you remember?"

I nodded my head. The mention of my father and our times together made my eyes burn, and it took everything inside of me to hold back the tears. Dad was the easy one, the nice one. I never imagined he'd die before I got the chance to say goodbye before I could figure out how to make it work with Mom.

"Well," she said, "there are more things he wanted—he needed—to say. Now, I'll be the one to talk to you, and some of the things in those boxes are things we'll have a talk about. It isn't time, though. Your father and I had many conversations about this. I made promises. And I'm not ready. Do you see where I'm coming from?"

As soon as I opened my mouth, the tears began to flow. "It wasn't like I tried to be disrespectful or snoop. I needed information for my paper—for school, and I remembered where you kept pictures and stuff." My voice shook and broke the more I spoke and tried to hold back the tears. Then I said, "I'm sorry."

She stepped toward me and touched my shoulder. My body moved involuntarily away from her touch—a touch I once loved more than anything else. Then she moved back to the counter to refill her glass and sucks down another drink. "I understand you have a paper, but some things are private. I'll pull out a couple of things for your paper." Just like that, she dismissed me and my feelings as trite.

"Thank you, and sorry." *I guess.* I grabbed my books and took the stairs two at a time.

My words were apologetic, but they didn't quite reach my heart. Things were different. It was schoolwork, and I didn't do anything wrong. Her over-the-top reaction made me even more curious about the contents of those papers. I love my mother, even with her being unreasonable. Mom missed my Dad, and she got a job. It all makes her edgy. Not my fault by any means. I *would* look through her stuff again. It was my Dad's stuff, too.

But when I passed her bedroom and cast a glance at the trunk, she added a new padlock. Giving my fingers a wiggle, the lock fell open with a thud. My little heads up for her—she would have to do better than that to keep me out.

* * *

Soccer season started. Meaning the boys, Joaquin and his brothers, would be playing every afternoon. Our after-school visits would be slashed to a bare minimum. Not wanting to miss any available time with him, I stayed for their practices. Sitting in the stands, I worked on my homework. Even aluminum bleachers and homework were better than the sour looks and drunken spats from my mother. To make a place work, I took a seat where I could put my feet and my books on the seat in front of me, like a desk. This meant I could stop on occasion for a quick glance at his drills on the field—just a little thrill, and totally worth it.

Marisol and Alyssa would come some days. It seemed like Marisol came because she didn't want me to sit alone all the time, and Alyssa came because of Marisol. Not that she liked me, the sour looks on her face proved it to me, along with her aloof attitude, made me wish she'd just skip the whole *I'm here out of obligation* thing and just go home. She flopped down and flipped through her cell phone. Nothing she did could be considered caddy or mean, just cold.

"Watching practice, again?" Marisol asked.

"Hi, Maria," Alyssa said.

They settled next to me with a vibrating bump. I tried to feign interest in my schoolwork, but as Joaquin stripped his T-shirt off and tossed it to the fence, my breath caught. The small intake of breath didn't go unnoticed. Marisol giggled, and Alyssa huffed. Not that I cared what anyone thought. Joaquin without a shirt was a pleasant sight, with his defined back, small waist and the tight rippled muscles that stretched across his stomach. Enough, it'll make me fall of the end of the bleachers.

"Yum! You're the lucky one today," Marisol said. "No. No, wait."

Micael walked over to the fence in front of us. He removed his shirt with the skill of a male model revealing another muscular body. With a wink at Marisol, he hung his shirt over the fence and ran back toward the group.

"Thank you, baby! Got to love the fact that they are hot natured. God's little gift to my eyes," she said.

Marisol's eye sparkled as she watched her boyfriend with what I can only describe as pure teenage hormonal lust. The fact that she was unashamed was admirable. I could really start to like this girl.

Personalities aside, one might assume these girls were twins, or at the very least sisters. Flawless skin and makeup applied to perfection, giving them a more mature look than the other students. With outfit styles more like *Vogue* than *Seventeen*. With all that perfection, Marisol always seemed to find something about me to compliment, even if it was my bag or jewelry. A more authentic version of Cindy.

* * *

On our way home from school on Friday, Joaquin reminded me he wanted me to come over for a cookout with his family. Busted. No more avoidance. I would meet his parents. The thought of it brought burning bile up into my throat, and my hands started to sweat.

"Should I ask your mother?" he asked.

"No, I'm sure it'll be fine. She pretty much trusts you over me," I tease.

As he turned on my road, a smirk spread across his face. Much sooner than I hoped, we were in front of my house. He sauntered around to my side of the car. The sun slid below one of the five hills, leaving our neighborhood in a dusky shade of darkness.

The absence of my mother's car gave me an odd chill. Joaquin, with all his chivalry, came inside with me to check things out. His caution gave me a Zen-style peace. As we walked through the house, I wound my fist into the back of his T-shirt. We traveled from room to room. He even checked the upstairs, the dreaded place branded off-limits—according to him.

"Do you mind staying until mom makes it home?" I asked.

"No, I don't mind." He gave me a full-on wrap-around hug. "I hate the thought of you here alone. But I do need to call home."

He called home, and my hand hovered over stuff on my desk, moving things around while he had his conversation. As he hung up the phone. I threw my arms around his neck, catching him off guard, and he staggered back a step. But he righted himself and slid his hands to the small of my back. His cheek pressed to mine, he slid his arms further around my waist, crossing them behind me, and lifted me into the air. My body almost becoming one with his as I melted. And then, he quickly dropped me to my feet. Strong hands slid to my hipbones, urging me to let go.

"Come to my room," I said.

"Not a good idea," he said.

"It's about time you cut out worrying about how things look. Nobodies around. Just come to my room and wait for me to change. Five minutes, tops."

He agreed. I grabbed his hand and led him to my room before he changed his mind, then I stepped back out to the bathroom.

In my bathroom, I threw on flannel pants and a T-shirt. When I stepped back into my room, he'd settled down on the side of my bed. His eyes opened a little wider when I touched him. The smile on his face turned serious.

I moved toward him. I let my knees bump his like a guy fist bump. His warm hands slid down my arms from elbows to hands. Our fingers weaved together; I squeezed back. This is exactly where I wanted to be. I couldn't take the anticipation any longer. My body leaned into his. He stilled but didn't pull away; his hands gripped mine tighter. Warm lips met mine, and the kiss started out with a soft feather touch. Freeing my hands, he wrapped his arms around my waist, pulling me in tight. My arms flew around his neck, and I pressed my body into him harder and harder until we fell backward onto my bed. The warmth only increased the need to be close to him. Our embrace tightened; his strength just short of painful.

We stopped kissing for a moment, catching our breaths. I pushed up on my elbows and basked in the warm attention of his eyes. He let down his guard and allowed me more than one kiss. But the need was clear in his eyes; he straightened up and pulled me sideways onto his lap. Like many times before, he caressed my face with his fingertips. Over my forehead, down my temple and cheek. The trail continued to my jaw, and he pulled my chin toward him for another kiss. Next, he pressed his lips against the skin on my neck under my ear, sending a jolt down my body.

He whispered, "I hate to spoil the fun, but we need to go downstairs. This could turn bad really quick." My head dropped. He urged me to look at him. "I care about you. I don't want to mess up and tick off your mom." He touched his forehead to mine. "Plus, I want to keep this special. You and me."

All the years of *worth the wait* classes in Catholic school ingrained restraint in me, but I never realized how difficult he would make waiting.

He grabbed my hand and led me to the living room. I switched on the TV. Then, I curled my legs under me on the couch and laid my head on his shoulder. I couldn't believe how strong his shoulders were or how comfortable.

He kissed the top of my head and whispered, "You're killin' me—you know that, right?"

His eyes blazed a wildness that made it hard to look away. I picked at the nonexistent lint on my pajama pants. Trying to hide the blood rushing to my cheeks. It was kind of nice knowing this whole restraint thing was hard for him as well. He leaned into me.

We heard keys rattling in the lock of the front door. Just like that, the moment was stymied.

Mom. She thanked Joaquin for staying. We all stood at the door saying our goodbyes when a knock at the door startled us. Mom peered out, then opened it.

Lexi stood there, distraught. "There's police everywhere," she said.

"What? What do you mean?" My mom let her enter. She explained that there were police searching up and down the road to her house and multiple sheriffs' cars in the driveway at their home.

"I couldn't even turn into our drive. There were patrol cars from like three counties," she said.

Mother made a perfunctory sound of surprise and then excused herself to bed. Her behavior came off so glaringly rude that even Lexi noticed. I shrugged. I couldn't explain why she seemed almost unaffected by the situation, either. The smell of mints and a hint of alcohol told me there was more to her rage than the news about patrol cars.

"Let's get you home," I said to Lexi.

I rode with her to her house, and Joaquin followed close behind us. Things seemed to have calmed down. A few patrol vehicles remained. We crawled our way down the drive to her house. I got out, and she gave me a big hug.

"Jim has been sick," she said, out of Joaquin's hearing. Honestly, I hadn't even noticed he missed school.

"What's wrong?"

"They have done tons of tests, but none of them are coming up with any answers. It has something to do with this cut he has on his shoulder—some kind of weird infection, maybe from the lake. They have him on antibiotics, but I can't even visit. He's an ass, but he's my cousin."

For the first time, concern for her cousin showed on her face. They were family, and on that level, I could sympathize, even if I didn't like him or his best friend. I hugged her again. Then, I jogged to Joaquin's car, and we pulled out of the drive. Looking back at Joaquin made me wonder if driving onto the land Jim lived on bothered him.

Joaquin took my hand, seeing the look across my face.

"Jim's sick," I said.

"He hasn't been to school for a while," he said.

My mind spun. Flashes of him coming out of the water, bleeding. In my half-conscious state, I'd sworn something bit him on the shoulder.

* * *

Lexi and I each spent time wrapped up in our new relationships, we neglected our friendship. When she called me to talk, we engulfed ourselves in conversation. Mom had been *working* late all week and still hadn't made it home, and Joaquin had to do something with his brothers. I needed some girl talk.

"I'm going over to Joaquin's for dinner," I blurted out without stopping to breathe.

"Well, this is getting interesting. You better call me the minute—no, the exact second—you leave his house and tell me everything," she chirped.

I laughed.

"No, for real. That family is perfection—so be on the lookout for something out of place. A crooked towel in a bathroom, a crack in the wall, or a body in the closet," she insisted.

"Shut up."

The front door rattled and flung open. Mom literally stumbled into the kitchen. "Hello!"

I asked Lexi to hold on and talked to my mother with the phone clutched to my chest.

"Another meeting?" I growled.

"Yes. We stayed for a safety meeting about all the animal attacks."

I prayed she would stay in the kitchen to hide the smell, and that Lexi didn't notice her slurred words.

"It took longer than I expected," she said.

"Oh," I said.

"Sorry. I'm back. Mom had a late meeting about those animal attacks."

"Uncle James told me the attacks are due to mating season. And that they have to come in close to town because of the drought. He said they are more ferocious this time of year and become out of control if they're hungry. They attack other animals and people. He says it'll get worse."

I rubbed my neck where Teo left me a little reminder mark of his attack. The line was faintly pink, but there was a real scar on me—one that wouldn't fade.

"Lex, I better go," I said.

"I'll see you soon," Lexi said.

"It was nice talking to you."

"Yeah. This was nice. Later," she said.

Mom basically said goodnight and staggered up the stairs, and I followed with my hand hovering around the middle of her back—just in case.

In my room, I open my email account and sent off a quick email to Theresa, letting her in on Joaquin's invitation and leaving her with a promise to write again soon. I fell back onto my bed and let myself slink into meditation.

Theresa sunk deep into depression and closed herself off from me, and I missed her, but before I could get down on myself, my cell phone started to buzz. Theresa. I picked it up and expected a fun conversation about my upcoming visit with Joaquin's family, but her voice sounded almost frantic.

"Slow down! What happened?"

"Are you upstairs? Away from Mom?"

"Yeah, I'm in my room."

"Something's wrong. I mean, like big-time wrong. This creepy guy came to the door three days ago. I checked the peephole. He told me he worked for the census bureau, but he started to ask all these personal questions about us—me and you. Who our grandparents were and about our *real* last name. I told him Richards, of course, and told him to get lost. But he seemed adamant that I gave him false information. I told him to leave, or I'd call the cops."

"What? That's freaking crazy."

"The creep left. Problem is, I keep seeing him prowling around, and this horrible sensation sinks into the pit of my stomach when I see him. Maria—I know he's around before I see him. I—I sense him. And tonight, I swear he peered through my window."

"Did you call the police?"

"No. I have this fear that they can't help me. Dad used to be all freaky about strangers, and this makes me understand him a little more."

"T, what does he look like?"

"It's weird. If I didn't get this bad vibe, I would consider him handsome. He has black hair and dark eyes—muscular, tall, but not too tall."

"How old does he look?"

"In his twenties. Older than me."

Not Teo, I told myself. But all of this sounded too familiar. "I don't want you to be alone. Let me call Joaquin, and we'll come up to visit. I'll tell mom you invited me to a festival. She came in piss drunk, so it'll be a breeze."

"I hate for you to have to do that for me."

"T, I am coming. I will call you right back."

I hung up the phone and called Joaquin. He told me his cousin lives in Austin while he attends The University of Texas. He would send his cousin, Jose, over to her apartment. I gave him the address, and Joaquin said he would come right over. While I waited for Joaquin, I called Theresa back and told her to let Jose in as soon as he got to her house.

Joaquin arrived at my door in minutes. I told my mom I wanted to go visit Theresa and that I would stay the night. Mom gave a sloppy wave, as usual. Too tipsy to notice the time or ask questions.

* * *

On the way to Austin, Joaquin reached over and took my hand. His warmth calmed me, but we didn't talk during the drive. At the apartment complex, Joaquin stiffened and told me to wait in the car. He slipped to the side of her building, and I watched someone bolt across the parking lot. Then, Joaquin casually strolled out to the car and opened my door. Inside, Jose sat on the couch, consoling Theresa. Looking jarringly similar to Joaquin, they could be brothers. Theresa sat clutching her knees, crying. As soon as I entered, I fell onto the couch beside her and wrapped my arms around her.

"What happened?"

Theresa shook her head. Jose said, "When I got here, he scurried away from the door. I came inside, and she fell apart."

I asked her if she wanted to come home with us. She shook her head. I understood. Coming home to no dad and an absent mother wouldn't help her forget her problems. But I promised that Joaquin and I would stay the night with her. She rented a two-bedroom apartment. In light of the possible danger, Jose offered to stay until we figured out this situation and identified this whack job. However long it took. She didn't hesitate for a moment to agree. Since Joaquin and I were here, Jose went to his dorm room to pack up.

After I'd made some tea and played with her hair for a while, Theresa stopped crying. We talked about everything from the whack-a-do stalker to her classes this semester. She joked, "It's nice to have you visit—but too bad it takes a psycho stalker to bring us together."

Jose returned with Chinese food and a DVD. He picked out *Step Up*. We were happy enough with his choice. Besides what girl doesn't like Channing Tatum? Theresa and I slipped into the bedroom to change into comfy clothes, and we ate around the coffee table. Joaquin's usual tense nature began to melt away.

At bedtime, Theresa and I took her room. Jose settled into the extra room, and Joaquin took the couch. The boys' presence exuded safety and made me glad Joaquin's cousin could help my sister. My dad gave us safety, these boys gave me a peaceful feeling—and my instincts gave me a special little inside.

In bed, I whispered, "Jose is super hot."

Theresa elbowed me. "Ya think."

We both giggled but covered our mouths, keeping the boys from hearing. Then, we heard a scratch at the window. We both stiffened. The bedroom door flew open. Joaquin sprinted to the window with Jose on his heels.

They looked at each other and told us to stay put. Without another word, they sprinted out the front door. Clicking the lock and sliding the chain behind them, theresa peeked out of the window to figure out the situation. Me, I stood back and started a chant—one my dad taught me for protection. Eyes glowed in the window, and an outline of a limb or a body moving in the shadows. Then heavy footsteps moved away from the window.

In a few minutes, the boys knocked on the door.

"Well, they're gone," Joaquin said.

"They?"

"He recruited a friend. They won't be back for a while."

"Are you sure you don't want to come home?" I asked Theresa.

"I have work and school. I can't," she said.

Jose said, "I'll take care of her if she stays here." He reached over and hugged my sister, who seemed to dissolve into him. And he squeezed her tighter. It reminded me of the night Joaquin saved me from Teo. Hoping he gave her the same safety.

Before we settled back into bed, I went to the kitchen with Theresa. My abilities were the strongest, but dad had taught her potions. She was awesome at it. We pulled out the clear bottles and got to work. Twine was wrapped around a bundle of lavender—all we had to do was dip it into the oil we mixed. Lavender was actually for love, but the oil was the important part. Plus, while Jose was here—two birds, one stone. Lighting the end with the oil, we waved the bundle around each room, and I whipped ash around the windowsills and door frame. This, along with Jose's presence, made me feel better. Joaquin decided to sleep on the floor under the window in Theresa's room.

In the morning, Joaquin and I left. On the drive home, I asked him, "Can Jose *really* protect my sister?"

Joaquin took my hand and squeezed. "She's safe. Trust me."

Nothing else was needed. I sensed it. Jose would be my sister's protector—the same as Joaquin guarded me.

* * *

I needed to find an outfit for my visit with Joaquin's family—something to impress a family who owned a palace on more land than the eye could see. In the end, I decided to take my mother's advice and be myself—hard to believe. I grabbed my best pair of jeans and threw them on my bed. The app on my phone said it would be cool, almost cold. I pulled out my belt, boots to match, a black tank top with lace along the bottom and a black turtleneck. From my jewelry box, I selected a silver butterfly necklace—a perfect match to the butterflies that fluttered in my stomach.

The moment I checked my outfit in the full-length mirror, the doorbell rang. I grabbed my short black leather jacket and bounded down the stairs. Joaquin stood there, beaming. With a yell, I told mom we were off and that I loved her.

These days, we held hands like they were Legos made to fit together.

"You look amazing. Nervous?" He asked.

"Ya noticed, huh. I hope I don't pass out."

"I'll catch you," he said. He pulled past the fountain in front of his *hacienda* and glided into a spot near the garage.

"Are you sure my outfit is OK?"

"It's lunch and a day on our land, not some kind of formal dance." His elbow gave me a gentle tap. "Come on, lighten up. It's all good. They're dying to meet you."

91

I gave a partial smile. "A dinner with eight people's eyes scrutinizing my every move—opportunity of a lifetime."

"I'm the one you need to impress—and that's done. My family is excited that I found someone that makes me happy. They don't have any crazy expectations. You don't howl at the moon or anything, do you? Oh. Wait. That's me. I guess you're good." He squeezed my hand and pulled it toward him for a kiss. "They'll agree that you're great."

I entered the *hacienda* for the first time. In the entryway, one object, in particular, caught my eye: a painting of a wolf. A brass plaque beneath it reads,

> *In Africa, there is a folk story about the lion and the antelope. It says that in order to survive, when the sun comes up, you better be running.*
>
> *On our continent, we take our lessons from the wolf. In a pack, it is the most dangerous animal in the world. That is why in America, and especially in Texas, we don't run—we stand and fight. (Painting by J. Brown.)*

J. Brown was a famous Central Texas artist. That should have been my clue of things to come, but he asked me, "Are you ready?"

I sighed. I said, "Mm-hmm. My howl is almost perfected."

He laughed. "C'mon, you."

We slipped through an arched door and into a massive living area. I tried to take it all in, the Spanish style fireplace, the mix of Texas and Mexican décor, the large, room-length island/breakfast bar with multiple stools, and the oversized leather furniture with the huge cowhide rug on the floor. The family stood in a semicircle gawking at me like I was a freak show exhibit.

His father broke the stare fest. "Hello, I'm Alberto." From what I remember of those horrid days after my father's death, Alberto seemed stiff with stress lines over the bridge of his nose. On the television, next to Jim's dad, he appeared to be of average height, but today, he seemed taller—enough to tower over me. Also, he looked younger, minus the creases and the suit, which was replaced by jeans and a smile—he was simply Joaquin's dad.

His mother hugged me and kissed me on each cheek. "I'm Annette, welcome. We're glad to finally meet you."

I had met the rest: Micael and Marisol, Enrique and Alyssa ("She's the grouchy sister," Joaquin whispered), and then the younger brothers—Alejandro and Gabriel.

"I'm Mom's favorite... Everybody's favorite," Gabriel added.

They all scoffed at him. Then, each of them smacked him on the back of his head.

"We're still working on dinner, and we might be a bit," Alberto said. "Why don't you take Maria for a tour of the house and a boat ride?"

"OK." He touched the small of my back to guide me. He pointed out the obvious rooms but seemed to dwell on one in particular—the one he and his brothers used as fodder for teasing their mom. "This is Mom's girly room," he said, and swept his hand across the doorway.

A beautiful room with white shelves loaded with books. There were two fluffy chairs on either side of the room. A white fainting couch sat front of the French doors leading to the patio. The drapes were light pink silk with white chiffon coverings. Powder and hot pink throw pillows decorated the couch and chairs. To the right were a desk and craft table. All the pens were in soft pink containers and a Tiffany floor lamp was at one corner of the desk.

"Well, I love it," I pronounced.

He rolled his eyes. "All the girlfriends do."

The word *girlfriend* gave me a jolt of electricity.

He showed me the bedrooms—each brother had his own, which included a bed, a desk and a bookshelf, but each style was unique to their taste. Three bathrooms were shared between the five brothers. Joaquin held his arm out, inviting me into his room, careful to leave the door open. "The rule of the house is when girlfriends come to visit, doors stay open." He shrugged, but I didn't care—he'd said it again.

Joaquin chose rustic polished log style furniture. His comforter and curtains were an imperial shade of purple. Everything was in its place. I was a little embarrassed thinking that he'd seen my disaster of a room. He opened the doors by his bed and led me out to the bricked sidewalk that encircled the house.

He held out his hand, and I took it. We trudged into the wooded area at the far end, away from the house. I looked from the wooded area and to the house, trying to keep my eye on the opening—my flashbacks of that night in the woods with Teo urged me to locate the nearest exit.

"It's fine, Maria." He tugged at my hand. "I'll keep you safe. I promise."

The pounding of my heart against my ribs made it hard to breathe, and I heard every beat ring in my ears. A long line of sweat trickled down my spine as if I were hot, but it caused me to shiver. The air seemed thicker. We crossed a line of trees and emerged into a clearing. The clearing was filled with lavender, chamomile, echinacea, hawthorn and calendula. Water rushed in the creek, adding its whisper to the sound of wind in the grass. I bent down, touching the tops of the flowers and waved my hand to pull in all the aromas. These aren't indigenous—they were planted. Then, I spotted a little wooden dock with a canoe waiting in the water.

"I can't swim," I stood and pulled back. "You heard, I almost—almost drowned."

"The water's not deep. Promise." He tugged at my hand. I didn't budge. "You can stand up everywhere. Plus, I can swim like a fish." His hand ran across my cheek and gave me a feather lite kiss on the lips. "I wouldn't let anything happen to you. Face your fears head on with me by your side. It'll be different. I promise."

I slowly made my way to the canoe. Joaquin bent down on one knee to steady the canoe and took my hand. I stepped in and took a seat. He stood up and stepped inside. The canoe wobbled. Then he leaned over to untie us and picked up the paddles. He sat in the back, which he said was reserved for the more skilled position and let me sit at the front. "Keep us going. It's easy. Paddle on either side or both sides—whatever."

"It's beautiful here," I said. My eyes darted everywhere, trying to distract myself from the water.

He looked at me and grinned. "Do you want to hear another story?"

I could listen to his deep, melodic voice all day. "Shoot."

He shot me a brilliant sideways smile. "My family is from Mexico, but we migrated long ago to Texas and settled on this land. Way before the white people or Anglos reached Texas, the Tonkawa Indian tribes lived along the Cowhouse Creek. My family are descendants of the Tonkawa, and this is Cowhouse Creek."

I looked behind me at the path of the creek.

"The word Tonkawa…"

"Means wolf," I interrupted.

"Yes. A-plus to the lady in the front of the boat." He smiled and continued, "They believed they were descendants of a mythical wolf. They decided to farm because of their beliefs against harming animals. They tattooed their bodies and some, their faces. Each clan claimed its own mystical creature as their guardian."

"The eagle?" I asked.

"Ding. Ding. Ding. Right again."

He pointed up at the sky. A massive eagle, whose wingspan reached eight or nine feet, flew overhead. It was a golden eagle, which somewhat resembled a hawk. Flashed with a golden color, and its golden-brown feathers layered its upper body and amber brown feathers beneath. It swooped down low enough for me to see the scaled yellow feet with jet-black talons. Its hooked beak parted in a cry, and as it veered upward again, a gush of wind poured from its wings and stirred my hair.

"What's this about you almost drowning?"

"It happened at the beginning of school. Jim and Teo were there—figures. Well, we were in paddle boats, and Jim rammed us."

"Us?"

"Ugh. Me and Teo."

I heard a low growl and saw his knuckles turn white around the oar. I glanced back, and he didn't make eye contact.

"Anyway, long story short—I fell out, hit my head and went under. Teo pulled me out of the water."

Joaquin kept rowing. He didn't ask any more questions and went back to his stories. Having him for a boyfriend made me happy. He let me lead with any questions, and when I needed to talk, he listened, but he didn't push.

"The eagle stays over this land still. The Tonkawa were a peaceful tribe. We joined with the Caddo tribes and the Anglos to fight back against the Apache." He tapped me on the shoulder, and then pointed to a fish coming close to the surface to snag a bug skimming across the water. I smiled back at him.

"The Apaches, on the other hand—well, their name means enemy."

My mind flashed back to my time with Teo. Him clawing at my chest and then shifting into the growling wolf with blood-red eyes right in front of me. He told me his history, too, but left out all the bad things about his tribe. *Tomato, tomahto*—yeah, right. It all made sense. No wonder he made me sick to my stomach as soon as he drew near.

"Because the Tonkawa were outnumbered, we were almost wiped out. Today, they say there are about thirty-five left in Oklahoma, but they also say there are a few that live in secret around the Austin and Bastrop areas." He smiled. "And they will live in secret because they are the true descendants of the wolf people. Some call us shapeshifters." The river came to a fork. Joaquin began to turn the canoe around.

I pointed at the fork. "What's that?"

"That's the Bee House Creek. We don't go there," he said.

"Why?" I asked.

"The Apache hold down a strong camp on Bee House Creek."

The wind stirred my hair around my face. The clouds were broken and low here, and a stray drop of rain hit my cheek. I closed my eyes and turned my face toward the sun, drawing on my deep understanding of the gods of the sun, wind and earth—and of course, the healing spirits. This place exudes a magical aura, pulling you in, causing all else to melt away like ice at the touch of spring. I could almost visualize the old village stretching along the creek banks. As my eyes traveled up the steep cliff on the opposite bank, visions of where the men stood guard, keeping a protective eye on their families below, played like I was there with them.

Then, where the creek forks, the foliage changed, growing dark and dense, a place where something sinister could stalk close to its prey without being noticed by the guards above. It could lie in wait for the unsuspecting woman working a mere step or two too far away from the safety of her tribe.

"They took women from the Tonkawa tribe, hoping to have a son with the shapeshifter gene," Joaquin said, mimicking the words inside my head.

I looked back at him, and chills ran down my spine as I visualized my attack—these women experienced savage rapes, and their children were ripped from their arms after birth. "Some were successful, but they were not true shapeshifters. They are something very different. Werewolves and they were cursed." His breath deepened to a growl, and he started to row harder, putting the intersection behind him.

"I read a little about it," I said.

He paddled back in the direction of the dock. "These werewolves carried the shapeshifting skill of the Tonkawa, but the evil, warlike mind of the Apache. The Apache bloodline weakened, and some of the skinnier shapeshifters looked more like wererats." He laughed out loud. "At least that's what we call them."

"Wererats?" I asked.

He kept laughing, and the laughter held a spiteful edge, directed behind us, at the Apache ancestral land. "Wererats are these things that stand upright as a half man and half wolf. They're scrawny, and they look like big rats. They even have red eyes and long teeth—sharp incisors. They can sort of talk and go for the scent of blood. Disgusting, mutant things."

"An Apache werewolf can produce a wererat? Do you believe that is true?" I asked. "I mean, have you seen them with your own eyes?"

"*No hay nada que no pueda existir.*" He translated, "*There's nothing which can't exist.* Because the tales are handed down by word of mouth, things are lost, and things are added. Folklore, legends and myths start with the truth."

My mind shook off the story. I tried to take in the view and tried not to visualize the legends that replayed in my imagination. Not only did I unequivocally understand that my boyfriend shifted into a wolf, but there were even more sinister monsters within the borders of this small town. I didn't want to try to separate the real from the false. Even though it seemed crazy, I accepted it all. Joaquin held strong to his belief, and I trusted him enough to take it as truth, too.

"Hey, that drowning thing? When Jim came out of the water, I swore, he transformed into some kind of animal. The murky water washed over him, and he looked rough and dirty—and then something grotesque. His body crouched, his hands were claws, pointed ears and fangs. They were long and skinny. It sounds crazy, and I was barely conscious just moments before, but do you believe—is it possible that Teo bit him? That he is one of those—"

"Possibly." His voice took a gravelly tone.

"I mean, Jim's creepy and a little mean, but now he's more aggressive—if that is even possible."

"Until they learn to control themselves, yes, they are aggressive—vicious. You need to steer clear of him. And you might want to watch out for Lexi."

I nod.

"I'm serious. Maria. Be careful with him."

"I will. I promise."

We floated down the creek between tall white cliffs, bare native stones overhanging with low trees. Along the waterline, the foliage grew lush and green. The beauty overwhelmed me—hard to consider that bloody fights happened here not long ago. This land would be worth a battle.

We passed the dock, but he turned around to head back. He laid our paddles in the canoe, and we drifted back down the creek toward the dock, near enough for him to grab the pylon and pull us close enough to tie up. My knees slid between his, and he cupped his hands over my calves and pulled me into him. Unable to help myself, I threw my arms around his neck. Our foreheads were touching, but his eyes were down, and he began drawing circles on the top of my thigh with his finger. We sat in silence. He pulled his head up and kissed me. I clung tight to his neck.

"I need to see you," I said.

"You can see me whenever you like," he said.

"No, I need to see you—as a wolf," I said. "I want to believe it in the way you do."

He tensed and pulled back, and then he pushed me back onto my seat. "Next time we go to the park together. Can we do it then?"

"No, now. Out here. On your land."

"It has to be now?"

I nodded.

He stared deep into my eyes. "What do I get?"

"What do you mean?"

"You see my secret. I want to see yours."

"Wh—What?"

"Just stop. You know I saw you at the library. And some hints here and there. You, my beautiful girl, are more than you seem."

"OK. I want—no, I *need* to see you. But you first."

He stepped onto the dock and helped me out. His eyes went straight to the ground, and his hands were in his pockets. He stood in front of me, unmoving and silent. I couldn't understand his reluctance. My love for him burned through every inch of me; it filled my mind, controlled my body and consumed my soul. This wouldn't change things. I would be able to take it. This wouldn't scare me off. I reached out and put my hand on his stomach, then tugged at his shirt.

"Please."

He kissed me three times fast as if to agree to my request.

As I moved toward the path, his arms circled my waist from behind. He pulled me back into him, holding me tight and extra-long like he didn't want to let me go. His warmth consumed me, but this was a distraction. I looked over my shoulder and his lips met mine. I turned around and pulled him even closer. Our hearts and his body were even hotter than usual. I laid my cheek against his chest and held him, rubbing his back.

I whispered, "It'll be OK."

When he pulled back to look at me, sadness filled his eyes, a distance I never wanted between us. No smile. With resolve, he took a step back, pulled off his shirt, and handed it to me. My heart accelerated at the site of his smooth bronze skin stretched across a rippled abdomen. He slipped off his shoes, leaving them at my feet. Each step a hesitation. What I needed to see would be difficult for him. But no more secrets. Tangible proof, not something I read at a restaurant or on the internet.

I gave him a reassuring smile. "I need this. I'm sorry."

"I get it."

He turned and slumped into the woods out of sight. A rustling, and then quiet. The quality of the silence shifted, and then I heard a thud, and the earth moved all around me. Time stopped, and the moment lasted longer than it should, too long. My nerves snapped with a fierceness, and I tried some breathing exercises to calm myself. My emotions wound like tangled fishing line, impossible to separate. I squeezed his shirt in my hands; I held it to my face taking a deep breath of his scent.

After what seemed like forever, a mammoth wolf prowled toward me. I sighed and tensed, but the terror or horror one might have expected was absent. My hand went out, looking for something to steady myself. I found nothing. I stared at him. He ducked his head and swung it side to side, and sauntered up to me. The wolf's coat shined a chocolate brown with streaks of golden brown down the ridge of his back and on his paws. His beautiful face with gold under his ears and under his chin gazed back at me. The top of his head was marked with a golden patch, the shape of an arrowhead. His head stood taller than me, and his back was twice as wide as me. My heart urged me to reach out and touch him, but my mind said to run, envisioning that night in the woods as Teo transformed into a beast.

Still, I stood ready to take his head in my hands and gaze into his eyes, but I couldn't—I froze. He stepped even closer to me, keeping his head low. My heart could not take it anymore; I put my hand out, trembling, and lifted his muzzle. Looking into his eyes put my mind at ease. In my heart, I recognized him—in his eyes, I found a gentleness and familiarity. The most beautiful brown eyes, and without a doubt, my Joaquin stood before me. The need to run deserted me. My hands were steady, my breathing slowed, and my heart pounded against my ribs, out of excitement, not fear. He nuzzled my hand with his head, and I reached up and ran my hand down his side. The rumble reverberated under my fingertips as he made a noise, half cry and half sigh. I threw my arms around his large neck, and he laid his head against my shoulder. Tears came to my eyes as overwhelming warmth grew inside of me. The moment wasn't long enough.

He pulled back, and I squeezed, wanting to hold him a fragment of a moment longer. My arms slipped off him as he moved into the woods, not taking his eyes off me.

Joaquin emerged, buttoning up his jeans and shaking his hair. I handed him his shirt, and he slipped it on as he slid his feet into his shoes.

"Well, you're still here," he said, not connecting with my gaze.

"You believed otherwise?"

He nodded. "I was afraid."

My heart twisted at the pain I must have caused him in that moment, but we made it through the worst part.

"The strange thing, I still pictured—you," I said.

He made his way back over to the dock. He pulled a small package out of his pocket and laid down a small pile of food—small, round and red-brown, some kind of seeds. They were larger, like pumpkin seeds and berries that resembled cranberries. After he strolled back to the path, the eagle screeched and swooped down behind us and landed on the deck.

"Your turn," he said.

I took his hand and led him back to the flower-covered field. Handing him a lavender flower, I backed away. He cocked his head. My mouth parted and moved quickly over silent words. Hands raised, and my face pointed toward the sun. The silent chant became barely audible. Leaves tumbled from the trees on the perimeter, and the wind whipped my hair. As I slowly turned, the wind followed, spinning the leaves into a mini-tornado. Stopping my spinning, I gave a twirl of my hand, and the leaves fell to the ground. Unable to resist, I bowed and stunned my boyfriend.

He laughed, "You're cleaning that up."

I sighed, swooped my hand, and the leaves jumped into a pile under one of the large pecan trees. I smiled.

"There you go. All clean," I said.

"So, are you a witch?"

"No. I mean, I am just in touch with nature. Dad says, said, I'm one with the Great Spirit. He listens when I ask him to help me with the air, water, earth and healing."

"Healing?"

"Yeah. This is where it sounds a little weird. My sister and I can do natural remedies, but it seems to work better when I apply them."

His head dropped, and he slid in close to me. One hand around the back of my neck, and then walked his fingertips down to the small of my back, drawing me closer to him. "That settles it. We are meant to be together."

I stopped in front of him and stretched up, giving him a long passionate kiss. He pulled back to gaze deep into my eyes for a moment. The corners of his mouth turned up. Then, he picked me up and swung me around. I laughed until he set me back down.

* * *

When we got back to the house, the outside fireplace held a glowing fire, and a large banquet table was positioned in the center of the patio surrounded by ten chairs. The girls came through the open patio doors with the last few items for the table. Everyone walked to the table, and the men pulled the chairs out for the ladies. We thanked them, took our seat and then the men were seated. In unison, everyone bowed their heads for prayer. Their thanks were brief but sincere. Then, the fun began: plates of juicy tenderloin, grilled chicken slathered in marinade, corn on the cob with seasoned butter, grilled mixed vegetables, stuffed peppers and a garden salad with huge slices of tomatoes. I'd never seen such a well-prepared meal, not even at my family's Thanksgiving dinners. For dessert, they filled a small rolling cart full of sweets—peach cobbler with crystallized sugar sprinkled on top of a flaky crust, homemade banana pudding and vanilla waffles. Annette announced that the Blue Bell vanilla ice cream to go on top of the cobbler was in the freezer.

Annette turned to me. "Well, Maria, would your mother let us steal you away for a family wedding?"

I said, "I am not sure. I've never spent more than a day away from home before."

"Oh, I understand that's a long time. I would imagine you're a big comfort to her."

"Some days," I said, wondering what Annette would say about Mom's wine, "she could be doing more things that make her happy, though." I looked down and wiped my mouth off with my napkin.

Annette smiled. "That's sweet. Would you mind if I spoke with her?"

"I would hate to be any trouble," I said.

"No trouble," she said, waving her hand in the air.

Someone asked for a bowl of cobbler, and the conversations around the table started again. Everyone appeared happy with one another, and I absorbed their cheerful nature. In a few hours, they pulled me into all the conversations like I belonged. His family welcoming me was like sitting in front of a fire wrapped in a blanket—and at the same time, a little guilty. We used to have a family like this, a smaller version, more broken and fragile.

The end of the evening came way before I was ready. I said my goodbyes, and we left.

We turned out of the driveway, and onto the highway and I gave out a long sigh. "Did I pass?"

He tilted his head, frowning. "Of course. But something's making you sad."

"Your mom said that I'm a comfort to my mom. It made me realize my family hasn't been happy in a while."

He touched my hand. "You can talk to me about it—if you want to."

I looked down, trying to force the lump in my throat to dissolve. I exhaled. "Our family used to be close. We did everything together, a lot like you are with your family. My father worked at a bank, and he loved to fish and hunt. We went to church together every Sunday. He took my sister and me shopping, even though he hated every minute of it. Dad took me to all my softball games. You couldn't ask for a better father." I took a deep breath. The tears started to burn at the edges of my eyes. My lungs constricted, and my emotions flipped out of control. "Last year, when my father—when he died, it devastated our family. More than I realized until tonight."

I looked out the window, unable to look at him or speak for a moment. Tears rushed down my cheeks, hot and quick. My vision blurred, and my voice cracked.

I said, "It makes me—*angry.* They ran into some trouble with the evidence. They couldn't hold his killer. He went free. I'm sure your father has way more information. You probably understand it better. Anyway, he's dead now, and there's nothing fair about it."

I wiped my nose and face. I took a couple of breaths and looked out the window, watching the dark scrubland speeding past in the Texas night. "I lost everything that day. I changed schools. Stuck in this new life, one without a father and with a drunk mother. My friends were left behind, and new ones came into my life. You—" I looked at him "—you went from being some guy waving at me in the library to the closest person in my life." I looked up to see his eyes widen, and I dropped my gaze back toward my lap. "I am nowhere near the same person as six months ago. I have learned tons—about how to appreciate and hold tight to the people in my life. In a moment, your life can morph into something poles away from its start. Plus, dad was my connection to this—," I swept the wind, stirring the things in Joaquin's cup holder.

Joaquin's reflection appeared in my window. He kept quiet. Watching and holding my hand. My body started to do that shudder thing that happens when your lungs can't keep up with your sadness anymore.

Joaquin pulled the car over to the side of the road. Empty fields and a lonely highway sprawled in front of us. He wiped the teardrop hanging from my chin, held my face in his hands, kissed my forehead and then touched his forehead to mine. We remained motionless with our foreheads pressed together. For the first time, I pulled back first. I wiped my eyes with both hands, not able to raise my head or look into his eyes. My insides were raw and out in the open—I kept my head turned toward the window, hiding the nakedness of my emotions from the person I cared about most. Since my father died, I hadn't spoken about it until now. Joaquin must have suffered from these same sensations revealing his wolf to me. He did not deny my request to see him no matter the cost, bared his true self in front of me despite his fear of loss and rejection. And he sat beside me.

He said, "I'm sorry." He ran his hand through his hair; I could hear a rasp in his breath. "I have wanted to talk to you about that day for a while and to be there for you." He shook his head. "You see, I watched you at mass. Many times, I wanted to go talk to you, but something always held me back. I regret it to this day." I looked up, and our eyes met. "When they shot your dad, I needed to go with my dad. I needed to be there, even if you didn't realize I came for you." His hand tightened around mine, and I could almost see his strong heart pounding in his chest. "I carried you to the car and stood back out of the way. I went to the hospital. I came to your house that night and brought food. I went to the wake and the funeral, but I've never experienced such helplessness." He leaned in close to me, our faces millimeters apart, and his breath warm and moist on my skin. "I wanted to be there for you, but I had never even introduced myself to you."

He ran his hand over his forehead and took a deep breath. "I wanted to do something, even if I only stood there. No matter how painful your grief became, I could do nothing. I couldn't hold you or comfort you." His forehead met mine, and he closed his eyes. "I'm sorry about everything. I've never felt so helpless."

We waited for a long moment. "Can I give you a kiss?"

It's been a while since he asked permission. I didn't reply—I leaned toward him. When he cups my face in the palms of his hands and kisses me on the lips, tears hung in his eyes, too.

His hand found mine, and all the way home, we held on to each other.

At my house, he opened the door and bowed like you would to a queen—his attempt to lighten the mood and make me laugh. He held up his hand to help me out. Instead, I slid past his hand and hugged him tightly. We entered the circle of light that spilled from my porch, but I still couldn't let go of his waist.

"Do you want to come in? Mom's gone."

As we entered the house, he turned to lock us in and then did a full inspection of the house. "All clear," he said, as he came back downstairs.

I tugged at his shirt and pulled him toward me. "Do you want to go to my room?"

"Not a good idea." He tapped my nose.

"Yes, it is," I said.

"It's not that I wouldn't like to, but it's better if we stay down here."

"I understand, but I would like to curl up next to you and go to sleep."

"One day, we will," he said.

"One day soon?"

He threw his head back and laughed. "Soon enough. Let's go to the living room and wait for your mom."

I ran upstairs and changed first. He stayed in the living room, arranging pillows and blankets. I came back, and we flipped through the channels together and settled on *Animal Planet*. Joaquin righted himself on the couch. I curled my legs up under me, hugged his muscular arm, put my head on his shoulder and drifted off to sleep.

When I opened my eyes, I lay curled up in my bed.

CHAPTER 9

We made it through half of the week. Joaquin and I strolled out to the parking lot with his brothers. Gabriel said, "Maria, you haven't lived until you go to a Mexican wedding." He patted his chest. "We do it up right." He grinned and puffed his chest.

We all laughed at him. And it brought me back to my first dance. We attended a family wedding, and my father led me to the dance floor. He lifted me up and put my feet on top of his. I couldn't have been more than five-years-old. I wore a white sleeveless dress with a yellow silk ribbon tied around the waist. Dad stood tall and handsome. He smelled of musk and the outdoors. He smiled at me as he danced me around the floor. At the end of the dance, he twirled me around and gave me a big hug.

I smiled to myself. The memory filled me with tender visions and sad emotions, but I never wanted to forget it. I forced myself to rejoin the conversation and even laughed. We loaded up and started back toward the house.

* * *

Joaquin turned down my street, going slow to avoid a game of basketball happening beneath a curbside hoop. An unfamiliar car was parked in our spot. Joaquin let out a laugh, covering his mouth with his fist.

"What?"

"Oh, you'll see." He tried to hide the hint of laughter in his voice.

He parked and opened my door, then pulled me up and whispered with a laugh, "It's my mother." I jerked back and caught his eye. He laughed. "You said she could ask your mother. Well—" He nodded his head toward the door.

"No way! Your mother is in there right now, asking my mother if I can stay with y'all for the *entire* weekend?"

He pursed his lips together and said, "Hmm, yep."

"Hey kids, we're in here," my mom called as we entered the house. Her laughing tone assured me she got a big kick out of this, at my expense, and I shot Joaquin a burning glare. He laughed at me. Not able to hold back any longer, I smiled and headed back to see how the big first meeting went.

"Hi, Mom," Joaquin said. He moved toward her and kissed her cheek.

"Thank you, *mijo*," she said.

"Annette came over to invite you to a wedding with their family," my mom said. She gave me a sideways smile. "It's nice of her to make the invitation in person."

I looked at Joaquin, and I couldn't contain my smile. I am pretty sure my mother agreed to allow me to spend an entire weekend with my boyfriend and his family.

"Kids, have a seat." Annette pointed at the open seats. "We've got a few ground rules, being it's an overnight trip."

We did as we were told.

Annette patted my hand. "We ask that you stay with the group." Joaquin and I nodded. I could've told her that she didn't need to worry about him, and my biggest desire would be fulfilled by being with him all weekend.

"No leaving the hotel at night—without us. Also, be smart. Don't put yourselves in bad situations. Assume we have our eyes on you at all times." She smiled and looked at my mother. "Did I forget anything?"

My mother smiled. "Nope. I think you got it covered." Mom added nothing. What could she say? "Do you both agree?"

I answered first, "Yes, ma'am."

"Yes, ma'am," Joaquin said.

"We'll pick her up Friday morning." She patted my hand one last time. "We're flattered that your mother would trust us with such a precious package." She swept her hand down my cheek and caught my chin in her finger and thumb. She smiled at me and then excused herself. "And pack plenty of clothes! We're going to have lots of fun."

* * *

"He has four brothers? Wow, I can't imagine. Life with you two girls seemed chaotic." Mom walked to the fridge, searching for milk. She still wore her pajamas because the whole school district was on holiday. "Are you hungry?"

"No, thanks. I need to do some homework." I fumbled with the hem of my shirt, already packed and nervous about leaving. "Do you have any more rules for me? Joaquin is respectful. You don't need to worry."

She turned and faced me with an "I'm-not-an-idiot" grin.

I blurted out, "I mean, what I wanted to ask—are you going to be okay by yourself?"

She popped me on the butt and said, "I'm still the parent here. Don't worry about me."

I hated leaving her. She still seemed lonesome and troubled. As I rinsed my cereal bowl, I checked the wine rack by the stove to check for missing wine bottles. Possibly one. What would prevent her from driving to the store? My mother had her own car, and she was over twenty-one, making it easy to buy more. I needed to trust that she would be fine. For the first time, I wondered, *what will she do when I leave for college? Will I be able to leave?*

"You're not my babysitter, honey. You need to enjoy being seventeen," she said.

"I'll call you every night." I kissed her cheek and went upstairs to finish packing my suitcase.

The day before, I finished up my family tree project for class. Mom pulled out a few black and white photos of my grandparents. Memories of my grandmother were of an older woman, but I connected with those eyes, even without color, the warmth jumped out at me—my eyes. I resembled my father's family the most. Mom gave me birth certificates for my sister and me and a creased marriage certificate for her and my father. On the marriage certificate, some of the words were blurred and illegible. Part of my dad's name and birth date were worn away. I closed the folder and admired my work through the clear cover. It might fool my teacher, but it didn't fool me. My mom had a secret.

* * *

My overnight bag was a gift from Dad for my overnight softball games. He made a big deal about me going out of town with the team, even though he or my mom always went along. I ran my hand along the leather strap, and the pressure of memories took my breath away. No wonder my mother suffered. She must have tons more of these memories, all crowded in the house around her.

The doorbell rang, and I turned my head like he would appear through the wall. My stomach did a little flip from excitement. I hurried downstairs to my mother and gave her a big, long hug. I guess I tried to stock up for all the ones I would miss.

"You're going to keep yourself busy, right?" I asked.

"No plans, a little work and staying around the house. Maybe I'll clean out that closet upstairs. Or maybe not." Her laugh seemed a little too exaggerated.

"Maybe I should stay," I said.

"I told you not to worry about me. I'll be fine. I've taken care of myself for a few years."

Joaquin offered her the usual reassurances at the door. After a round of goodbyes and I love you's, we turned and headed for the door. He took my hand again, but as we headed for the car, I worried. Sometimes, I become more like the mom or the caregiver. I stood for a long moment looking back at the house. I pushed through the dread to go on like she said, I am seventeen. I should enjoy it. I let Joaquin close my door for me and drew the seatbelt across my chest. The rest of his family rode in two cars in front of us. One of the cars carried his parents and younger brothers. The other car carried Micael, Marisol, Enrique and Alyssa. I took a deep breath, and we were off.

Not being able to shake how my mother looked or the thump of my heart after riding for a few blocks, I picked up my phone and texted Theresa. I told her how worried mom made me and stopped short of begging her to come home for the weekend. My worry ran twofold about my mother and the creepy stalker that chased my sister. Having both at home together would loosen me up and allow me to enjoy the weekend. Theresa said she didn't want me to leave mom alone. It took me two blocks to send all the information. She wrote back immediately. She said she would be there Friday night and stay until after church on Sunday. I shot back, *Promise.* In a second, she wrote back, *I PROMISE.* I texted her a thank you, sighed, and got ready for the weekend.

Remorse over my selfishness washed over me. I typed, *What about Jose?*

It took a minute, then she wrote, *He will be with his family.*

Are you OK with that?

She wrote back, *I have to be.*

I'm sorry.

It's fine. I need to help with Mom. My turn.

Thanks. Love u.

Love u 2.

I sighed and dropped the phone into my purse. "Where to first?" I asked.

He peeked over at me. "The hotel, first. We'll check-in and unload."

I leaned as close as I could to him and put my head on his shoulder. We listened to the radio. When one of my favorite songs came on, I sang along. From time to time, he would press his lips to the top of my head. He put his hand on my leg and squeezed—the warmth radiated up my thigh, giving me a sense of comfort. He smelled good, and it almost made me forget about all the horrible things that happened that night at the campfire—almost. Then, with a tender shake of my leg, he caught my attention.

"Maria, we have to stop for gas. Would you like anything?"

"Coke, please," I said.

That small question sent prickles running up and down my spine. Teo's perverted misgivings wouldn't spoil my time with Joaquin, but my brain held tight to that memory. And really, I didn't want to forget. It served as a reminder of what happens when I didn't follow that inner nudge of instinct. I was gifted with an ability I needed to use.

Joaquin kissed my cheek. When he came out of the store, he'd brought a Coke, a bag of beef jerky and a carton of Goldfish. "Road trip food. How can you resist?" I laughed, returned to a more favorable time—the present.

The engines roared in unison, and we were off. And this time, I fell asleep with my head on his shoulder.

Joaquin and I visited our favorite spot at the State Park. Yet something seemed off; a mist crept across the field in our direction. The sunshine choked out by the rolling, thick shadow. Not a cloud, more like long creeping fingers inching their way toward us. We stood together. Suddenly, a hideous monster stood in front of me. The monster came almost close enough to touch me and the lukewarm moisture of its breath on my face. The thickness in the air around me made it impossible to breathe. My stomach clenched. I turned to Joaquin for protection, but he shifted into his wolf form. Something growled from the trees in front of us. The sound vibrated, guttural and cruel, and it sucked me back to reality.

When I awoke, we were in Austin. I shook my head, hoping to erase the images from my mind like the sands on an Etch-A-Sketch.

"You okay, sweetheart?"

Joaquin turned on his signal, and I looked around a little disoriented.

"Yeah. Dreaming." He said we would drive to the hotel first, but instead, he turned downtown. We headed off the highway and turned on Brazos. The convoy stopped in front of huge, red-carpeted stairs. Valets in black pants and white shirts hopped to the curb and opened the door to greet us. Some porters were already wheeling a luggage rack down the ramp. The sign said we'd arrived at the Driskill Hotel.

My head spun. I never stayed anywhere this nice. The architecture looked old, a hotel restored from a massive mansion. The original façade faced Sixth Street and looked to be four stories—two enormous balconies extended over the steps that brought you to the double door entryway. The hotels I stayed in were the ones booked for our softball team—motel rooms in a strip off a dusty Texas road. This one looked like a hotel for royalty. The lobby was furnished with such magnificence that the outside seemed insignificant. With my hands stuffed into my back pockets, I turned a circle inside the door. A huge longhorn skull mounted over an immense fireplace. They decorated with dark leather furniture and a plush looking rug—the sitting area in front of the fire.

Mr. De Luna brought us our key cards, and we headed up a few stairs to the elevator. Gabriel punched the button for the fourth floor.

The boys gave us the corner room: a suite with a large living area and rooms with private baths on either side. Our room contained a balcony that opened right onto Sixth Street. Marisol and Alyssa headed to the right, and I shifted to the left. Joaquin set my bag on the suitcase table and took my overnight bag to the bathroom. When he emerged, he joined me on the balcony.

The sun started to set behind the skyscrapers. Light bounced off the mirrored facades with flashes of blue and gold. It lit the multitudes of people scurrying around on the street below; all of them occupied with the business of drinking. I hated being around my mother when she drank but seeing the entire street full of people celebrating to excess was more than difficult. Several people whistled or yelled something unintelligible at me. The nauseating twist in the pit of my stomach came back, making me scan the crowd for anyone who might wish me harm.

Joaquin slid up behind me, and the heat from his body draped around me. I leaned back into him, taking both of his hands and wrapping his arms around my waist. Everything subsided, all except safety and tenderness. As soon as I turned to face him, his lips met mine. They were warm and moist. "We're going to have the best weekend," he promised.

"Big plans, hmm?"

He took my hand and pulled me inside, toward the common area.

Micael came out of the bathroom, drying his face. "Hey, you two. We're supposed to freshen up for dinner, and we might even go dancing. If we're good." He grinned and elbowed Joaquin and Gabriel. They started laughing.

I changed my blouse, brushed my hair, reapplied makeup and brushed my teeth. I dressed faster than the other girls and found Micael, Enrique and Joaquin seated in front of the TV, all fresh and smelling fabulous.

"Hey!" Joaquin held his hand out to me. "You look beautiful."

Sitting surrounded by testosterone gave me the impression of being out of place, but Joaquin pulled me off the arm of the couch and into his lap. His arms encircled me, filling my heart with tenderness.

Marisol and Alyssa came out together, making a striking pair—long silky black hair and amazing outfits that looked tailored. Alyssa asked, "Are y'all ready?" She smiled and slid her arm around Enrique's, hugging him close. She gave Marisol a cool smile, too, and passed by me without a word. Overwhelming unease leftover from my nightmare in the car swirled in my gut. Staring at her back, I reminded myself of Joaquin's promise. We would have a good time, no matter what.

* * *

Alberto and Annette picked the restaurant because none of the rest of us could make up our minds. The restaurant's location happened to be within walking distance, even in heels. We headed out past the row of cabs and into the evening.

We hadn't been on Sixth Street for more than a minute when that familiar tug caught my attention. Then, through the crowd emerged a familiar face. I squeezed Joaquin's hand and pointed. He let go of my hand and pushed me behind him.

Jim stopped in front of us, chest puffed, and arms crossed, looking strong and muscular. Lexi told me the other night that he fell ill, but he didn't look like someone sick—if possible, he looked stronger. His chest looked as if it exploded like he'd lifted with the wrestling team, and the veins running down his arms were plump with rushing blood. His once handsome face took a hard turn, though, with an almost greenish pale sheen. The pupils of his eyes were twice their normal size—and here's the kicker—had a red glow. The twist in my stomach sent bile up into my mouth.

"Hey, Maria. Lexi told us you would be in Austin." He shot Joaquin a smirk and the glint of fangs shined under the blue glow of the streetlights. The sight made me reach out to take hold of Joaquin's waist. "You slumming it?"

Teo slipped in from behind him and said, "Hey, are you two-timing me?"

Through clenched teeth, I said, "Um, us dating? Are you drunk or stoned? You're freaking lucky the police weren't involved!"

Joaquin squeezed my hand and looked back at me, urging me to stop. "Maria," he said.

I pushed myself in front of him, made courageous by my outrage. "You're freaking kidding, right? Seriously?" Courage rooted in the protection of my new family helped me step forward. Joaquin caught both my arms and held me close to his chest, and then wrapped his arms around me. "You—you're not even someone I want to be in the same room with after what you did." Joaquin squeezed me closer to him with a slight jerk, and my body got hot. Forgetting we were with his parents. This behavior wouldn't give them a very positive impression of me.

I could hear growls in front of and behind me. I slunk back into Joaquin, a little afraid now that things escalated, and we were in a public place—but my fury raced, getting the better of me.

"And Jim, who are you to me?" I said with a bite in my voice. "Being my best friend's cousin doesn't make you anything to me. Back off."

I swear I heard several growls and a shriek. Then, Annette pushed past her sons, with Alberto stepping behind her, letting her take the lead. She put her hand up in the air like only a mother can do, saying, "Boys, this isn't the time or place." She glared at them. They all took a step back and held their hands up like they were surrendering.

Jim said, "Okay."

Her voice rose an octave. She sounded almost happy. "That's better. Now, go and behave yourselves." She swept her hands like she shooed an animal off the porch.

Jim and Teo ducked their heads like they'd been spanked. Then they turned and swiftly disappeared in the crowd. As she turned, her shirt inched up some. That's when I noticed it: a spot of purple ink on her lower back. A tattoo?

I tugged at Joaquin's watch. An ornate purple "D" marked his wrist. He didn't seem like someone who'd have one, neither did his mother. I tried to catch a better glance, but she'd already straightened her blouse.

Gabriel looked around at his brothers. "Well, are you going to let a couple of sewer rats spoil your appetite? C'mon. I'm hungry."

* * *

After a dinner of crab legs, corn on the cob and red potatoes, we strolled a little farther up the street and entered a dive bar called Chupacabra. The kind of bar that didn't bother to card its proprietors. The name sounded familiar, but my memory didn't volunteer anything but mere recognition.

Inside, there was a small wooden dance floor in front of an elevated stage for the band. They filled the back of the building with mismatched round and rectangular tables and folding chairs. Gabriel came up and asked Joaquin if he could dance with me. He reminded me and everyone else at the table that he danced better than anyone in the family.

"I have to tell you, I'm not good," I gave an embarrassed face.

He pulled me up out of the seat. "I'll show you! It's easy!"

He actually told the truth—he danced fabulously. He turned and twirled me until my head spun, and I could not stop laughing. By the time we got back to the table, my face hurt from smiling. He tried to ask me again, but Joaquin pushed him to the side and pulled me out of my chair. "Find your own girlfriend, little brother." He gave his brother a playful growl.

Gabriel didn't have any trouble finding another partner, and even Alejandro danced. Joaquin held me tighter and closer than Gabriel. Gabriel may have been a good dancer, but Joaquin had him beat. He led with strength, making it easy to place my feet where they needed to go. My head spun from all the excitement.

The music stopped, and we made our way back to our seats. A group of middle-aged men to the left said, "*Hombre lobo.*"

The boys shot glares like bullets.

Then a woman spat twice and glared at Micael. "*Maldito.*"

A loud, guttural growl answered her.

I looked up at Joaquin and mouthed, *What*? He shook his head at me. Micael put his hand on his father's shoulder and whispered in his ear. Alberto looked in the direction of the men and shook his head. "Ignore them," Alberto murmured and gestured for his sons to return to the table.

One of the men got up and strode past our table, growling, "¡*Hombre lobo!*"

"What's your problem, man?" Gabriel asked, obviously agitated.

"You are, boy! You give us a bad name," he said.

"You must be mistaken."

"No mistake," he said.

Gabriel stood up and slammed his hands on the table. "Would you like to take this outside?"

"Meet me out back," he said.

The other brothers looked disappointed but ready to defend Gabriel. His parents flanked and spoke into his ear with expressions of anger across their faces. They headed outside and down a side alley to a fenced-off parking lot. As we followed them outside of the club, I asked, "What's going on?" Joaquin touched his finger to his lips and slowed down to fall back a bit from his family. "It's some crazy old man."

"What did he mean? I don't know that word."

"Werewolves. He called us out as a pack." He half laughed. "I'm not that hairy, am I?" He looked at his arms and tried to make me smile. I grabbed his hand back and held tight.

We rounded the back corner, taking a small alleyway into the parking lot. Other people were already waiting. I should've known. In the hard light of a single, brilliant security light, Jim, Teo and Thomas's features were cast in sharp shadow—they looked like demons. And they weren't alone. They brought friends, younger and sturdier than the middle-aged men in the bar. Teo slapped some money in the guy's hand, and as he passed us, he bumps my shoulder.

From the alley, Annette's voice said, "Girls, come here."

Reluctantly, we turned with heavy feet and traveled the sixty feet back to the street and waited in the bright lights of Sixth Street. I couldn't believe how easily she accepted her boys fighting; either it showed weakness or great confidence in their skill as fighters. Over the loud music coming from the clubs and laughter of passing college students, I heard snarls, growling and crashing. The ground vibrated under my feet at one point. An animalistic whine made me want to run to the back. My legs wobbled, and I leaned against the wall as I looked toward the fight. Annette grabbed my arm.

"Everything's fine. They're strong. The boys can handle this problem. They work well together. And Alberto is with them," she said.

Alyssa tapped her foot and looked at her fingernails. "This is all her fault," she mumbled under her breath.

"My fault?" I said.

"Shut up! It's not her fault," Marisol said, and she pushed Alyssa.

"Yes. It. Is. We were all just fine until she came around. No fights. No—,"

"Girls," Annette said as she stepped between them.

Marisol leaned against the wall with her arms crossed. I paced with purpose like the movement would reveal my reason for this fight. But the wait seemed like it was shackling me to the concrete. Finally, Alberto came out and whispered to Annette. She clasped her shirt in her fist over her heart. Micael came out next and stayed with the girls, and Annette dragged me along to the back alley. My feet tripped along the uneven bricks, not moving as they should because my mind wanted to go even faster.

When we got to the lot, Enrique ducked his head as he stomped his way back to the street with the girls. Joaquin slumped half-hidden in a shadow, sitting on the ground in front of Alejandro and Gabriel. They stood behind him in a protective stance, scanning the area with their eyes and noses. This time, there wasn't the slightest tinge of playfulness on their faces. I ran over to Joaquin, sliding down on my knees in front of him. He slumped over with his knees up and his arms propped on his knees. Four deep rips across his forearm. Blood and some kind of yellow discharge oozed out and dripped off his arm onto the ground, covering the tiny pieces of gravel from the old crumbling blacktop. My hand went up, and I wanted to touch it, but I didn't have the courage.

Before it occurred to me, Annette knelt beside me, and she took a roll of bandages and a small bottle of alcohol out of her oversized bag. I looked at her, puzzled at how or why she would have these things in her purse. She must have sensed my stare because, without a glance in my direction, she said, "Five boys."

She poured the alcohol down his arm. The liquid turned crimson as it passed over the wound. He squinted and took a deep breath—and at the sound of his breath, I realized I held mine. Then, Annette ripped open a square pad with her teeth and laid it on top of the wound. It soaked up blood immediately, turning the weave dark in little outward spreading squares. She wrapped the sterile white bandage around it until she covered the wound. She passed her hand across the bandage with the palm of her hand. A deep crease between her eyes and the corners of her mouth turned down as she patted his shoulder.

"Hold on," I said.

With one finger, I drew a circle in the gravel around Joaquin. Chanting my healing spell under my breath, I rubbed my hands together then wrapped them around the bandage. Joaquin flinched. But I held tight. Speeding up my chants, a shock went through me and knocked me out of the circle.

Wiping my pants, I looked around the lot. Widened eyes stared at me. But nobody spoke a word. The silence burned my ears, and tears stung my eyes. Not really how I wanted my boyfriend's family to find out about my abilities.

Alberto held out his hand and gripped Joaquin's good wrist, then pulled him to his feet.

"Good job, son."

I leaned back on my heels and stood up beside him. Tears spilled over and were starting to fall. Joaquin wiped the tears from my eyes and leaned down to kiss me—didn't it figure, he tried to comfort me while he nursed an injury.

"I couldn't heal you," I whispered.

"I'm fine, sweetheart. I'm a quick healer. Don't worry. I gave them a fight they'll remember." His words said fine, but his eyes showed a deep concern I hadn't seen since I asked to see his wolf form. Something seemed wrong.

* * *

Together we moved toward the street. Joaquin's arm around me seemed even heavier with each step we took back toward the hotel. Not noticeable to the crowd, his feet drug and his steps slowed. My body ached, too. They hurt him because of me. I hated how one bad choice and the inability to say no, rippled into the best days of my life. He put his arm around me, leaning in a little heavier than normal, and he held his bandaged arm across his body with his hand clasped to the waistband of his jeans. The police were out patrolling on horseback, more of them than usual, and the intersections were blocked off earlier, keeping cars from traveling down the street. Joaquin tried to be strong and caught up to his brothers, but I could see the pain escalating instead of decreasing. Halfway to the hotel, the sweat on Joaquin's face gave off a dull glow in the streetlights. Blood oozed through the bandage. My anger started to bubble—the other girls seemed almost giddy. They enjoyed their healthy boyfriends.

Finally, we reached the room sometime after midnight. "I got it from here," Gabriel said and started to take Joaquin from me.

Patting his wounded arm, Joaquin said, "Hey guys, I'm tired, and I'd like to say goodnight to my girlfriend, in private." He threw up his good hand and said, "I understand the rules."

"Go ahead, we'll do the same," Marisol said, waving her hands for us to go ahead. She seemed to be more concerned about the fight than anyone else. After the fight, she understood my guilt. She cut off anybody else's protests, and I loved that she could pull it off with ease.

We entered my room, and Joaquin parked himself on the edge of the bed. I closed the door as close as I could without shutting it and then plopped down beside him. By the look on his face, what happened in the alley must have been worse than what I imagined, and he searched for the words to describe what he wanted to tell me.

"Be honest with me," I said.

"Things may be a little more extreme than we anticipated."

I pulled my knee under me, facing him and making eye contact.

"He still wants you," Joaquin said. "He won't stop."

I clutched my stomach. He leaned in to kiss me, but it didn't give me the comfort I needed. My stomach churned, and my head throbbed. This injury—Joaquin's weakness—this turned out to be way more than some territorial fight over land and birthrights. It started with me.

"He's bitten a couple of *friends*. You weren't seeing things. He did bite Jim. Thomas, too. There were two other guys I didn't recognize. They transformed, making it even harder to guess. When we passed the wooden fence enclosing the private parking lot, Teo recruited four wererats to support him. He wanted to be dramatic and gave a little speech before it started." Joaquin gave a huff of a laugh and wiped away the streaming sweat from his forehead. I stood up and flipped the switch to the ceiling fan and grabbed my hooded jacket. "He said he would pay you back for ditching him. I told him it was your choice. He shifted, giving us no choice, but to fight."

The cool air from the fan gave him no relief. Sweat streaked his cheeks. He coughed, and his voice became raspier as he spoke. "We shifted. With Dad, we outnumbered them, and the wererats can't match our strength. My brothers pinned them down within seconds, leaving me and Teo to fight it out. Teo down on the ground with both my feet on his chest, and I hesitated. I told myself, maybe I shouldn't deliver a final blow." He smacked his forehead. "Stupid! At that moment, I heard something from behind the cars—two more wererats. Dad cut them down with one swoop, but as I looked away, Teo bit me. He wiggled free and ran. We let the others loose, and they followed after him with their slimy rat tails between their legs."

I brushed my hand across his brow. His skin burned my hand. "You should be healing. And my spell didn't work." Tears stung my eyes and fell in long lines down my face.

"Don't worry, I will," he said and then kissed the palm of my hand. "Anyway, that's when you guys ran back to us, and I fell to the ground with this." He held up his battered arm.

"It is all my fault. Alyssa was right."

He clenched his teeth. "Alyssa needs to keep her mouth—" I could hear his teeth grind together. "That's Alyssa. Don't worry about what she says." He pushed my hair out of my face and kissed my forehead. "I will always fight for you."

"I don't want you to. I want you safe."

"And I want you safe. I will do whatever it takes. That is a promise."

I stood in front of Joaquin. He tucked his finger inside the waistband of my pants and pulled me toward him. He kissed me softly on the lips and said *goodnight*, his lips still against mine. As we approached the door, I stole one more kiss goodnight and hoped that he would be better, healed, in the morning—that he would be back to my healthy Joaquin.

CHAPTER 10

A gentle knock on my door woke me. I grabbed the bed in search of a pillow to pull over my head. I identified the footsteps that drew near my bed. Joaquin removed the pillow from my head. He stood beside the bed with a huge grin on his face. I moaned.

"Are you okay?" he asked.

"No! I don't want you to see me."

He laughed, "How did you sleep?"

"Ugh," I said. "How do you think?"

As I stood, I noticed his arm hung in a sling. "Your arm looks worse."

His natural tan looked several shades paler, and he had a thin sheen of sweat on his face. In the sling, his arm appeared to have swollen to twice his size.

"Thanks," he said. "But you're right, it is. We are going to try to figure something out today. Get dressed and ready to go to the wedding; after we run some errands."

"Joaquin—"

"Maria, it's fine. Now, get into the shower."

I wiped the sweat from his face. The fever from his forehead burned my fingertips. I pulled back. An overwhelming sensation of guilt washed over me; tears threatened. Teo hurt him to get to me. Joaquin saw my reaction and pulled my hand to his warm, smooth lips and kissed it.

"It is fine. I'll be fine. We need to leave in a hurry." He leaned in and kissed my forehead. I stood there until he left. I slipped into the bathroom and turned on the shower. There, I washed the tears from my cheeks.

Pull yourself together, I told myself. *Joaquin needs you strong.*

* * *

Joaquin's arm was harnessed in a sling, and he has even less color in his face than before. He couldn't pick up his feet as he entered the room and speaking seemed to pain him. When he noticed me, he shuffled over and took my hand—his fever grew to an alarming temperature. The heat and infection wracked his entire body. And over his cologne, I could smell it.

"Are you sure you shouldn't go to the ER?"

He patted my hand and shook his head. Everyone in his family seemed stubborn. We left the hotel and made our way down the long busy street. My head swam, watching all the people rush past us. It took us quite a while to make the trek to wherever we were going. All the shops and people in downtown Austin distracted me that I almost stumbled over Joaquin—he stopped in front of an almost hidden alleyway. A small slit between two tall buildings. We took it. My chest tightened, and my stomach clenched. My feet were reluctant to enter this dark, tight spot. The hairs on my arms stood on end.

"Joaquin…"

With these huge walls on either side of us, the air stood still; I put my hand up, and my nose curled from the smell of damp mold. He pointed. At the end of the building hung an old sign over a door. It swung back and forth, squeaking without wind—*The Poisoned Pen*. In the middle of the day, this place gave the illusion of night.

"We'll keep watch," said Micael. He and his brothers stayed outside.

Alberto opened the door for Joaquin and me. It made a loud, long creak. Dispersed light illuminated the inside of the shop, and the faint luminosity gave a bluish glow. Sitting to the right, was an antique desk with an old cash register; behind the desk stood a bluish shelf with crackled paint full of candles. The smell of incense and jasmine filled the air. This place believed in the *Keeping Austin Weird* theme. The walls were lined with tall uneven bookshelves full of books. My gaze touched on each for a moment. Some of the shelves were stained wood, but others were painted in purples and blues. They were mismatched. Yet somehow, they fit together in a perfectly imperfect way. The books that filled the shelves were labeled with the same symbols and archaic writing embossed or written across the leather spines. Symbols were painted in bright red on the ends of each shelf; some no more than odd shapes; some notable native American symbols like howling wolves, Kokopelli, arrowheads, men and birds. One shelf crammed full of leather drawstring bags filled with who knows what. Native American symbols were painted on some of the bags.

A noise caught my attention and caused me to turn to Alberto. He went to speak to the lady in a doorway at the back of the room. His dress shoes struck out a sharp note on the floor. She motioned with her finger for him to follow her inside. Beads in the back doorway clacked together, and the two of them disappeared into the darkness beyond.

The shortened bookshelves were lined down the center of the room. My fingers slid down the row of books, reading the titles as I passed. They were first edition translations of Native American folk tales. The shelves were lined with books on the Nahuel, a Native American dream walker. A large book on the North American Chupacabra, I smirked a bit. Toward the back were books on werewolves. There were also books on the wererats. I pulled one off the shelf, and it smelled musty and old. It fell open to the beginning of a chapter: *The Curse*. The words spoke to me—I literally heard them in my head, but the voice wasn't my own. I glanced around the room to see if anyone else could hear.

The last line of the page jumped out at me, and a cold chill ran down my spine.

Suddenly, my stomach lurched, and my eyes darted around the room, looking for the cause. The door creaked, and a guy about our age dressed in jeans and a hooded sweatshirt entered, prowling around the bookstore, moving straight toward Joaquin. Quickly, I replaced the book and slipped over to Joaquin and snatched his hand. He looked scary pale.

"We have to go," I whispered. "Now."

He stiffened as we recognized the figure moving toward us. I kept hold of Joaquin's side, but I took a more defensive stance as the new guy moved toward us with silent and swift steps. As he got close, my hands came out. You could see the space ripple in front of us. I heard a shrill cry escape from inside his hood, and he flew across the room into a bookshelf. He scrambled to get up. His head showed a wound forming, and he drew in a long whiff. With a smile, he fumbled his way out the door. Fear traveled through me. This would get back to Teo.

"They're testing me," he said. For the first time, he looked afraid.

I ran out the door. Outside, his brothers were nowhere to be seen. I returned to Joaquin and started to pick up the fallen books, which helped me hide the streaks of tears sliding down my face. I wiped them away when I heard Alberto's voice from the rear of the store.

Alberto came back out holding a book. He paid and thanked the woman for her time. She looked beautiful, with long curls swooped back on the sides. Her clothes were interestingly different, flowing and sheer with a skirt down to the floor. Bells along its hem gave a slight jingle each step she took. Her sandaled feet revealed some rings on her toes and an ankle bracelet with tiny bells that chimed to the rhythm of her steps. She smiled at me, but when her eyes met Joaquin, her face fell.

"Wait. This, too," I said and grabbed the book that spoke to me. "Can you tell me the price of this one?"

She dropped her head and did not meet my gaze. "Please, take it. And good luck to you."

I thanked her and fit the little volume into my purse. When we exited the shop, all my senses heightened. "Heads up," I said. "They're still around here somewhere." The goosebumps clued me in.

As soon as we all gathered outside, Micael and Gabriel came running up. "We chased a bunch of them off. But we need to move out. I don't like this."

"Me either," said Alberto as he searched the sky. He nodded.

As I peered into the sky, a large bird soared past. It must have been what caught his attention. "We need to go, now," Alberto said.

Joaquin remained silent about the scene in the bookstore—I guess he didn't want to say anything that would throw guilt on the shoulders of his brothers about someone breaking through. He didn't want to add any more stress to the day.

Teo sent them. These guys were creepers—lurking around corners and behind buildings, hiding in the shadows, bent on keeping us on the run. The wererats were scared, and they couldn't beat him, even in his weakened state, but they would keep harassing us, taking the information back to Teo.

We were being followed. I kept my voice low and steady. "I read something in the bookstore." I looked down and cleared my throat. "And when I found out about—you, I did some searching." Joaquin lagged behind his brothers, where only he could hear me.

"What did you read?" His voice fell raspy and low.

"It's because of the Apache Curse. I started to read something— we'll have to look at it closer. But it said something about needing to be bled by an Alpha without the curse."

He slumped, silent. His eyes were on Micael. I tried to weigh whether his brother would bite him or not and if it would be harmful. "At least there's something to be done," he said weakly. "That's good, right?"

When I looked down at his arm, it bulged inside the sling. If I stared at it, I swore I could see the beat of his pulse.

Obviously, we would miss the wedding. Alberto called Jose. He would meet us at the hotel. We packed in record time and met Jose downstairs. He drove Joaquin's car back to the De Luna's house. I sat in the back thumbing through my new book.

I asked, "How is Theresa?"

He gave me a gentle smile and said, "I'm taking good care of her. Promise." He ducked his head a little. "I miss her this weekend."

Joaquin tugged back and forth at his tie, loosening it until he could slip it over his head. Next, I helped him pull off his jacket and laid it in the back window. He unbuttoned his shirt and let it fall open, the sweat soaked through his undershirt and dress shirt. Jose looked back and turned the air conditioning on as high as possible and pointed the vents toward the middle, letting the air flood the back seat. Joaquin sprawled out limp, and his breathing slowed. I combed my fingers through his sweat-laced hair, and tears fell onto my dress—I feared all my emotions would be revealed. I cried until my eyes stung with rawness.

Finally, Jose swung the car down the gravel drive. Each bump caused Joaquin to moan. Jose opened the door and was pulling Joaquin out. His legs weren't moving, so Jose and Alejandro carried him. The toes of his shoes left uneven furrows in the gravel behind him.

Theresa sat on the edge of the fountain out front with her black kit on her lap. When I got out, she ran over to me.

"So, you know?"

"Werewolves and shapeshifters, yep. I'm up to speed."

We went straight to the patio table and unloaded our kit. Alberto lit the fire pit and turned on the patio lights. Theresa asked him for the molcajete, a Mexican stone grinder. Flipping open the book, we started with the mixture.

"Okay, Jose. We need you. It's like in the olden days where they bled people to rid the body of infection. This involves a little of the supernatural. Bite him near the sight," I said.

Theresa gave Alberto a vial. "Fill it all the way up. Milk the cut if you have to. And Jose honey, we need a little from you, too." She wiggled a second vial at him.

"Honey," I asked.

"Focus," she cut me short.

"Move your ass," I screamed.

Joaquin sat crumpled in the yard. He slumped down on his knees and couldn't raise his head even to look at Jose. They stripped him of his undershirt and sling. His arm blazed as red as the taillights of a car and twice its normal size. There were streaks moving up his biceps toward his shoulder. Theresa read the book about the curse to me. And we finished the antidote—all but the blood. The poisonous bite turned a normal human into a wererat—but to a werewolf, it meant death. The books confirmed this to be a known cure if we weren't too late.

Jose meandered out to the yard and backed up in a straight line from Joaquin. He threw his shirt and pants to the side. Standing in his shorts, his head went up, his arms went out. It started at his feet. The tremors were slow at first, building into more violent shakes. His back arched, and he fell forward onto all fours with a thud that shook the ground under my feet. His back broadened, his waist narrowed, and chocolate brown fur sprang from his flesh. His jaw began to grind back and forth as it elongated into a fanged snout. Then, his head shook back and forth.

I couldn't control my scream of terror, afraid he would make things worse. Theresa hugged me close. Jose's head turned to me—but the eyes didn't belong to a vicious animal. Jose stared at me with pain in his wet onyx eyes. This terrifying wolf standing in front of us about to bite the love of my life possessed the soul of a gentle cousin filled with guilt for what he must to do. Pounding his massive paws into the ground, shaking the earth beneath our feet, it seemed brutal and primal and dangerous.

"I'm sure this will work, Maria. If he doesn't bite Joaquin, there is no hope at all. Please, don't make this any harder for Jose," Theresa whispered.

As he charged, I closed my eyes and held my breath. I heard the pop of flesh being pierced and heard something snap wetly. Joaquin screamed. All the contents of my stomach rose to my throat. I fell to my knees and threw my hands over my face. Theresa guarded me, half protecting me, half making sure I stayed out of the way. My legs wobbled, weak and tingly, like they'd fallen asleep. Finally, she hugged me close to help me stand.

Jose shifted back into his human form. I pulled away from Theresa and ran over to Joaquin, and slid down on my knees beside him. With both hands, I turned his arm over to observe the wound. Above the bite from Teo, at his elbow, Jose's bite looked cleaner and looked more like a cut from a knife than an animal bite. A river of blood and putrid fluid flowed from the new wound, purging his body of the infection. Alberto filled the vile.

From the corner of my eye, I saw Theresa pull out a knife and slice Jose's forearm. She filled the test tube and then called me over. On my way over, I rubbed my palms together. Then I held the wound tightly. When I pulled back, the wound had almost disappeared, and I wobbled a little from the exchange of energy.

Theresa and I finished the concoction and brushed it on Joaquin's wound, then I wrapped it with a bandage. We held hands and began our chant.

"Curar la mordedura. Toma el veneno." The English translation is *Heal the bite. Take the poison.*

Lightning struck the ground in the center of us, knocking us backward.

CHAPTER 11

They lifted him up, and slowly, grabbing under his arms and knees, carried him into his room. He lay still and quiet on the bed while I stared at his chest, watching for movement.

I took his hand and held it against my cheek. The heat in his skin began to wane, and he smelled of perspiration, but not disease. The swelling in his arm subsided enough that I could see the deep tracks of Jose's bite, one right below his elbow and one right above it. The flesh from the first bite was torn away and left hanging loose. His intact skin looked less stretched and shiny, though.

Alberto put his hand on my arm and helped me to my feet. He told me Joaquin needed to rest and that sleep would make the healing process progress faster. I kissed Joaquin's forehead one last time for the night, and then Alberto and I shut him in his room to sleep. The door closed like the lid of a tomb closing on my heart.

Theresa and Jose drove back to Austin. My bags were already in Micael's room. They told me he would stay in the guest apartment over the garage. I went into the adjoining bathroom, washed my face and collected my nightclothes. My head spun, and my heart ached. The not knowing was excruciating. In the shower, I let the hot water pour over my head. It sluiced some of my grief away. This painful sensation seemed too familiar, but also different—not like the shock and agony of losing my father, but more fraught with uncertainty. I couldn't slow my mind from racing over every worst-case scenario. I dried off, changed into my nightclothes and cried myself to sleep.

* * *

The De Lunas woke me up for Mass before the sun was up. I dragged myself out of bed and to the bathroom to shower. At church, I lit a candle for him on the way into the sanctuary. I knelt and said a long prayer before Mass, pleading with God and the Great Spirit to take care of him.

Micael drove me home after lunch. As I entered, I yelled to let my mother know I made it home and jogged upstairs, not up for questions, nor did I have any answers. We hadn't done more than grunt at each other for a while—she had given hints she wanted out of this town. I ignored her earlier rants, but Joaquin having an *animal* bite would be the cherry on top of her argument. I went straight to my room and powered up my computer.

It clunked, and with a couple of pop-up screens, the internet service connected. I did a Google search on werewolf viruses. Nothing good. It came up as *Curse of the Lycanthrope*. I read and read. Searching for the tiniest shred of positive news or truth—everything I read seemed infused with exaggeration and guesses, even to me, a novice. But I had to trust my ability.

I washed my face and brushed my teeth. I looked at the clock—it was almost midnight. Tomorrow, I'd return to school. I turned off the computer. Finally, I lugged my body over to the bed and fell over, drifting into a restless sleep.

* * *

The next morning the doorbell rang. My heart jumped. With a bounce, I ran down to the front door and flung it open. It wasn't Joaquin—Gabriel stood at my door. My heart sank, and I let out a sigh.

"Don't look so disappointed," he said, grinning. "Want a ride to school?"

I sighed and said, "Sure."

We drove to school in Joaquin's car, and I could still smell Joaquin's scent. His jacket and tie were where he left them on the way back from Austin. Despite Gabriel's joking around, I could tell he took his assignment as bodyguard to heart. We entered the building side by side.

Jim and Teo stared at me from across the hallway. Teo's voice stung my ears: "Where's your boyfriend? Did you trade him in for a newer model?"

I shot him an "I hate you" stare and scrunched up my fists. Gabriel tugged at the sleeve of my shirt and shook his head; it took everything within me to continue on my way.

At lunch, Gabriel scooted in next to me, too. After school, he met me at my locker to take me home. He kept close; scary close. We went straight to the car and drove away quickly. The massive lump in my throat made it impossible to speak. It stayed there all day, making the five words I'd spoken today painful. In the car, I stared out the windows telling myself to breathe. No longer involuntary. Then, I realized we drove past my street.

"I thought you might want to check on Joaquin."

"Absolutely. I want that more than anything." My emotions were mixed; would he be sicker? Or would he even be awake? My body ached, unable to fathom the shape I'd find him in. Gabriel gave me no indication of Joaquin's recovery or how things progressed through the night. He patted my shoulder, and I pushed out the breath I didn't realize I was holding.

As we entered the house, my eyes fell on Joaquin slumped across the couch. He leaned back against the couch arm, looked at me, and then reached his hand out. I ran to him. Smiling at me, he said, "I missed you, sweetheart."

Those words exhilarated me. He wiped my face with the back of his hand. "Please don't cry."

I shook my head and smiled. "No promises," I said. "I'm relieved."

He told me he wanted to be at school tomorrow, but he was too weak. Gabriel would take me to school again; Gabriel would keep me safe in his absence.

Looking him over, he was dressed quite casually. He wore a white, loose fitted tank top with his Umbro soccer shorts and bare feet. Everything inside of me wanted to snuggle with him, but should I? I tossed a bag of chips and a couple of empty soda cans out of the way before I made room next to him, making sure to move with care to avoid any unnecessary pain. Scrubbing his stubbly face over my cheek and pulling me close, he threw a heavy arm around my stomach and put his chin on my shoulder.

"Mini vacay?" I asked.

"Something like that," he chuckled and squeezed me. Seconds later, his breathing evened out, and his arm became heavy.

Evidently, I fell asleep, too. Gabriel startled me awake hours later with a tap on my shoulder. "I should get you home."

"Did my mom call?"

He looked confused. "No. No, but it's almost nine."

The ride was dominated by a heaviness—a long gloomy atmosphere. Promises were sacred. Gabriel walked me to the door. Tomorrow he would be at my side, again.

"He needs rest." The love he expressed for his brother filled my body with warmth.

"It's a wolf thing," he told me with a wink. A side hug, and he was gone.

* * *

Same time the next day, Gabriel arrived at my door. Today, he accompanied me to all my classes, appearing before I stepped even one foot into the hall. He followed me to lunch and even through the lunch line. At the table, he protectively situated himself beside me. The bodyguard thing was kind of adorable.

At their house, Joaquin waited outside for us—all showered, shaven and wearing a crisp T-shirt and clean blue jeans. A fresh hunkier version of himself, if that could even be possible. As soon as I approached, he hooked his arm around my neck and hugged me close to him. Lifting me until we were face to face, he pressed a fierce kiss on my lips. I deeply inhaling his intoxicating woodsy scent. The smell of the infection had disappeared. I wrapped my arms around him and squeezed tight with my head buried into his muscular chest. His thumb brushed away the tear that trickled down my cheek. Relief washed over me, and I rewarded him with a smile. As it was any other day, he asked, "Want to take a walk?"

The bite scars glowed bright white on his tan skin. I ran my fingers along the raised lines.

"It's fine. Thanks to you," he insisted. The ball in the pit of my stomach didn't believe him. Maybe the heaviness came from the possibility of further harm. I reached out and touched it. A mild keloid scar still raised and warm.

He took my hand off his arm and started to play with my fingers while he led me out back. Stopping under a tree close to the water, I settled down with my back against it and my knees bent. He positioned himself down by my knees.

"Trust me, Maria. You did it. I'm stronger. I get more powerful after each battle. Look."

Leaning back, I could see the rippled muscles, and his gaze intensified like he wanted to consume me.

"Stronger, like Thomas and Jim. They're wererats?"

Trying to make me smile, he flexed his muscle. It didn't help the burning in the pit of my stomach. He grabbed my ankle and pulled me down until I laid on my back on the ground. The forcefulness took my breath and made my body tingle. He crept toward me and slid between my legs. My heart pounded against my ribs, and my hands trembled. Moving toward my face, his body hovered inches off mine. He kissed his way up my neck, and his breath tickled my skin. Then his breath caressed my face, and he placed tender kisses on my lips—sweeter than before. Just like that, he jumped up, grinned and tugged me with him.

I dusted off my pants, and he wiped down my shoulders and back, then his lips met the curve of my neck and moved down to my shoulder. He was my Joaquin—a more intense version. He yanked me close, gave me a deep kiss. His soft laugh flooded me with warmth. Did something seemed off, albeit good or bad?

* * *

Today, Joaquin drove me home. Mom made it home from work, but she withdrew to her room by six o'clock, and the house looked completely dark except for the one porch light; her little way of saying, "I love you." Even though we hadn't spoken to her in days, Joaquin and I stood under the yellow glow of the light, holding each other for a long moment. My face buried in his chest, and his chin on the top of my head, the world around us fell away. I visualized him with his amazing smell and the strength of his arms wrapped around me. I pulled myself back and pushed myself on my toes to kiss him—he seemed taller.

"You seem different. Bigger. Stronger."

"I'm fine."

"Let me in. I may not be *la familia*, but this affects me. I want to get it. No. I need all the information, so I can get it. So, I can help. That book gave me only the slightest insight. Besides the information from the internet, and everything on the internet is true. Right?"

"You aren't officially *la familia*, yet." He rubbed his nose to mine. "But we aren't keeping anything from you." He hugged me a little tighter. "Some things I don't have the answers to. Yes, I'm stronger. Taller. Bigger. If I had all the answers, I would tell you. Seriously. Can you trust me a little bit?"

"I trust you. I do. I need to be a part of all this, and I've had a short time to absorb everything. I'm a little—it's hard to pinpoint, *nervous* about all this. I don't want to lose you." I hugged him tightly.

He exhaled and returned the embrace. "It's tough. But it gets easier with time. I promise. And you're not completely without an understanding of the supernatural."

Reluctantly, I went inside and got into bed, excited about the day to come. He would be back by my side.

* * *

As it turned out, others noticed Joaquin's return, too. When he opened his locker door, waiting for him were two of the biggest rats I'd ever seen—dead and hanging by their tails from the coat hook. My stomach heaved. Whoever left them also left a note, a yellow piece of paper impaled next to the rat. *Welcome Back*, it said, scrawled in blood. At that moment, Jim and Teo passed by, pointing and laughing.

Gabriel heard the commotion and walked over. He pulled them out, holding them up by the tail near Jim and Teo.

"Hey, *raton,* these look like your relatives!"

The rats drew an immediate crowd, and now the students erupted in laughter. Teo flipped a finger and stormed off. Leave it to Gabriel to turn a joke around and piss those guys off.

As I got close, I realized the rats were fake. Gabriel swung them at a group of girls who squealed and scurried away. He laughed, chucked the rats into a garbage can, returned to our group and made a playful swipe of his hand across his shirt. Then he wrapped his arms around me and Becky.

"What's up, ladies? Anything exciting in your lockers?" He chuckled in a way that is signature Gabriel.

In the afternoon, we walked out to the parking lot near where an eagle perched on a fence along an open parking space. Teo stood between us and Joaquin's car door. He puffed his chest and balled his fists, ready for a confrontation. Joaquin took several aggressive steps toward Teo. But before a fight could ensue, the eagle spread her wings and resettled between Teo and us. This gave Joaquin plenty of time to load me into the car and click the door locks. No one noticed the almost altercation—they pointed at the eagle and took pictures with their phones. At the sound of the door closing, she took flight, and her talons struck Teo square in the chest, knocking him to the ground. I laughed, along with about a hundred other of our classmates. Joaquin got into the car and took my hand. We ended up laughing until tears flowed down my face.

I looked back, and all the brothers stood in a circle around Teo. Micael talked. Then, Gabriel—being himself—held his belly and laughed out loud. Teo leaped to his feet and, within seconds, stepped up into Gabriel's face. Immediately, Gabriel's smile vanished, and he looked ready to fight. Their mouths moved in what appeared to be a heated argument. Teo tried to bump Gabriel with his chest, but Gabriel didn't fall back even an inch, and Teo stumbled backward. I could hear a loud "Whoa!" erupt from the crowd. Teo fumed, then slipped through the circle between Enrique and Alejandro. Gabriel's sweet smile returned, and his hands went in his armpits to wave his elbows like a chicken. Some of the guys in the crowd around started to pat Gabriel on the back. He loved it, but this would not be the end of things. Joaquin shook his head and sped up.

We got to his house first and settled on the couch in the living room, flipping the channels, not addressing the scene that happened a few moments earlier. Finally, his brothers made it home after dropping off the girls. Joaquin stood. They replayed the conversation from the parking lot.

Micael turned to me and said, "You're safe, for now."

I kept my eyes on the TV, but my mind replayed the words *for now* over and over. Joaquin pried the remote out of my hand.

"Honey, you've watched ten straight minutes of commercials." He caught hold of me. "Are you okay?"

"Fine. For now, I guess."

"I'm here, sweetheart. Don't worry."

A fog fell over me as we got into his car, and he drove me to my house. Again, Mom slept upstairs, and the porch light lit my path. I kissed him and held him extra-long, even more pensive than the day before. Things were not fine, and I needed his embrace. After a quick kiss, I walked inside the house and took the stairs one at a time. When I fell asleep, I started to dream.

We were in a field of high grass that swayed from side to side like waves in the ocean. Yet abruptly, the beauty drained away—the loss of color, only shades of gray. I waved my hand across the grass, dipping them up and down until something approached. At my side hulked a huge chocolate colored wolf. The fur along his front leg was absent, revealing scarred skin beneath. He ducked his muzzle and nudged my shoulder, and I slid my hand down his side and laid my head on his shoulder. He stood taller than before, and the sight made my heart flutter. A wonderful sensation enveloped me, like someone's arms wrapped tight around me.

The moon turned red, sending an orange glow over the field, and the stars were hidden behind roiling clouds. The wind picked up and swirled. Paper and leaves flew past. Something cracked overhead, and I ducked to avoid a large branch. On the orange horizon, a funnel cloud started to form. It came down to a point, almost touching the ground, and then it tilted back up at an angle to the clouds. I could smell the rain coming, too—the smell of dirt and moisture.

Teo stepped through the grass flanked by a hideous guard. Already shifting into his hideously, terrifying wolf form, he lumbered toward me in a crouched position. Behind him were two others; they stood upright and were hairy and grotesque, making it impossible for me to place their identity. Fangs grew and distorted their bottom lips. Wererats.

I heard growls from behind me. Joaquin's entire family shifted into wolf form, but there were extra wolves that I didn't recognize and couldn't place. The wind kicked up, and the rumble of thunder and sparks of lightning filled the air. A bolt of lightning struck in front of us; a wildfire kindled to life in the grass. Then a larger strike hit the top of a tree. I ducked and covered my head as sparks sprayed and crackled to the ground.

We were dangerously close, too close to Teo for my liking. His nostrils began to flare, and he dug his feet into the ground. He coiled, then sprang forward—his paws struck me in the chest.

Then our doorbell rang.

CHAPTER 12

The holidays came around too fast. Joaquin and I shopped a couple of weekends and got little things for everyone, but I didn't have a chance to buy anything for him. At lunch, I asked Lexi and Becky if they would go with me and give me some ideas. I never had a boyfriend—Joaquin was my first. I wanted to get him something special. They were super excited. We would go after school today since Joaquin practiced soccer, and Friday, we were out for the break.

"I need a little girl time," I told Joaquin.

"Call me when you arrive at the store, okay?"

He would be at practice, making it impossible to understand why he wanted me to call. Sweetly, he added that it would please him if I did. With everything going on, he needed to be protective. He made me safe. It reminded me of the ride home from the hospital after my dad died and before I met Joaquin for real. Sitting beside him soothed my nerves.

"I'll text you," I said, and that satisfied him.

I met the girls out front, and we laughed and enjoyed being friends. We drove to Killeen; Cove being too small for a mall. Becky turned up the radio, and we sang along. Right outside of Killeen, she turned down the radio and asked about ideas.

"This is why I needed you! Give *me* ideas!"

"Cologne," Lexi said.

"He already smells great," I replied.

"A shirt? Something for soccer?" Becky said. They were all good ideas.

Before we went into the mall, I sent out a quick text to Joaquin. He sent back, *Have fun, mi amor.* It made me smile as we set off on our search. First, we looked for shirts. Nothing seemed right. He owned tons of clothes. We went to the men's cologne—still, nothing caught my attention. Then we went to another store with fancier men's clothes. I wrinkled my nose and shook my head. "They're just not him," I said.

When we wandered out into the mall, I could smell cinnamon. Then I found it: a little kiosk with cinnamon coated peanuts. We bought some and took a break, sitting on the bench and enjoying the atmosphere. The mall was filled with Christmas lights and trees. Huge Christmas balls were hanging from the ceiling. Holiday music played over the intercom. All the sights and sounds reminded me of past holidays. Of course, my father lingered in the center of all my best memories. I remember taking this exact path on my way to sit in Santa's lap and putting my letter in the special North Pole mailbox. I tugged my father along by the hand. Always a calm and easygoing guy, and every Christmas, I pulled him at almost a run as we trekked down the mall.

Unaware of my sadness, Becky sprang up from the bench and waved for us to follow. We made our way to the mall's center court to Santa's workshop, where he posed to take pictures. Becky stepped in front of us, clasped her hands together and stuck out her bottom lip in a sexy pout. Lexi and I looked at one another, then shrugged. Becky grabbed our arms, dragging us over to the little house. We went inside. Lexi took one arm of his chair, and Becky took the other. I stood there, looking, and Santa patted his knee. I shook my head. Lexi pulled me over by my arm.

"C'mon, party pooper!"

"You owe me big time for this," I told her. We laughed and got our picture taken with Santa. Becky went over and ordered some pictures. She handed one to each of us and said it would help us remember her while she skied in Colorado.

"Showoff!" I teased. I looked at the picture. We were all smiling, and I placed it on my chest. I took a deep breath and let a little more of the holiday's bittersweet magic into my heart. Pictures reminded me of all the ones taken over the years with my sister. Dad talked Theresa into taking a picture with me every year, even with her being four years older. I figured I'd put it in her stocking this year; she would get a kick out of it and tell me that karma returned to bite me in the butt.

Right then, I heard my name. I turned to see none other than Theresa herself, waving and trotting toward us. I sent her a quick text saying I would be hitting the mall with some friends, but the sight of her gave a joyful shock. I ran toward her and hugged her tight. I dragged her by the hand to introduce her to my friends.

"What are you doing here?"

"I wanted to see you and buy some gifts. Is that okay?"

"Of course. Where's Jose?" I nudged her with my shoulder and smiled.

"Actually, he is with your boyfriend. He's watching him practice soccer or some kind of sports thing. I didn't pay close attention. Boys."

Still looking for a gift for Joaquin, we roamed the mall. We inspected a jewelry kiosk, and something caught my eye: a silver dog tag with an engraved black-and-white soccer ball. The clerk said he could have it engraved with my boyfriend's number. The perfect gift. I asked him to add the number seven. He said it would be ready in about fifteen minutes.

Theresa perused the counter and pointed through the glass to a silver Christmas ornament that said, "In Memory of Dad," with a place for a picture. I threw my arm around her shoulder, and we called another salesperson over and bought the ornament on the spot. She wrapped it up tight in white tissue paper and placed it into a square red velvet box, then handed it to us. Theresa rubbed her hand across the top of the soft box and wiped a stray tear from her eye.

"Well, enough of that. It's girl time. What's next?"

While we waited for the engraving, we ordered pretzels, cheese and Cokes. The smell of the cooked dough wafted through every part of the mall, and it made my mouth water. We found a table toward the end as far away from the congestion as possible.

"Theresa, is Jose your boyfriend?" Lexi asked.

"Is he friends with Joaquin?" Becky asked.

Theresa and I looked at each other and began to laugh.

"Oh, she wants him to be her boyfriend. They are taking things slow. Like, tortoise style slow." I elbowed my sister, and her face turned bright red.

"We are close friends." She elbowed me back. "Yes. We are taking it slow. And he is Joaquin's cousin."

"Oh. My. God." Lexi fanned herself. "Is he as hot as Joaquin and his brothers?"

Theresa answered the question with another blush.

"Jose and Joaquin could be brothers. Believe it or not, he is even more muscular than Joaquin," I said.

The girls looked at Theresa.

"Nuh-uh! And you haven't jumped on that yet? You better watch out," Lexi teased.

Theresa choked on her Coke. "Hey," I patted her back and laughed.

"Your friends have no boundaries, huh? Yes. He is an amazing looking guy. He has bulging muscles. Plus, he is the sweetest guy I have ever met, but I am afraid I may be stuck in the 'friend zone.' We hang out like all the time, but nothing. He has never even tried to hold my hand. I guess he's not interested."

"Have you looked in a mirror? I am sure he is interested. If he's anything like Joaquin, you may have to make the first move." Becky turned to me. "How long did it take Joaquin to kiss you? Seriously. These guys are the hottest guys on the planet, but they take forever to make a move."

Theresa looked at me; my cheeks were the ones glowing. I shrugged.

"Me and you have got to talk later."

I smiled and played coy.

At that precise moment, my stomach lurched, and as if in tune with my pain, Theresa turned a little green and looked around.

"Ugh!" Lexi sighs and then stands up.

Hot hands landed on my shoulders and made me flinch. Theresa looked up and slid her chair away from the table.

"What the hell are you guys doing here?" Lexi asked.

"It's Christmastime. Shopping. What else?" Jim answered.

"Well, go to it and leave us alone."

"Who is this?" Teo asked.

I stepped in front of my sister, blocking his view of her. "None of your damn business."

"That's right. Move along." Becky said.

"Or what?" Jim asked.

Timed to perfection, two muscular security guards showed up. One tattooed with words around his neck and a snake tattooed on his forearm. The other appeared clean-cut but with muscles found in bodybuilder mags. They may have caused me some alarm a few months ago, but these uniformed guys were exactly who I wanted to see at that moment.

"Are these guys giving you ladies trouble?" the tattooed guy said. He leaned against the table and put himself between the boys and us.

"We were about to leave, man," Jim said.

"And don't come back in a few minutes when these nice gentlemen leave us," Lexi said and hugged the tattooed guard with the blonde spiked hair. It struck me a little funny watching this burly guy stutter at her boldness. The boys backed away. Lexi offered the guards a seat. They refused because they were working but said they would stay close to keep an eye out for us. The blonde one handed us a card with a cell phone number in case we wanted them to escort us to our cars. The second guard hadn't taken his eyes off Becky the entire time, but she did her best to avert her eyes. He padded up close to her and offered her his own card. She grasped it in a less than composed motion.

"This is my number. If you need anything, my name is Ben." He held the card for a moment after she reached for it. "Seriously, you can call me anytime."

When they got a safe distance away, I could not resist. I looked at Becky, who tried hard to ignore the recent events.

"Okay. Are you going to call him already?"

"Stop. He was just being nice."

"No way. Even I can see those signs. He wants *you* to call him," Theresa said.

"I couldn't," Becky said as red blotches spread to her neck.

"And why the hell not?" Lexi asked.

"I've never called a guy before—I just couldn't."

"Here," Lexi held out her hand. "Give me your cell and that card."

Becky handed it over, "Why?"

Lexi dialed the number on the phone. While she waited, she tapped the card on the table.

"Hello. Is this Ben?" Becky grabbed for the phone, and Lexi batted her away. "You gave my friend your card. She is super shy and would never call on her own. I wanted to help you out. This is her number. Her name is Becky. She is super sweet and super available. Call anytime."

Becky's mouth gaped open, and her hands gripped the edge of the table. Lexi slid the cell and the card across the table to her.

"You're welcome!"

We all burst out into a roar of laughter. Finally, Becky closed her mouth and picked up her things, tucking them back into her purse, as the sides of her mouth inched up into a full-blown smile.

"Thank you."

"Okay, let's go!" I said.

We picked up our things and finished shopping. We didn't have to call the security guys when we were ready to leave because they stayed close. Darkness fell, and we didn't want to make the trip to our cars unaccompanied. Lexi gave a two-fingered whistle like someone fresh off the farm and waved the guards over. They were at our sides in seconds. Ben almost pressed himself against Becky, his hand settled on her elbow. They didn't say a word to each other, but Lexi had the blonde guy in stitches. Becky drove us around to Theresa's car.

* * *

On the way home, Theresa and I laughed about the day. The short time with my friends and Theresa filled me with overwhelming happiness. Then came a brief pause in the conversation.

"Is that *the* guy?" she asked.

"If by guy you mean, the world-class jerk? Yes."

"It's crazy. I sensed them before they arrived. It's what happened to me before when those guys stalked me."

"I understand. It was the same with me, but I tried to dismiss it as new school nerves. Only, it never let up."

"No, they do give off the creep vibe. Steer clear of those two."

"Not. A. Problem."

"Okay. Change of subject."

"Yeah?"

"How long did it take Joaquin to make a move?"

"Forever. He would touch my face, kiss my cheek, but nothing more. It took weeks, maybe even a couple of months."

"Whew! I thought I was a freak or something. I like Jose, but I'm getting nothing. Like Joaquin, he will push my hair back or kiss my cheek, but that is it. He lives in my apartment with me, for goodness' sake. Still nothing."

"You ever consider making the first move?"

"It may come to that."

We both laughed and enjoyed the rest of the ride home. I sent out a text to Joaquin when we pulled into the drive and told him we were home. I added, *Tell Jose hi from Theresa.*

The glow from the front porch light was absent, but one light glowed from the back of the house. Mom slumped at the kitchen table with a half-empty glass of wine and an empty bottle in front of her.

"You girls decided to come home." She slammed her glass into the sink. When she swung around, she corked a wine bottle with maybe an ounce of liquid inside, sloshing its contents around at us.

"Sorry, we were doing some last-minute shopping."

Theresa pulled out the ornament we bought for Dad. She went to show it to Mom, but Mom shoved it away. She went over to the sink, and dropped her glass in and went upstairs without saying goodnight. I looked at Theresa and shrugged my shoulders. I wanted to say, "Welcome to my world," but it was such a wonderful day, I had no intention of spoiling it.

We watched TV on the couch, cringing as mom banged around upstairs. Relief came from the creak of her box springs, and knowing she would sleep it off. We didn't want to be under the hammerhead of her wrath as it came down. I pulled out my phone, and she did, too. Both of us wanting to be with the De Luna's, even if it was through a text.

* * *

The next few days passed too quickly. Theresa worked up until Christmas Eve. She went back to her apartment, but she called a couple of times. This made my holiday start off on the positive. She would be here Christmas Eve and Christmas, but she needed to go back to work.

The sun set long before my sister made it home Christmas Eve. Joaquin and Jose were spending time with their families, making it girls only. Mom made a fire and hot chocolate, and we watched *The Santa Clause One, Two* and *Three*.

"Where's Joaquin?" Mom asked.

"Oh, he texted to say he's doing family stuff. I'll go over there tomorrow." Theresa elbowed me. "They invited all of us to come for dinner. It might be nice to leave the house for a little while."

"That's—nice," Mom said. Then she went upstairs to bed.

"Jose will be coming, too," I told Theresa. "He's driving in from visiting with his family."

"Seriously?"

I nodded my head, and we finished watching the stack of videos on the coffee table before heading off to bed.

Christmas morning grew chilly. We got up with the sunrise and opened our gifts—bath stuff and pajamas that could have been for anyone. We thanked mom and gave her a hug. Theresa and I got Mom the two books she said she wanted. We rested on the couch, staring at our gifts. We remained in our seats like we were all waiting for something, maybe for Dad. Joy stayed far from this room; silence and sadness were all that remained. As I stood, I moved with cautious steps over to our thrown-together-in-a-rush tree and touched the ornament my sister and I bought at the mall. My sister chose the perfect picture of my father, one of him laughing.

Our Christmas lunch was absent of our traditional big spread with Dad carving a turkey. We put in an order for a meal from a local restaurant. Hoping to shake ourselves out of our funk, my sister and I drove to pick it up. Of course, in Texas, not a hint of snow, but the temperature dropped severely. On the way to the restaurant, we passed my dad's old bank—that's what we needed. One more brick to sink us even deeper into our grief.

As soon as we finished our unremarkable meal, we went upstairs to dress for our evening with the De Luna's. Annette had found out that Theresa came home, Jose would travel up after lunch with his parents, and she invited my mom and Theresa to come along, too. Maybe it would be what we needed to rid ourselves of the black cloud looming over our day—spending a little time with a "normal" family.

* * *

We arrived, and the smell of food hit us as we stepped out of the car. Mom brought a bottle of wine for the De Luna's; who would have imagined? My mother with a bottle of wine. That didn't matter. I couldn't wait to see Joaquin. Because of the little lecture about not leaving mom alone courtesy of Theresa, I spent the past two days at home. Now an excitement over seeing him again overcame me.

Gabriel met us at the door with hugs and a huge smile. He took our coats and told us to make ourselves at home. As soon as we stepped into the living room, Joaquin and Jose met us with more hugs, with Annette nearby ready to greet my mother. Mom gave her the wine, and Annette went to the kitchen to open it. Theresa and I gave each other a quick look and took a deep breath.

The boys ushered us into the living room, where they pulled out a stack of videos to watch. We chose *The Grinch*. Nothing too sappy and no "great fathers" to pull us back into our funk. Micael, Marisol, Enrique and Alyssa crowded onto the love seat, snuggled up close. The fire blazed, and we settled into the extra-large sofa. I noticed Theresa slide in close to Jose as he wrapped his arm around her. It seemed like he wanted a more-than-friend's relationship.

Dinner arrangements were casual. We ate in the living room watching TV, while our parents ate at the table in the kitchen. After a couple of glasses of wine, we decided it was time to take our mother home.

"Mom, you ready to go home?" Theresa said.

"Yes. I'm a little tired." Mom said.

She insisted we stay and have a little fun—she didn't seem drunk, and for the first time in a while, a spark of life lit her eyes. Theresa and I exchanged glances, then shrugged and agreed. We drove her home, and the boys followed us.

Theresa climbed in back with Jose. We drove to Belton to see the show—scenes with lights all around Belton Lake. Santa in a rocket, blinking candy canes and a helicopter with spinning propellers. A beautiful sight. I never in my life imagined there would be this many lights. We pointed out some of our favorites—mine happened to be the tunnel of lights at the end because it reminded me that every one of us has a brilliant path to follow in life if we choose to accept it.

On the way home, someone drove hazardously close to our rear end. Joaquin edged to the side to let them pass, but they continued on our tail. I noticed Jose pulling Theresa closer holding her with both arms. Bright lights flooded the car and made it impossible for Joaquin to see out of the rearview mirror. Joaquin placed both hands on the wheel, and we all got quiet. I grabbed the door handle, holding on exceedingly tight. Finally, they made their move to pass and drove up beside us. But they swerved into us. Joaquin jerked the car to the shoulder. Gravel sprayed in the air. Then they turned on the interior light to reveal themselves.

Jim yelled out the window, "Freaks!"

From the backseat, I heard, "They don't have room to talk," and then Theresa started to laugh. The headlights faded into the distance.

"Were those guys the ones from the mall?" Theresa asked and leaned forward.

"Yes."

"What? The mall?" Joaquin asked.

"We were fine," I said.

"No. It's not fine. You can't keep things from me!"

"I'm sorry. They showed up, per usual. These two security guards ran them off. Luckily, the one crushed on Becky, and they stayed close. A calm washed over me the whole time. If I hadn't, I would've called you. I wasn't trying to keep anything from you. I promise," I said.

"Cool down, cuz. Be glad our gals can handle themselves in a pinch," Jose said.

Joaquin's knuckles turned white as he twisted them around the steering wheel. He took a few deep breaths and said finally, "You're right. Okay."

"Of course, I am." He clasped his cousin's shoulder and shook him roughly, giving a little levity to the serious situation.

The boys took us home. Joaquin guided me to the door with a slight push to my back and kissed me goodnight. Jose and Theresa stayed close to the car. He leaned against the car door, and she stood in front of him. He ran his hand up her arm and leaned in—this could be it, the first kiss. I held my breath, but I caught his eye as he kissed her on the cheek. A smidge of sadness fell over me, but I understood. The perfect moment might not be standing against a car with Theresa's little sister gawking at them. Joaquin's face blocked my view as he kissed me again, and Theresa and Jose approached, fingers entwined. I tiptoed up and kissed him several more times before they left.

Once inside, we decided to go upstairs. Mom slept in her room with all the lights off. I went to the bathroom to clean up for bed. When I stepped back into my room, Theresa parked herself on my bed, startling me. She frowned and picked at a loose string on my comforter.

"These guys, the ones from tonight and the mall are bad news?"

"Yes," I settled in beside her on my bed. "That's why I was so glad you had Jose."

"Does it help having Joaquin around?"

"Yes. But Teo believes he still has a chance. He's nuts—like, certifiable."

"You love Joaquin, don't you?"

"Maybe, I guess I do. Do you love Jose?"

"It's new, but with him, it's different."

"Enough of the gushy stuff. We need to ask for protection. I'll get my bag."

We sat on the bed together and called on the Great Spirit asking for strength and protection. Swiping my room as we did Theresa's apartment.

* * *

The vacation days passed too quickly. Joaquin and I visited with each other every day. New Year's Eve came, and the plans were to spend it together at my house. Joaquin asked to come over to my house with me since I didn't want to leave Mom alone. We watched a movie, and then at midnight, we flipped the channel to watch the ball drop. Mom gave me a kiss on the cheek and said her goodnights.

For the first time, I looked at her. As she climbed the steps, Mom looked skinny. Her clothes hung on her, cheeks hollow, and she had purple crescents underneath her eyes that looked black in the shadows. She seemed to conceal them for work, or else the holiday hit her harder than it hit us.

Joaquin and I stayed up a little longer. Then we heard the crackle and pop of firecrackers outside, and we stepped out into the backyard. A few fences over, kids in the neighborhood were igniting fireworks. He took a seat in one of the chairs, and he pulled me into his lap. He slid his hand between my knees, and we started kissing underneath all the shooting lights as they whistled and buzzed past the house. With all the changes Joaquin endured since the fight, I liked this the most. His physical restraint lessened. Our kisses were more frequent and passionate. He didn't jerk away when our touch became too sexual. But I feared our relationship might lose its voice of reason. If he lost control, then we were going to be in big trouble.

Too soon, the time for him to go home arrived. I pulled him by the hand toward the front patio. I wrapped a blanket around my shoulders, and instead of leaving right away, we spent more time together out in the chairs on the front porch. Without the porch light on, the darkness flooded us, except for the occasional perforation of lights across the sky from fireworks all around the neighborhood. He took my hand and pulled me over into his lap. We started kissing again, and my thigh tingled as his warm hand moved under the blanket and up the side of my leg. It exhilarated me. Then, his hand traveled up my side and to my back. He pulled me close to him. Sweat started to form on my skin, giving me a hot yet cold sensation. As my hand slipped under his shirt and up his warm taut skin, an overwhelming need to pull him into me flooded my body. Smoothly, he slipped his hands under my legs, stood and placed my feet on the ground. And like that, his restraint flooded back. He gave me one more long, sweet kiss and trotted in a half jog to his car.

From the door, I watched him drive away. I fell against the jamb, and a sense of sadness struck me like when cool air from the north slams into the warm air of the south—watch out for the tornado. I pressed my hand against my chest, and my heart beat strong and steady. A huge lump settled in my throat, making it hard to breathe. On the way upstairs, my mind told me I acted silly, I would see him in a few hours—yet my heart broke every time he left. I wanted more, needed more, more of his touch, more conversation and more time.

Since the weekend in Austin, I sensed a change. I ran up the stairs and flopped on my bed. My body raced with my need to hold him. Life seemed such a mess—my sister lived far away, and my mother lodged herself in the denial phase of grief. All these things pushed me further into Joaquin's arms. Fear gripped me; fear for my family, threaded with anger at all the changes, at my age and the limits on my time, and my crumbling ability to resist my need to have Joaquin. I never realized love could be this hard.

With this increasing pain each time he leaves for a few hours, how severe is her pain? Dad will never return. Tears welled in my eyes and exposed a gigantic hole in my heart that even Joaquin's love couldn't fill. I tried to swallow the lump in my throat. Then, I pulled my covers up tight, closed my eyes, and prayed for sleep.

* * *

The next day we were back at school. Joaquin dropped me off at home after his soccer practice. He gave me a kiss in the car and held my leg tight. In the darkness, we stayed there, kissing for a few minutes. "School tomorrow," he said into our kiss, and pulled away. "Gotta go get your beauty rest."

I sighed, laughed and backed out of his embrace.

I attended his practices all week, sitting in the bleachers in his heavy coat, doing my homework. He played like a professional, and his brothers were good, too. Maybe I'm biased. They were fast and played well together, like they possessed some type of weird telepathy.

The game coming up this Friday would be the most crucial game of the year. We played the Eagles, an important rival team that ranked right below us in the standings. The practices went a little longer, and Joaquin and I didn't have enough time together in the evenings—a quick kiss and goodnight. I found myself being a little sad, crazy right, being jealous of soccer. But I wanted to see him kick butt in Friday's game.

On the big day, the school walls were plastered with all the "Good luck!" and "Beat the Eagles!" signs. The cheerleaders organized a pep rally for the team, too, being such a big game and the team being un-defeated. The players all received ribbons from the cheerleaders to wear. A school tradition was for the players to pass the ribbons along to their girlfriends to wear, and I wore Joaquin's. It hung, pinned to my chest, and I ran my fingers down the blue and gold ribbons. They were attached to a plastic soccer ball, his number in glitter on one of the ribbons and his name on another. My fingers traced each letter of his name. We were together, and everyone was aware of it. For the first time all year, I belonged here.

* * *

We planned to eat dinner at the *taqueria* in town at four o'clock. The boys wanted a little time to digest their food before the big game, and they visited their parents all week.

Alberto and Annette waited for us when we arrived at the restaurant. We all made our way through the double glass doors together. People stopped and stared. They recognized who the boys were and wished them good luck. If you are an athlete in a small town and your team is doing well, people recognize you from the local paper.

During the meal, Alberto told everyone about his soccer days. He bragged about his glory days and how many goals he scored. He told everyone that he taught his boys every skill they used on the field, including all the little foot tricks. He spent many days in the backyard coaching and playing with the boys. Most of the time, the boys agreed with everything he said, but Gabriel seemed pretty good at giving him a hard time. He said things like, "Yeah, try to keep up with us now, old man."

"You are like my dad," I said. "He loved coaching me in softball. We would practice out in the backyard for hours. Dad would even persuade Theresa to come play, which took some convincing because she hated sports. We would play for hours. I can throw a mean curveball because of his persistence."

The smile stretched across my face. Everyone stopped to hear my story. Annette tilted her head a smidge to the side and clutched her napkin against her chest. The girls, even Alyssa, showed a softness in their eyes over it and the boys looked over at me. The truth being, I'd never been able to talk about my Dad in a group of people until today.

"He was a great dad. I wish you all could have met him. He would have been right here trading stories. He would have loved to see y'all play."

I ducked my head, and my chair made a squeal as Joaquin pulled me close to his side with his arm around my shoulder. He kissed my forehead.

Alberto said, "Your dad would have loved to be here. Did he tell you we went to school together?"

The lump forming in my throat prevented me from speaking. I shook my head. He reached across the table and patted my hand, and with a smile, he said, "I will have to tell you some stories one day. When you're ready."

I nodded and smiled.

Gabriel grinned. "You play softball, huh? Maybe someday you can show off your so-called skills, little girl."

"Little girl? I'll show you *little girl*." I picked up a small chip and tossed it at him. Everyone laughed, and the conversations started again. I laid my head on Joaquin's shoulder and smiled at the memories of Dad—and all the memories I made in that moment. Like that, I became part of a new family. *La familia.*

Until today, I never paid attention to Annette and Alberto's looks. Under the *taqueria's* bright fluorescent lights, you should have been able to see every wrinkle, but both of them looked young. Alberto seemed a few years older than the boys, except for some dignified silver in his hair. He must have been younger than my dad. Or was he? Annette didn't have any fine lines around her eyes at all—her skin looked flawless. The way she dressed, trendy but subdued, gave her the illusion of additional maturity.

We finished up our dinner and did the usual sorting of who drives who's car to the game. Joaquin kissed the top of my head, and they left. We were two blocks from the field. Joaquin rode with his brothers to the field house, leaving me to drive Marisol and Alyssa to the game in his car. Driving his car made my stomach tumble—a stick, in an expensive sports car.

I inched my way to the soccer field where Alberto and Annette were out of the car waiting for us when I pulled into the parking space. We headed for the stands then took a seat on the bottom bleachers at midfield.

Alberto greeted tons of people. Between being a lifetime resident, the DA, and the father of five super athletes, he knew everyone, and everyone knew him. He talked to the people around us. He retold some of the stories from the restaurant and bragged about his boys. Deep down, his pride over them playing "his" sport showed.

The game began. Joaquin kicked off. He sent a screamer all the way back to the other team's defenders. The boys lined up: Micael, Joaquin and Enrique were positioned up front on offense, and Gabriel and Alejandro were defenders. They were amazing. One of them would dribble the ball down the field, and without even a glance, they would send a perfect pass right over to one of their brothers. In seconds, they would rush toward the goal and try for an open shot.

About halfway through the first half, Joaquin broke out with Micael at his right, one step behind. With every stride, their muscular legs flexed, revealing hard lines in the stadium lights. They were at the top of the goal box, and Joaquin passed to Micael. A perfect pass shot about two strides out in front of Micael. Micael sent the ball to the goal, flying right across the goal, and without missing a step, Joaquin headed the ball in the opposite top corner. It looked like a perfect Z. The goalie couldn't even come close. The fans erupted in celebration. We jumped to our feet.

The referee set the ball for kickoff. The Eagles took a different route, going for the short pass across to another team member who sent the ball flying downfield. They made their best effort, but Gabriel and Alejandro were there, and they weren't giving an inch. Both teams stayed on our end, passing back and forth. This went on for a little while until Alejandro intercepted and sent the ball sailing back to midfield. Enrique turned to make a break. He zigzagged a few times, dribbling through defenders, giving his brothers a chance to catch up. Once Micael closed the gap, he started sprinting past Enrique toward the goal. Enrique slipped a little forward pass between the defenders. Micael dug deep for enough speed to put a foot on the ball. Like a bullet, Enrique centered on goal. Instead of shooting, he did a heel pass and sent the ball back to his brother, who blasted the ball in the upper ninety. The stands screamed in an even louder celebration.

The Eagles kicked off using their same short kick, but then they dribbled the ball in toward our goal. Again, they were no match for Gabriel and Alejandro. They fended them off until the halftime whistle blew. Our boys were up two–zero. They went to the benches for some instructions and a drink.

My face hurt from smiling, and my hands were hot pink from clapping until I heard Lexi scream.

It came from up high in the stands. Lost in the game and conversations around us, I hadn't seen her arrive. As I looked up, Jim grabbed her and shook her by the arm. They started yelling. I went into defensive mode and started leaping up the bleachers to help my best friend. I sensed a presence as Alberto fell in step behind me.

"Hey!" I shouted, half friendly, half ready to break up a fight. "Hello! What's up?"

Things seemed to disperse a bit. The spectators started to clear away from them. Alberto stepped up right beside me, and Jim would not like this to travel back to his dad, the sheriff. Alberto gave Lexi a polite invitation to come and sit with us.

"Yes, absolutely." She pulled away from Jim without looking at him and marched down the stairs to where we were sitting. At our bleacher, she caught hold of my arm. She didn't smile, and she shook. I looked around for Xavier.

Marisol and Alyssa pretended they didn't hear the screams from the fight and pulled her right into their conversation. It took a little time, but she returned to her old self. Maybe not all the way, she kept looking back up in the stands.

I leaned in close to Lexi's ear, "What is going on?"

"He wants me to date Teo's cousin. That guy is a beast. Look at him. Not to mention, I don't want anyone who might have Teo's genes." She gave me a look, and I understood what she meant.

"Did you break up with Xavier?"

"No. Jim wants me to, but it's not happening. I'm falling in love with Xavier. Plus, I am sick of Jim pushing me around. I hang out with him enough. Can you imagine what it would be like if I dated his friend? Ugh!"

"Is it his way of keeping you away from me, too?"

"Yes. No. I don't know. Probably. I hadn't considered that. He is such a pest. I can't wait for him to go off to college."

"Soon, enough." We laugh and turn to watch the game.

Annette spoke to Alberto, in Spanish and they laughed. I looked down, a bit out of place. My father spoke fluent Spanish, but I didn't speak it much outside of our home. Thinking about my heritage made me ache for dad. He was everywhere, and the grief I kept hidden gripped me.

Annette rubbed my back. "I still miss my dad every day," she said.

"Does it get better?" I asked.

"Yes, but it doesn't go away." She talked about her family. Through her father, she belonged to the Tonkawa tribe. But her mother belonged to the Caddo tribe, and her grandmother was white. She said her mother was fair-skinned with green eyes. Looking at her, I realized she didn't inherit the pale skin, but she did have dark green eyes—green eyes like mine.

"Well, you're beautiful," I confessed.

Annette laughed and hugged me.

The game's second half began. The ball flew down the field toward Gabriel and Alejandro. This time Gabriel sent the ball to midfield in an almost perfect pass to Joaquin. He took a shot on the goal in two strides, and it sailed into the net before the goalie could put a hand on it. Everyone in the stands gasped and rose to their feet in jubilation. Nothing like you'd ever seen before, but Micael appeared unhappy. He went straight for Joaquin, and the conversation appeared serious. Joaquin ducked his head. Joaquin showed more of his newfound strength than should have been possible. It was crazy important to keep their little secret safe. Micael put out his fist, and Joaquin bumped it, then they lined up for the kickoff.

Even with all the opponents' effort, they could not move past Gabriel and Alejandro. With one playing stopper and the other sweeper, they bottled up the middle. Each time, they slammed the ball back up to Micael. They were up by three goals. Micael dribbled through the midfield, waiting for a perfect opportunity. A short pass to Joaquin, who saw Enrique streaking past him. One soft pass later, Enrique shot low at the corner post.

Micael passed to Joaquin, who took a short stride, sensing that Enrique set himself, and passed it off. Enrique took a low shot to the corner post, and it cruised in. The crowd jumped to its feet again. People started to clear out a little bit, but I stayed put. I wanted to wait for the boys after the game. The whistle blew, and the game ended, four–zero. The boys lined up to wish the Eagles a good game while they filed down the line. Then they headed for the field house to change and shower.

Lexi stayed with us. I asked her, "Do you have your car?"

"Yeah, I came on my own tonight. I'll be fine. Jim's already gone."

We hugged, and Alberto escorted her to the car. As she disappeared toward the parking lot, a vision of her fight with Jim flashed before me. I shook my head as my knees weakened, and Annette's arms whisked around my shoulder to steady me. In that instant, it became all too clear that Jim would not stop. He would worm his way in between us. More determined than ever, I would have to fight for my friendship with Lexi. The words may come out of Jim's mouth, but Teo was positioned at the root of the problem. I would never let Teo steal anything from me. If Lexi suffered even a little bit for being my friend, then he better watch himself.

* * *

When the boys emerged, we hugged and congratulated them all. That's a pretty long congratulations when you have five boys. We all made our way out to the parking lot together and got into our cars.

Joaquin drove me to my house, and in the car, the uneasy rumble in my middle intensified after my goodbye with Lexi.

"Would you mind coming in and checking the house?" I asked.

He grinned. "It's Friday. I'm not going to waste the chance to spend extra time with you."

We drove up to the house, and all the lights were off. Mom didn't leave the porch light on for me—I wondered if I made her mad for some reason. Joaquin looked over at me with a frown, and I shrugged. We hurried to the door, and I turned the knob and pushed it open. The glow of the television flickered, lighting the house, every other light extinguished. The low light being the one thing that kept us out of pitch dark. I looked up at Joaquin.

I yelled, "Mom?"

The silence sent prickles through my body. Joaquin stepped in front of me, but he kept one hand back on my stomach. We stumbled toward the living room. My eyes adjusted. In the weird glow of the television, my mother's sleeping form appeared on the couch. Relief washed over me for a moment. Joaquin flipped the light switch. I made my way over to the couch, and something looked wrong with her face. I realized she was unconscious, and vomit was smeared all over the pillow.

I shook her and yelled, "Mom, Mom?"

She didn't respond. Her head fell back limply. Out of the corner of my eye, I noticed an orange and white bottle sitting on the coffee table. I shook it…silence. I read the label.

"Oh my God. Call 911!"

CHAPTER 13

Red lights flashed, people scrambled in and out of the wide-open front door. They placed my mom on the floor to work on her. I kept a tight grip on her hand as six men and a woman in uniform ran around my house looking in the medicine cabinets, trash containers and recycling bin. I heard the clink of empty wine bottles in the kitchen.

My stomach tightened, and my heart picked up its pace. Two of the men tried to revive her with CPR. Pump, pump, breath, and check... nothing. They would start again. She'd stopped breathing at almost the same moment the paramedics rushed through the front door. The woman tried to start an IV. Two other men talked behind me, and I heard Joaquin's voice respond. "What time did you arrive home?" "When did you leave?"

I turned back in time to see them tilt her head back and drive a tube down her throat. I heard, "Got it!" Then they pulled something back and attached a bulb to the thing sticking out of her mouth. Each squeeze of the bulb sent her chest up as the air filled her lungs. Then the man started back with the compressions.

The other two men came in with a long, orange board. The woman took me by the shoulders and pulled me back. Slowly, I lost my grip on Mom's hand. They slipped the board under her. "One, two, three," they lifted her from the floor, never stopping the compressions or the puffs of air. My knees buckled as I watched. The lady caught my elbows. They put the board onto a gurney that someone rolled into the hallway. I rushed over to her side and took her hand again. I kept pace on our way out into the dark, toward the flashing lights, my eyes going blind for a moment. I looked back down at my mother's hand. I held tight, but her hand remained limp and chilly. I heard some clicks as they dropped the gurney.

"One, two, three…" They lifted her into the back of the ambulance, pulling my hand loose again.

A masculine hand landed on my shoulder, and I turned to see Joaquin standing there. He told me to go with her, and he would meet me at the hospital. "You'd better call your sister, too," he said. "Or if you want to wait until we arrive at the ER, I'll sit with you while you do it."

"I'll do it."

"Are you sure?"

I nodded. One of the men helped me into the back of the ambulance. The double doors slammed, one and then the other, hard. As we pulled out, I watched Alberto, Joaquin and the two officers talking at my front door.

My mother was pale, but some of her color had returned to her cheeks, and the paramedics continued CPR. The lady worked beside me, drawing up something into a syringe. She pushed the plunger forward a little causing a drop to bead up on the point, and she flicked it. The liquid flew across the ambulance. Then she shot the syringe into the valve on the IV tube. In the front seats, two men talked into a radio spouting important information to the person on the other end—I heard "prescription overdose" and "quantity of wine" and "CPR" and "pupil response."

I could do nothing but sit there, feeling helpless while I gripped her hand like I was a five-year-old crossing the street. My mind reeled at all the things I needed to do. Theresa was the closest thing I had to adult advice. The ambulance walls squeezed me tight, building an invisible partition between me and everyone else—no one to talk to me, no one to tell me anything. The paramedics worked hard and fast.

The sirens were loud, and its lights made the tree branches outside the ambulance windows flash red in the night. Lightness filled my head like helium expanding a balloon. The lady next to me said, "Are all right?" I nodded. She returned to work, writing things down on a clipboard.

Then I heard the lock on the doors clank open, and all together, we moved out of the ambulance. I kept up with them. When we got to some double doors, one of the men punched the button on the wall with the side of his fist. The double doors flung open with a slam against the walls. The lady stood in front of me with her hands on my shoulders, blocking me from entering.

"You have to stay out here," she said.

"What?" I asked.

"You can't go back here. A doctor will be out soon."

I stood there frozen. My knees hit the floor. Someone tugged on each of my arms and pulled me back to my feet. Annette and Marisol stood on either side of me. They led me to the waiting room full of people, and I remained motionless with my head slumped and my hair covering my face. I went numb. I couldn't even cry.

"Here you go," Marisol handed me a bottle of water. My mouth sucked dry of any moisture, I took a drink and set it down on the floor beside me. Sure that any movement would cause me to break into a million pieces, I slumped in my chair. Hospital smells of chemicals, blood and sickness overwhelmed me. That all too familiar smell of death. I tried to force the dry lump down my throat that was making me nauseous. Finally, I reached down and grabbed the water bottle and took a quick swig, and that's when the weight of my phone in my sweater pocket caught my attention.

I took a deep breath. I pulled out the phone, pressed a few buttons, and staggered outside to give my sister the news.

"What's up?"

"It's mom. We are at the hospital. It looks like an overdose."

"Where were you?"

Her tone revealed anger and accusations. If I had been home, it wouldn't have happened. Like, I wasn't blaming myself? I remained calm and replayed the events for her. She sobbed uncontrollably.

"Theresa, let me speak to Jose."

The line cut to silence for a moment. Then a husky voice said, "Hello."

"Jose?"

163

"Hey, what's going on?"

I retold the story. I asked him to please drive Theresa to the hospital. I gave him directions and told him where to enter the hospital.

"Jose?"

"We are locking the door now."

"I will see you soon. Thank you."

"No problem. Are you okay, sweetheart?"

"I am. Take care of T. She needs you."

"You worry about your mom. I've got your sister."

"Thanks."

I went back inside and took a seat, ignoring everyone around me. Sipping from the water bottle and watching the clock on the wall above the check-in station. Time dragged.

The glass entrance doors of the emergency room shuffled open, and Joaquin and Alberto were there. I stood up with my arms tight across my chest, shaking my head back and forth. He pulled me toward him and hugged me tightly. No tears fell. I stood in place. Numb. Then, I pushed back.

"Theresa?" Joaquin asked.

"I called her. Jose is bringing her to the hospital. They will be here soon."

He whispered, "I'm here." Then he kissed the top of my head. I closed my eyes tight, holding back; breaking down would come at a different time. Mom needed me, and I would need to speak to the doctors soon and understand what they said. The strength to push on came from somewhere deep inside me. At that moment, my body held tight to the inner strength I inherited from my father.

I fell back down against the chair, trying to catch myself with the chair's arms. Still numb. I couldn't cry. Strength was needed. The clock on the wall held my attention, watching every tick of the second, minute and hour hand. A flashback to the first time I waited for my sister to arrive gives me a chill. The previous emotions broke loose and flooded over me. Looking at my father's lifeless body lying in a hospital bed. The nurse standing before me jolted me back to reality, "Miss Richards?"

"Yes?"

"You can come back."

I started to follow her, but then I looked back and noticed them all waiting. I turned and kept my forward pace. We, the nurse and I, proceeded down a long white sterile hallway to a big room full of areas sectioned off by curtains. We passed them all on our way to a large room at one end of the large bay. She was attached to all kinds of machines. An eerily familiar awareness stormed over me. She was reclined with her head elevated. Her chest went up and down with the machine's plunger. Two IV machines were hooked up, one to each arm. Circular stickers were attached to her chest with electrodes attached to a heart monitor. Wires and tubes running everywhere.

"She is stable for now. The doctor will be in soon."

My mind raced. I wondered how they expected me to understand what they talked about. "Wait, can someone come back with me?"

"I'm not supposed to," she looked me up and down and sighed, "but in your case, you can. Who should I ask for?"

It took me a second. "Joaquin and Annette."

She patted my back, "All right."

I moved over and settled myself into a chair next to the bed. *Déjà vu.* I took her hand and dropped my forehead down on the edge of the bed. Moments later, I heard Joaquin and Annette. They stood back for a minute; their footsteps lingered in the door. I put my head down on the bed.

"Thanks for coming back," I said.

"Sure, honey." Annette rubbed my shoulder.

When I heard more footsteps, I looked up—the doctor.

"I'm Dr. Pliego."

He shook Annette's hand and asked her name. She explained the situation and that they were family friends. "Alberto De Luna is my husband," she added, and at last, the doctor seemed to relax in her presence. He began to explain about medications. The word overdose reverberated in my ears. How the medications worked and what they hurt. My mother seemed to be stable but in critical condition. They would transfer her up to the ICU.

My phone buzzed in my pocket. I peeked at the screen—Theresa texting to say she and Jose were ten minutes outside of town.

He explained that transportation would come down soon and transfer her up to the ICU.

"Is she going to make it?" Annette asked.

Dr. Pliego's eyes cut to me and back down at the chart. "We're doing everything we can."

I dropped my head back down to the bed, and I didn't raise it again until I heard more footsteps. Transportation arrived to take my mother upstairs. They told us they were going to ICU five and we could meet them there.

We went back out to the waiting area and told everyone. They gathered their things, and we went down the hallway toward the elevators. Alberto pushed the up arrow button. With a loud chug, it stopped, and the doors banged open. We filed in. He pushed the number two button, and with a jolt, we started to rise. This time the walls flew wide open, and it was as if I were standing in New York City without a soul around. My stomach dropped with the stop of the elevator. We made our way into the ICU waiting room. I waited in a corner chair, biting my thumbnail and twisting my hair.

Finally, a nurse came out and said, "Richards' family?"

I stood up.

"You can come with me."

I followed her through a solid automatic door. A rectangular nurse's station stood in the middle of the room with glass walls and doors all the way around it, ticking off the numbers until we made our way to room five. Unmoving, Mom looked like she could wake at any moment.

I found a place next to the bed, held her hand and laid my head down on the side of the bed. Joaquin stood beside me, rubbing my back. "I noticed there's no cell service up here. Gabriel will keep an eye out for Theresa and Jose and will show her the way."

Reminiscent, I tried to find even one event in my life where I needed my strength alone. Dad strengthened our family. He paid the bills, worked and made all the plans. At every crisis, he positioned himself at my side. When I broke my arm, he scooped me up in his arms and whisked me off to the ER. Mom stayed home. She had no idea what happened. He stayed at my side, holding my hand, as I screamed while they reset the bones. He wiped my tears as they fell and watched while they wrapped the pink cast around my arm. Before we went home, he washed my face. He cleaned me up and bought me some French fries and a Coke, and then he presented a happy me, all smiles, to my mother.

When our grandfather died, we attended the wake. We stopped in the foyer and received hugs and kisses from family members. A little while later, he emerged from a back room, wiping his face with a white handkerchief. He smiled and took us to the hotel for a swim with the other kids. Cousins we'd never met. At the funeral, we stood at the back, and he held each of our hands. I remember him picking me up and hugging me tightly while he angled his body to block Theresa's view as the casket got closer. He sheltered us from school and people and all the things that were tough in life. I loved my father a great deal, but at this moment, I believed that his efforts were both good and bad. He should have been our guide through these situations, not our shield.

Here. Now. At this moment, I would hold it together for as long as possible. Teaching myself how to cope. Mom fell apart as I stood back and let it happen. Maybe I allowed this to happen, but I would have to take care of things and never again allow it. Try to make things right from this moment forward.

The next time I heard footsteps, they were Theresa's. I stood up and ran over to her; we hugged for a long time. When I stepped back, though, she scowled at me. Her eyes were bloodshot and swollen. She seemed to have lost some weight. She exploded with anger, and it must have come from more than this situation.

"I told you not to leave her alone!"

"Wait. What?"

"She's having a tough time. Why did you leave her alone?"

Her eyes flashed with rage. She wanted to place this all on my shoulders. I braced myself. The heaviness of guilt struck me, a guilt all my own. But, by no means would I accept all the blame. She shook from head to toe, and this ignited something inside me. That flight or fight mode arose within me. It was on.

"Seriously, Theresa? You visited mom, when?" I put my finger on my temple and said, "Hmmm. Christmas, for like a day?"

"You're here, Maria!"

"Yeah, you've got that right. I'm here. I live this—all the time. You're gone—all the time. You accept no fault."

Joaquin's body materialized between us. "Hold on, girls, you're a little upset. It's nobody's fault…"

"I'm leaving." I took off out of the room and hit the doors, slamming them into the wall. Annette stood up and hugged me, but I couldn't hug her back. Standing numb with my arms dangling limply at my sides, she let me go, and I headed out to the parking lot by myself. As I replayed my sister's hateful words, my skin grew a little hotter, and my heart beat a little faster. My steps were harder, and I balled my fists. I threw open the door to Joaquin's car and gathered things that needed to be thrown away. A trashcan—I needed to find one. My gaze traveled across the parking lot until I spotted one. I stormed over and threw things in the trash as if they were my worst enemies. A piece of paper clung to the lid. I gripped it and tore it to shreds, to symbolize my insides, and then I slammed the pieces into the trash. It didn't help. With both hands on the edges of the cement base of the can, I leaned over and tried to catch my breath.

Two hands slid around my waist, and my mood calmed. I leaned back against Joaquin and let him hold me. My breathing slowed. When I pulled away, his family stood behind him. Unaware of the extent of my tantrum they'd seen, but if they saw anything, they pretended otherwise. They said goodbye and Annette gripped my arm and gave me a forced smile.

"We are going to Maria's house," Joaquin said.

"Son, are you sure y'all don't want to come to our house?" Alberto asked.

Joaquin looked at me and turned back to his father. "No, she needs to be home."

Alberto nodded his head in acceptance and hugged his son. He leaned down and kissed my forehead. They all strolled toward their cars.

* * *

After leaving the hospital, I entered an empty house. There were tubes and wrappers scattered all over the living room floor. Since the night passed and the hour seemed late—or, early in the morning—and the house was left unlocked for hours, Joaquin came in to clear the house, making sure I would be safe. He started at the back, returned to the front, and then we went upstairs, checking each room until we came to my room. Theresa would stay at the hospital since she arrived a few moments earlier. We each needed space. Space to get my head on straight and learn how to apologize.

My body warmed, and my head pulled tight. I jerked open my drawer, yanked out my nightclothes, then slammed it shut. Stomping as I went, I made my way to the bathroom to change. I threw my clothes on the floor. As I looked in the mirror, I noticed my hair looked like I slept on top of my head.

"Why didn't you tell me my hair looked like this?"

I slung open a drawer and grabbed a brush, raking it through my tangled hair. My face scrunched and I groaned. "Ugh." I threw the brush against the mirror. It made a loud clank and then ricocheted off the counter, hit the tub and then fell to the floor. I leaned both hands on the counter and pressed my forehead against the mirror. Tears were running down my face and dropping into the sink.

Joaquin came into the bathroom. He pulled my arms around his neck and he held me around my waist. He said, "It's okay."

I pushed him away and started to yell. "NO! It is not! Are you serious right now? Nothing is okay."

"Maria, it will be. It'll become better."

"No… it won't." I pounded his chest.

"I promise you; your mom will be okay. You'll make it through this. I'll help."

"Oh yeah, you'll help. How the hell can you help? Give me a hug?" I threw my hands in the air. "You have no idea what I'm going through. What this is like. My heart is broken."

"Maria, please."

"NO! My dad is gone. Now, I am like this close," holding my fingers an inch apart, "to losing my mom. My sister is… You were there. I am alone!" I screamed. "Ugh!"

"Maria, you're not alone. I'm here."

"Oh yeah, you with your perfect little family. You are trying to tell me you understand. Right!"

His face turned red, and he huffed. Then he left me alone in the bathroom.

I followed him into my room, and the glow from my computer screen caught my attention. Joaquin typed away at the computer. Then he pulled his wallet from his pocket. With reverent care, he unfolded a piece of paper and ceremoniously straightened it out on my desk. He laid out several pictures. Then, he stood up and nodded to the chair. "Sit!"

Still angry, I planted myself against the wall with my arms folded.

"Please. Sit," he said softly. This time I decided I would go ahead, and I flopped down. He tapped the computer screen. "Go ahead, look at it."

I stared at him with a confused look on my face. This time his voice fell a tad softer, and he nodded his head at it, "Go ahead."

The page was set to an article about drinking and driving. It talked about a husband and wife killed by a drunk driver. They were survived by their two young sons. I looked back at Joaquin, confused. He nodded at the screen. I kept reading. I used the mouse to move the cursor, and a picture popped up. There were four adults standing dressed for some kind of formal event. Two were Annette and Alberto, and the other man looked like he could have been Alberto's brother. The caption underneath proved me right.

I went back to the article. As I read, my eyes filled with tears, and I grasped at my chest. Oh my God. I'm the biggest guilt-ridden jerk in the world sitting here, unable to apologize. The words caught in my throat like a dry pill. Joaquin waited silently, leaning against my dresser with his ankles crossed, and he nodded back to the desk. Alberto's brother died along with his wife.

My fingers grazed the pictures he placed in two neat rows on my desk. The first picture showed two pregnant women smiling with their bellies touching. Next, were boys that looked like a younger version of Gabriel and Joaquin sitting on a large rocking chair. The third pictured the man and woman with those same two young sons, all smiles for the camera. The last picture showed five young boys, all of them solemn.

I picked up the final clipping. Joaquin's eyes were glassy, and his jaw set tight.

The heading read, *Couple Dies in Drunk Driving Accident*. The text read, "The couple is survived by their two young sons." My heart squeezed almost to a stop, and I laid my hand on my chest. "Mr. De Luna, the boys' paternal uncle, will adopt the boys. 'Their aunt and I love them like sons, and they can grow up with their three cousins.'"

This time when I looked at Joaquin, he wiped a few stray tears from his eyes.

Standing slowly, I made my way over to him, shuffling my feet and pressing the top of my head against his chest. His heart sped, and I could smell his woodsy scent. His warmth drew me closer. Finally, he unfolded his arms and wrapped them around me. We stood there for several minutes, tears streaming down my face. He understood better than anyone else could. Suddenly, the utter loneliness began to subside. With one hand, I flipped the switch for the fan and pulled him over by my bed. We began to kiss, and my hand slid under his shirt, up his warm bare back, and I squeezed. I pulled off his shirt and dropped it on the floor. Then I made myself comfortable on the bed and pulled him down beside me.

I ran my hand across his chest. His heart beat faster, and mine chased his like we were both running a cross-country race. Lying back and sliding to the middle of the bed, I grabbed his belt loop to pull him along with me. He slid between my legs, but he propped himself up with his arms. I wrapped my arms around his back, and he tried to keep his weight off me. Finally, I pulled him to me and tangled my legs around his. We kissed and touched, becoming more and more entangled with one another. I skimmed his abs; they were muscular and defined. I kissed his neck and moved to his chest. He lifted himself up off me and kissed me several more times.

"School tomorrow," he said—his trademark way of stopping before we went too far, even though tomorrow would be Saturday.

I slid under the covers. He stayed on the outside, snuggling up close behind me. He put his arm around me and squeezed. "*Te amo*," he whispered.

Tonight, he stayed with me all night.

CHAPTER 14

When I woke up, I found that Joaquin left a note on the pillow. He drove home to take a shower and would return before nine o'clock to take me back to the hospital. I slid my hands underneath his pillow and pulled it in close. I took in a deep breath; his woodsy scent lingered. A smile crossed my face for the first time since this all began. I rose from the bed to check the clock; he would be back in twenty minutes.

I took a quick shower, threw on a sweatsuit, and pulled my hair back into a ponytail. I wiped the fog from the mirror to reveal a puffy face. Some work needed to be done.

Soon, I heard footsteps on the stairs. "Hello? It's me…"

Joaquin opened the door to the bathroom as I brushed the powder across my face. He came into the bathroom and put his arms around me. I turned around and faced him. He looked at me, kissed my nose and took my hands.

"Well."

"Yes?" I said.

"All the secrets about me revealed, and you still want me," he said.

"Why wouldn't I?"

"My secrets are pretty big," he said.

"True," I said. "But being able to shift doesn't change the fact you're one of the best people I know in this town—in the world."

He kissed the top of my head, "*Te amo*."

I cocked my head and that little crease formed on my forehead between my eyes.

He said, "It means, I love you."

My mouth dropped open, and I threw my arms around his neck. Something new bubbled inside of me, it fluttered in my stomach, and my scalp and cheeks tingled.

"I love you, too," I said into his ear.

He hugged me around the waist and lifted me up off the ground. He told me that after he said, *te amo* last night and he didn't receive any kind of response, he hadn't slept all night. He said he prayed I just hadn't heard him, not that I didn't return his love. Arms squeezed tight, he said, "I forgot your Spanish is a bit spotty. We need to practice."

I laughed. "No argument there!"

He kissed me again. "You ready to go?"

Back to reality. His confession swept me away until those four words rolled off his lips and dragged me down into the depths of a mucked-up reality.

When we got in the car, I found some breakfast burritos. My stomach growled, and I realized other than some popcorn at the game last night, I hadn't eaten for a while. As soon as I chewed one bite, I took the next one. I'd eaten it all before we got on the highway.

Joaquin also brought me a drink, and I took several big gulps in a row. Other than the crinkle of aluminum foil and the slurp of the straw, we drove in silence. Joaquin stole a glance at me and smiled. After I demolished the food, he took my hand and pulled it to his mouth and pressed it against his lips. He whispered, "*Mi amor*." Then he placed it over his heart, and it pounded against my fingertips. "My love."

I slid over until my hip bone pressed against the console and put my head on his shoulder. He loved me.

We drove up, and he turned off the engine. I stayed quiet in my spot. I stared at the enormous building and the blood drained from my face. Dread washed over me.

"Don't put this off," I said. We exited the car and strode toward the hospital.

At the ICU doors, I rang the buzzer. "Yes?" said a voice from the box.

"Maria Richards, here to see my mom," I answered.

"Yes, dear, come on back."

I heard a buzz and a thud. I hit the long bar and opened the doors into the vast white hallway. The trip to my mom's room took twelve steps, room number five. My sister scrunched up in the chair by my mother's bed, and Annette leaned against the cabinets in the back of the room. Mother looked the same as last night. No change. I heard a lot of beeps and whooshes, but no human noise from my mother. My throat wanted to close. Annette approached and held my arm.

She said, "I'll stay, you go talk with your sister."

I shook my head.

Then she informed me, "Not a question," and with her hand centered in the middle of my back, she pushed me toward Theresa. My feet shuffled forward, but my back pushed against her hand. Inside I was like a small child being coaxed to take an awful medication. Like I swallowed it without water or a spoon full of sugar.

Theresa stood. The rage was absent from her eyes, and she appeared to have gotten a couple hours of sleep. We rode the elevator down to the cafeteria without a word. As we got closer, I could smell the coffee and breakfast cooking. She ordered a plate of waffles and a cup of coffee. I got a Coke. We paid and found an open table.

There were plenty of tables available. People filed in to eat breakfast, yet they didn't stay. They were busy going somewhere else. The tension between Theresa and I tugged at me, but who or where should we start. In the meantime, neither of us make eye contact. I couldn't form the first words, and my sister did what she does best—avoid. She picked up her fork and took a bite. The fork dropped, and she began to cry. I reached for her hand. She covered her face with a napkin and then took a deep breath. It took her a little bit to compose herself. My heart ached for her and for the entire situation.

"I'm sorry!" she sobbed.

"Me, too," I said.

"The situation scared me."

"Me, too!"

Our relationship evolved. We learned to deal with each other in new ways—better ways, I hoped. We began to talk softer to one another. Grief manifests itself in different ways, anger being the easiest to show. I realized that now. Anger at the situation and at ourselves—it made us lose control of ourselves.

Helplessness inundated me. I wished I'd done things differently. What if we recognized the signs? What if we asked Dad to change his plans for the day? What if I tried harder to convince Mom to come to the soccer game with the De Lunas? Maybe we wouldn't be in this place now. Maybe we would still be one family—together.

"I want to go to the chapel," Theresa said. "We should light a candle."

"Sounds good." I took her hands like we were young again and ventured out to the hospital hallway together.

The chapel, if you could even call it one, turned out to be a tiny room with a stained-glass window and a cross mounted up front. There were three pews on either side of the room, and a table in the back held the candles. We lit one and made the short trip to the front of the sanctuary. I knelt and crossed myself, then took a deep breath and locked my fingers in prayer. I tried to make a deal with God. I would be a better daughter and sister if he would bring back my father and make my mother healthy again. I wouldn't miss Mass. I would be more active in the church, anything to have my family intact. Maybe if werewolves were possible, my prayer could be answered, too.

My heart told me better, but I needed to try. I needed to ask for everything with a remote possibility. When I opened my eyes, I still found myself in the hospital chapel. I hadn't been transported back in time.

This was my reality: tears, uncontrollable pain and fear. My mother's pain compounded mine.

My sister started to stand. I pulled myself up and stood. We lit another candle, then left the chapel. Theresa turned and grabbed me. She gave me the biggest and kindest hug. A lot of time passed since we were so close. We needed each other. I hoped it would get better. "I love you," I said, "and I miss you, and I cannot do this without you. It was hard to lose dad—I can't lose my best friend."

I couldn't let her go. I needed her, and she wouldn't let me go, either.

She took my hand and led me back to our mother's room. We both stayed at the hospital overnight. We slept on chairs. Annette and Alberto came in and out to visit. They were there when Joaquin went home to shower, but loneliness did not overcome me. Strength flashed through my body when we're together. We flipped through magazines. Mom didn't change.

The doctors decided she could be transferred to a regular room. Annette talked to Mom's boss for us. We stayed. Joaquin went back to school, but he came back as soon as he could complete his work, and he brought my homework for me.

Theresa said, "I've been gone a week. I need to go back to school for exams."

My breath became fast and choppy. I put my head between my knees.

She said, "You, too. You need to start back no later than Monday." She inherited the position of boss, but me back at school made my stomach churn. I couldn't tell you the day of the week. She said she would call every day or text. "And I promise to come home on the weekends, even if it's for one day. I *will* come."

My head wanted to believe her, but my body I couldn't control. I ran to the restroom and hung over the toilet, I wanted to throw up, but nothing came.

* * *

In the morning, I went down to the chapel and made my pleas to God. I asked him to help my family through this horrible ordeal. Sometimes I would throw in a, "What if…What if I'm perfect? Will you give me my mom and dad back?" Daily, I wished for Dad back, knowing it fell beyond the realm of possibility. I stopped with that request and begged for my mother back harder. I would be a better daughter, a good daughter.

My mind wandered to all the things I'd done wrong. It scanned for all the things I could have done differently, and it played out the entire worst-case scenario. Everyone pointed to how this came down to being my fault. From time to time, my heart would start to race, and I edged close to a panic attack.

Around four o'clock every day, Joaquin would come to the room with food and the schoolwork I missed. As soon as he arrived, I worked on it until I finished. Each night, I gave it back to him to take to the teachers the next day. I picked at the food he brought me; it always made my mouth water, but it sunk to the pit of my stomach. Then, I ran to the restroom. The food swirled down along with the emotions left behind after these two catastrophic events. Every couple of days, he would drag me home to shower. I would jump in and wash my hair once and rinse it. Then I would brush my teeth, change clothes and pull my hair back in a ponytail. I went out to the kitchen for a Coke and noticed the clean living room and the furniture positioned back in its original place. Annette.

Each time we left the hospital, Joaquin would try to find a reason to keep me out longer. He would stop by a store and buy a drink or run some kind of errand. But it made me grind my teeth until we started an argument.

When Joaquin returned to school, the time of day became easier to follow, and Sunday night came around too soon. I needed to go home. They placed my mother into something called a medically in-duced coma. They said her body needed time to recover. The nurses assured me I should go to school. They promised if she woke up, they would call.

Joaquin said it would be a good idea if I stayed with his family—and I agreed. I didn't want to be at home. I stopped there long enough to pack up six pairs of jeans, T-shirts and underclothes, enough for the week. I packed up my overnight kit and my makeup.

As Joaquin loaded the bags in the car, I locked up the house and then wandered down the sidewalk. I stared back at the door, not able to pull my eyes away from my broken home. In one year, this was the scene of a slow-motion catastrophe, and the tools to make it right again were buried along with my father.

* * *

The next morning, Annette's eyes widened a little as I emerged from the bathroom. I hadn't brought my hot rollers, and I didn't apply makeup. I looked the same as the past few weeks. Joaquin asked me if I need more time to get dressed and glanced at my loose jeans and sweatshirt—I shrugged and headed for the door. My clothes were stained and fell off me, but I didn't care.

School met me with stares, whispers and points. Nauseous and still unable to eat, I wanted to crawl into a locker. No one bumped into me in the hallway; it was as if I had contracted a disease they didn't want to catch. At lunch, I flopped down at a small round table by myself until Joaquin came over with a Coke and some French fries. I slouched in my chair and put my feet in his lap. He pushed the food in front of me.

"You need to eat something."

I picked at the food and checked my cell phone every minute like that would make it ring. Everyone still avoided me. They were teenagers, most never suffering through anything more than a breakup with a crush, or maybe they didn't get to buy designer clothes.

The bell rang. Joaquin tossed my half-eaten food in the trash. As we started toward our next classroom, I heard my name, but I picked up my speed. Becky caught up with us.

"Hey, Maria."

"Hi."

"Hey, I wanted to see if you wanted to stay with me for a while. My parents told me a sleepover might be—fun." She ducked her head; her body language didn't match her words.

My mother saw Becky's father, as a psychiatrist. She took most of his advice and seemed to make progress until he suggested she go to group grief therapy. Her pride got in the way. In her eyes, a shrink made her seem weak, and no way would she talk to a group. For once, I agreed with my mother. No one needed to be aware of what we went through. We could take care of things and keep it all inside.

"We all agreed, I should stay with the De Luna's for a while. But thanks."

"Well, if you need some girl time," she bumped Joaquin with her shoulder, "—time away from all the testosterone, give me a call, and I will whisk you away for a mani-pedi day. You, me and maybe Lexi, too."

"I'll call you."

She smiled warmly. I tried to smile but couldn't.

At the end of the day, we worked our way outside and started for the car, but not without incident. Teo waited at Joaquin's car. Joaquin's face grew red hot. I put my hand on my chest in an attempt to keep my heart inside my body. I huffed and moved faster, but Joaquin grabbed my wrist. My arm slung loose, and I stomped up to Teo.

"What's your freaking problem?"

Everyone in the parking lot stopped and turned to look at us. A hush moved across the crowd. The eagle screeched and landed on the school's roof, which gave me the semblance of an army behind me.

"Hey, I wanted to see if you were okay," Teo asked.

"Bullshit."

"You think?"

"You weren't worried about me when you knocked me to the ground at the party." I put my finger on my temple. "Or when you ripped my blouse, or when your disgusting hands were all over me, were you?"

"You're delusional!" he yelled.

I slapped him across the face. "You can kiss my ass!"

Joaquin grabbed my arms and pulled me back.

Teo passed by and made a kissy noise and whispered to me. "Anytime, babe!"

I lunged toward him, but Joaquin held fast, pushing me behind his back. He grabbed Teo's arm. Teo looked down at his hand. Joaquin growled, "You better keep away from her, do you understand me?"

"And what are you going to do?"

"Tear you apart."

"Time and date, man. Time and date," Teo said.

"Expect it." Joaquin let his arm go.

Teo straightened up his clothes and strutted away with unjustified confidence.

We got into the car and went back to the hospital. It took the entire car ride for me to decrease my heart rate and for my fists to unclench. My nails cut into my palms. This guy attempted to rape me and scooted around like my boyfriend.

We rode the elevator up to my mother's room. I took my place in the chair that had formed to my body. I leaned over and laid my cheek on the bed, and held mom's hand.

It happened. She moved.

CHAPTER 15

Tears spilled over and down my chin as I squeezed her hand. She tried to grip my hand, but she shook. Her eyes flittered to a blink and her other hand reached up to tug at the tubes in her nose. I stopped her hand.

"Mom, stop, you need the oxygen," I said.

"Wh-Where—"

Her throat was damaged from the tubes used to help her breathe, making it impossible to get out an entire sentence. My heart started to race, and I pushed the alarm for the nurse. Joaquin came over and put his hand on my shoulder.

"Hello, Mrs. Richards," said the nurse, relieved the emergency turned out to be a happy one.

My mom's eyes looked large next to her sunken cheeks. She moved her head side to side and tugged at the sheets. The nurse explained the situation saying that they admitted her into the hospital and were here to help her. Mom tried to lean forward to grab at my hand. I tried to smile and force away any trace of tears and told her to relax. She lay back against the pillow and looked to the side while tears rolled down her face.

As soon as the doctor came into the room and started to check her out, I stepped into the hallway and called Theresa. She didn't answer. I sent off a quick text. In less than a minute, my phone buzzed.

Joaquin texted a message to his parents.

"She's awake," I told my sister.

Theresa's voice cracked. "That's wonderful. You have to call back as soon as the doctor leaves and tell me what he says."

Before the doctor finished his exam, Annette and Alberto were at my side. "Let's go to the conference room," the doctor said, "and we'll let your mother rest for a few more hours."

He told us she would still be weak, and there would still be the danger of some organ damage, but we took an enormous step forward. Depending on the speed she progressed, she might be ready to leave here in two or three weeks. I smiled and squeezed Joaquin's hand.

"There is one catch," said the doctor. "She can leave the hospital, but she can't go home right away. She will need to be in treatment for at least another thirty days, maybe longer, with some physical therapy."

I gasped. Thirty days seemed like way too long to be without your mother. Annette put her arm around me to give me comfort. "It will go by in a flash," she whispered in my ear.

The doctor shook our hands, and we went back to the room. Alberto and Annette went back home and left Joaquin and me to wait for my mom to wake up.

When the nurse came in and said visiting hours ended, I nodded my head and worked my way over to kiss my mother's head, whispering I would be back tomorrow after school. I turned at the door and waved one more time before I left.

Her cheeks shook as she smiled and said in a raspy voice, "My baby."

* * *

The next day, the weather turned frigid. I reached for my sweats and UGGs. I didn't pull my hair in a ponytail, nor did I blow-dry it. It hung in wet ringlets all around my face.

Joaquin entered my room and grinned. "That's a new look." His tone revealed unhappiness, but this situation drained me. What did I want to fix myself up for? I wanted to stay at home in my room and sleep.

We drove to school. I didn't talk. I stayed in the seat and bit my fingernails. The silence was broken by the snap of my teeth together through my nails. Joaquin would try to hold my hand, but

I ignored him and kept at my nails. We parked at school and parted ways for most of the day.

I took notes and listened to my teachers. The hours flew by, and lunch came too fast. Lexi and Becky made me and Joaquin sit with them. They surrounded me with friends on all sides. I didn't miss the snide comments and whispers, but inside there was nothing—numbness—no anger or embarrassment. Nothing smelled good to me, and the colors on the walls and posters were dull. Sleepiness fell upon me. My life consisted of school, home and hospital. Sunday, I would go to church, and then I wanted to spend the day at the hospital. When someone asked me a question, I responded, but the responses were two or three words. That's all.

It occurred to me, maybe my mother's emotions were like mine before her suicide attempt, but like I said—numb. But I didn't care enough to want to die. I existed.

* * *

"Maria, you should lose this grunge thing you've got going. It's old."

I looked down at my clothes and adjusted them a little. "What you don't like my look?" I held my arms out to model my clothes and turned around. They all laughed. A great while since I last laughed, but I tried. Embarrassment, at least it was an emotion.

The bell rang, and we strolled toward class. Joaquin, Becky and I went to classes together every day. On the way, Joaquin noticed a sign.

"Hey, what about this?"

I squinted at the sign. "Softball tryouts. Hmm. Great."

"You should try out! You and Theresa used to play catch together, right? You liked it."

I shrugged. Then he pulled a pencil out of his back pocket and wrote my name down on the list.

"Wait a minute."

"What?"

"I haven't decided."

"I have. You're trying out." He took my hand and led me toward class. "Give me one week. I'll whip you into shape, and you can try out. You'll do great. If, in the end, you hate it, I'll take you to dinner every Friday for a month. Deal?"

I started to warm up to the idea—and then I spotted Teo with his finger on my name.

"What a joke!" he said in a boisterous voice.

"You're the joke from where I stand," I said. And in my mind, more certain than ever, I would try out and kick butt. At the end of the day, I asked Joaquin to stop by my house to hunt for my glove. He looked at me and gave me a huge smile.

I went into the garage and threw some boxes around. Then, I spotted it—the box marked with my name. I unfolded the top of the box, and right on top, I found my glove, as if it had been waiting for me all this time. I picked it up and hugged it to my chest. The smell of leather and oil was still strong. I held it up over my head.

"Found it," I called.

At his house, he ran to his room and came out with a glove. His family asked him what was going on. He told them I was trying out for the softball team. He beamed. Alberto suggested we go to the batting cages to hit this weekend. We went out to the backyard and threw back and forth for a while. When Joaquin warmed my arm enough, he backed up and squatted into the catcher's position. He smacked his glove with his fist and told me to show him my stuff.

I put my glove behind my back. I rolled the ball around in my hand until I found my sweet spot. Then, I twisted my toe into the ground in front of me. I snapped the ball into my glove and stepped back on my leg. I settled the ball and glove on my left hip, and then I took my right arm and spun it over my head. The ball slammed right into his mitt with a smack. I loved the smell of old leather, the stings rubbing across the tips of my finger, and the numbness shrunk.

Joaquin pulled his hand out of his glove and shook it. Gabriel watched from the porch, and he held his hands up to his mouth and yelled, "Dang, girl!"

We all laughed. A tingle sensation rushed through me, giving my body a new sense of awareness. I noticed a bird flying overhead, and I could hear the water from the creek; the world started to come alive again.

Joaquin tossed the ball back to me. "Send me another one."

Everyone came out to watch. I rolled the ball around in my hand again, then placed my fingertips across the laces, slung my arm over my head and let it go. This one smacked even harder.

Alejandro yelled, "You go, girl!"

I couldn't help it. My smile stretched across my face. I even blushed a little. More energy surged through me, and the weights strapped to my arms and legs fell off one at a time. We kept this up until the sun hid behind the trees and the dark shadowed over us. I should stop and let the exercise settle into my bones. It would make me even stronger tomorrow. I rotated my shoulder; it would be a little sore the next day.

Gabriel ran over and punched me on the arm. "Where did you learn to pitch?"

I smiled and bumped him with my shoulder. Joaquin put his hands on my hips and then got a look of concern on his face. He lifted my shirt a little. "Sweetheart, if you want to play on the team, you need to eat more than a French fry every two days."

I tugged at my pants, trying to raise them up to my hips. I pulled my shirt back down and smoothed it down. In fact, my bottom ribs protruded and made a dent beneath them.

We went inside. Annette agreed with Joaquin's assessment of my nutritional habits. She set dinner out on the table, ready to eat. The boys were excited that I turned out not to be such a girly girl. They asked how long I played. A bubbly sensation filled me as we talked about games with Theresa, and all the nights my dad practiced with us. The sound of my own laughter sounded strange to my ears. Breathing turned into less of a chore, and I *wanted* to talk for the first time in weeks. Some mystical phenomenon saturated me. It cast a spell to unlock the chains. I loved each clank as the links hit the ground one at a time. My body lightened.

We ate. With my shrunken stomach, I couldn't eat all my food. But I ate more than I'd eaten in weeks and didn't get sick. We went to our rooms and got ready for bed. Joaquin came in to be with me for a while. Of course, I talked about softball, but I talked. He stared at me as I talked and then gave me a big hug, one of those *where have you been* hugs. I reached up on my tiptoes and kissed him.

He pulled me back and looked at me. With a smile, he followed my lead. His lips pressed against mine. We didn't let go of each other for a long time, but I dropped down on my heels. Moving over, we positioned ourselves on the bed and started to kiss again. I stood up and pushed him back onto the bed, then laid down on top of him. The kisses came harder, stealing our breath. He kept his hands against my hipbones and pushed back against me a little.

He smiled through our kiss. "School tomorrow…"

As he started to leave, I tugged at the stomach of his shirt and leaned forward for one more kiss.

"I love you."

Joaquin pulled back and smiled at me and said, "I love you, too."

* * *

The next day, I wore my hair straight. I applied makeup and perfume. Then, I went to the closet and got my jeans, a blouse with long sleeves, and pulled on my boots and a belt. I strolled out to the living room, with freshness all around me.

At school, I got some looks—complimentary ones. Classmates watched as we passed by, but they didn't dare say anything. No one said a word except Teo and Jim, as usual. I could hear them across the hall, saying things like, "Looks like she decided to take a shower," and Jim, vulgar as ever, said, "No, it looks like somebody got laid."

Then he said, "Ow!" and rubbed his shoulder. Teo glared at him and punched him on the other shoulder.

In step with Joaquin, I squeezed his hand hard.

"You look radiant," Lexi said and stepped in beside me weaving her elbow through mine.

* * *

By the end of the week, my life sparkled like a fine cut diamond, precious. I practiced every day, and then Alberto gave me the biggest gift in the world. He said my glove looked worn, and he took me to restring it and buy a new bat. My bat could be used for little league, but not high school. I needed a new one. His offer made my heart leap.

In the sporting goods store, the man showed us the racks of softball bats. I stood back and looked for a minute, then picked up a couple and bounced them to check the weight. Then I caught sight of it, a silver one with a purple grip. I lifted it with one hand and bounced it to adjust my hand to the weight. I smiled. Both my hands wrapped around the grip and twisted back and forth. Then I stepped into an open area, pulled it over my shoulder, and took a slow swing. The action exhilarated me, and I swung full strength. "This is the one," I announced. Alberto grinned and waved me up to the cashier counter.

In the car, I said thank you over and over, but words didn't seem enough. In the backseat, I kept both hands on the bat and twisted my hands on the grip. I stared at it. Joaquin put his arm around my shoulder and hugged me close.

"You'll knock them out of the park tomorrow. Good luck."

* * *

On Saturday, we woke up early. I grabbed my bag, and Joaquin took it and threw it into the trunk of his car. Breakfast did not get any easier, but I ate a banana on the way to the batting cages. We drove up, and girls packed the place out. Everyone needed to prepare for tryouts.

I got my coins and then found a cage with the least amount of people in line. I clipped my bag on the fence and slid out my bat. It rolled on my shoulder. I twisted the grip and found a good spot. My time arrived. Inside the cage, my coin fell in the box with a clank. Then, I placed my feet into position, wiggling until my body found its groove. The first pitch went by, but I didn't even swing. I looked at Joaquin, then turned back to the mechanical arm. The next one flung across the plate, and I sent it to the back net. It went high into what would be left field. This time when I looked back, Joaquin smiled, and he said, go ahead. From there on out, I made contact with every ball—not perfect every time, but the movement seemed natural as if I never stopped. Two hours flew by.

A zip of my bag and my bat in place, we headed toward the car. My hands stung. I looked down; they were blood red, and I rubbed several blisters. As Joaquin started the engine, he looked over and took my hands. He stopped by the drug store to purchase some ointment, then he stopped at the sporting goods store to pick up a pair of gloves.

"You and your family have already done more than you should," I protested.

He pushed my hair out of my face. "Don't worry. It makes me happy. Your smile came back. It's worth every penny." I leaned in and put my head on his shoulder. This was the best day yet.

That night, we picked out a movie and took it to his room to watch it. Annette came in and left some popcorn for us on the desk. Tenderness filled me. We laid on the foot of the bed with our head closer to the screen. I kissed him on the lips and said, "Thank you." He leaned in and kissed me while holding the back of my head.

I slid my arm under him and tugged. He rolled over on top of me. Then he kissed my neck and moved down to my chest. My breath pulled deep into my chest. He moved his head up and kissed me on the lips. His hands moved up my side, and his fingers grazed more than my rib cage. The touch of his hands made my breath catch. Lips on my neck, around to my throat, and his hands moved down to my chest.

A howl erupted outside his window. His muscles flexed, but he continued brushing his lips across mine then moved his hand down the center of my body. When his fingers met the button of my pants, another howl tore from outside and distracted him.

He dropped his head to the bed beside my head, and he slid his arms under me. They howled again. He growled and jerked his hands out from under me. He said, "I have to go."

Almost before I could say goodbye, he left.

I rolled over and found four long rips on the comforter. It made me shiver.

I turned off the television and took the popcorn bowl out into the kitchen. Annette cleaned the kitchen and said they would be back soon, and I didn't need to worry. She scurried around. On the counter were some of the red berries and seeds Joaquin fed the eagle.

"What are those?"

"Pumpkin seeds and cranberries. I love them," she said. She tossed one into her mouth with a wink. Her teeth clicked as she bit down. My head tilted, and my mind rumbled. Then she tossed another handful into her mouth with a quick wink. Was anyone in this house normal?

* * *

I headed for the dressing rooms to change. When I changed into my shorts, I stuffed my school clothes back into the bag. Then I pulled the band from my wrist, wrapped it around my ponytail and jogged out to the field. The wet, earthy smell tickled my nose—clipped, bright green grass contrasted the white chalk lines marked around the diamond bases.

To warm up a little, I jogged over to the dugout. One of the girls from our lunch group asked if I wanted to toss a few. Ashley and I were introduced my first few days of school, but I didn't hang out with her other than lunch. Our group liked her, and she talked from time to time. She didn't seem to have one best friend; but she befriended everyone. The guys talked with her because she loved softball, and they talked sports with her.

She gave me a sense of guardedness and no-nonsense; our conversation consisted of questions about where I played before and how long. Her long, toned arms whipped the ball toward me, and even though this was a warm-up, her throws stung my fingers as they slapped into the web of my mitt—a good kind of sting. It rekindled something inside me, something lost.

The coach blew the whistle, and we all huddled up for instructions. We dropped our gloves and started to do some warm-up drills and sprints. She moved us to the field and started to hit some balls to us. A line of coaches with clipboards stood perched to take notes. One hit a few high flies and some grounders. Again, she blew her whistle for us to huddle up. We split into groups, pitchers with catchers, infielders and outfielders. We went to our designated spots.

Ashley caught, and they grouped me with her. It took her a minute to pull on all her gear. There were two other girls trying out for pitcher. I pulled off my glove and wiped my palms. Since there were two catchers and three pitchers, I decided to sit back and wait until last. Plus, I wanted to check out the competition.

As I waited, I noticed Gabriel came up to sit with Joaquin in the stands, and a few minutes later, every eye stared back at me—the whole family, plus Teo farther down in the stands. My stomach flipped, but I already lost yesterday's food before I came out onto the field. Nothing left to lose—literally.

Then the coach yelled, "Maria?" My turn.

Ashley tossed me the ball, and I hit it in my glove a couple of times. I took a deep breath and jogged over to the pitcher's mound. Ashley yelled, "You got this." Then she pounded her fist into her glove and held it out to give me a target. The coach said take two warm-ups, and then she would clock me. My toe shoved into the dirt right in front of the strip of rubber, making a place to push off. Then I put the ball and glove on my left hip and whipped it over my head. The moment I released it, out of nowhere, Teo yelled, "Freak!" I released the ball way too late, and the ball hit the top of the backstop. All the De Luna boys stood up and stared at him. He never turned to meet their glare; he stayed on the bottom step and smirked.

Ashley ran back and got the ball, and then she jogged out to me. She put the ball in my glove and said, "Shake it off. Forget about him. You good?"

I nodded and picked up the ball and pounded it into my glove. Back at the mound, I tried to wish away the first pitch. Set, I took the ball over my head and let it go. Bam! Right into Ashley's glove and she yelled, "There you go!"

When I turned to head back to the mound, I smiled. That went better. Out of the corner of my eye, I noticed the coaches talking and writing on their clipboards. One of the coaches yelled at me. "This one's for real."

In my zone, I took my stance on the mound and then rolled the ball over my head, my legs pushed me forward, and I let it go. Smack! Ashley shook her glove and said, "Do it again!"

They wanted me to pitch over twenty balls, and the rest of the team gathered to watch. All the adrenaline rushed through my veins.

They didn't say a word. One nodded and pointed for me to go again. They talked to each other and smiled.

Batting time came, and we went over to the cages. They told me to go first. Great! I retrieved my bat and slipped on my gloves. I wrapped the Velcro around my wrist. I took a deep breath, pulled on my helmet, and got into the batter's box. The machine pitched the first ball.

The ball hurtled toward me. As it got close, I heard, "Freak!" from behind me. This time it didn't faze me. I smacked the ball and it sailed into the nets. I turned and gave him an "up yours" smile and dug my feet back into my spot, tapping the plate with my bat.

The coaches let me hit around twenty pitches. Then one of the coaches said, "Next."

After almost everyone finished batting, one of the coaches came over and asked Ashley and me to pick up our gloves. We went back to the field, and she asked me to pitch a few more. She stood beside the mound with her clipboard in hand, and while I pitched, she asked questions. Things like where I played before, and I told her I made a select team here in Cove. Then she said she meant what high school I played for. I explained I'd gone to private school, and we didn't have a softball team.

She shook her head and said, "Welcome to the team."

I jumped up and down and whooped. She told me to be here tomorrow during last block. They would make the schedule change from PE to softball. I bounced up and down again, and Ashley ran over and told me I did a great job. The coach asked her to show me where the lockers were and to find me one.

"Yes, ma'am," Ashley said and then motioned with her glove for me to follow her.

Ashley stood five-eight, with dirty blonde hair fastened into a tight French braid, intimidating, to say the least. She had a tan that reminded me of one of those Coppertone models; you could see a hint of a bikini line when her shirt collar slipped to the side under her chest protector. Her green eyes with flecks of gold were stunning, and the few freckles across the bridge of her nose gave her a cuteness. Her physique included bulges at the thighs from well-defined muscles built by all the squats.

She made the team since her freshman year, and she loved it. We walked around the locker room, and she told me to pick an empty locker. Everyone else left after they took a turn at bat. After she tossed me the marker and tape, I made my choice. I tore off a piece of tape with my teeth, stuck it to the locker, then printed my last name across the tape. I stepped back and looked at it. My dad's surname, my hand yearned to touch it.

I ran out of the locker room and gave Joaquin a huge hug. He picked me up and swung me around. Ashley came out with me, and I introduced her to everyone. She smiled, then waved and went to her car. I told him I made the team. He said he could have told me that, and we loaded up to go.

On the way home, I texted Theresa, and she responded with *Congrats!* The quick response sent a warmth through my entire body.

When we got home, Joaquin ran ahead of me and tried to beat me inside the house. He told his parents. Annette and Alberto cheered and wrapped me in a group hug.

"We need to celebrate," Alberto said. "Get dressed and meet me at the car!"

We went to our usual spot to eat. Alberto told everyone I was a prized new member of the team. He bragged that we would have a winning team since one of his kids played on the softball team. *His kids.* He claimed me as family.

* * *

At lunch, Ashley replayed the events of our tryouts and summed up everyone's performance to her guy friends at the table. When she noticed me, she stood halfway up and said, "There she is!" Everybody stopped and looked.

"What?" I asked.

Lexi said, "Ashley told us we have a new superstar pitcher on the softball team."

"She exaggerates."

Ashley said I was trying to be modest and went on about it the entire lunch. Lexi and Cindy whispered at the end of the table. The bell rang, and we all went to class; Becky came over and gushed about how happy the news made her. She said she wanted a copy of my schedule. She wanted to be at all the games. I smiled and told her I would send it to her whenever I found out myself.

In fact, the first game on the schedule was for Friday. My stomach flipped, but I made myself breathe slower and calmed my heart—this stomach thing needed to get under control.

* * *

My mom entered the treatment center. We were allowed to see her on Sunday. I always called when we got home from church and lunch. She sounded happy that I played softball and said she remembered how I loved it—she almost sounded like my mom again.

* * *

Every day, I practiced hard. Joaquin and I added extra sessions at night and on weekends. Days flew by, and game day arrived all too soon. The cheerleaders put signs up all over the school. And our boosters put out signs with the pictures of each player in different businesses all over town. D & R Realtors displayed mine up in their window, and I passed it every day on the way home from school. Some of the businesses in town wrote "Good luck!" on their marquees.

The adrenaline rushed through me, but these days the tinge in my stomach was constant. It made me nauseous. We went to the locker room and got dressed. We were blue and gold; blue shirts, shorts and socks. The socks were striped with gold up the side, and all the letters were gold. We wore blue hats with Cove printed on them. I held up my uniform shirt and smiled. Then, I turned it to the back to see my name and number seven printed on it. As I traced the seven with my finger, Joaquin's image flashed in my mind.

The coach came in and gave us the normal pep talk. Then she took me to the side and said, "Do it like you've done in practice."

We ran out to the field, and everyone clapped. Joaquin, his brothers, their girlfriends, Annette, Alberto, and Theresa and Jose were all in attendance. My sister stood up and clapped. I jogged over to the fence and mouthed, "Thank you." She pointed at me and then held her hand over her heart. It brought tears to my eyes, but I wiped them away.

Ashley popped me on the back with her glove and said, "Let's do it!" We took our positions. I got set, looked up and Teo settled down behind Ashley. I swallowed. Of course, the creepy crew accompanied him; Jim, Thomas, Cindy and Lexi huddled with him. Since my mother had her incident and the softball tryouts, Lexi and I lost the closeness of our relationship. But she wouldn't even look in my direction; she kept her eyes directed at the ground, the outfielders or the group of people with her. Our relationship grew distant, to say the least since my mother got sick. I took some blame. After my funk, I let our friendship suffer, but this distance surprised me. When I made the softball team, an even larger wedge drove between us.

I took a breath and whizzed the ball to Ashley. Ashley strode out before the first batter. She told me to watch her. Nothing else around us mattered. The first batter came up. I hurled three strikes past her. Then the next one up grounded to first; easy out. The next one smacked a little harder, up two strikes to two balls. Ashley gave me the sign to send a changeup. I took stance, whirled my arm and pitched a creeper. The batter swung before the ball made it halfway to the plate. I clapped my glove and headed for the dugout.

Batting in the second position, I readied myself and moved to the on-deck circle. I took a couple of warm-up swings with the weights on my bat.

Our first batter struck out. With a bang of the bat handle, I dropped the weights and went to dig into the batter's box. The coach signaled me to take one. I let the first one by, and the umpire yelled, "Strike!" The other team's stands clapped. Teo called me a freak again, but what's new? I stepped out of the box and looked at the coach. She gave me the go-ahead signal. The pitch came my way, too high. I stepped out again. The coach gave the signal. This perfect pitch sailed down the middle, and I swung. The ball flew over the infield and dropped in front of the left fielder.

Safe. The first base coach hit me on the butt and told me good job. I eased off first base and got ready to run for second.

After the first pitch, the coach sent me to second base. The catcher over-throwed to the second baseman, and I made it to third. Our fans clapped and yelled. The next girl up to bat struck out. Now, Ashley geared up in the batter's box. She took the first pitch, but I could see by the look in her eye that they would not get passed her. I led off a little. She made solid contact, and the ball flew over the centerfielder's head and hit the top of the fence. I made it home, and Ashley took second. We hit one more single but didn't score again.

We took the field; three up and three down. We were up to bat again. We scored one more run. The inning ended two to zip.

The game went on without another score. The top of the ninth inning, and they were up at bat. The first two were easy outs. The first pitch to the third batter fell straight down the middle, a strike. The second ball, a swing and a miss. Third, a strike cracked off the bat; it flew over my head and right into the second baseman's glove.

"Out!" the umpire yelled. The stands were on their feet, going crazy. "Ball game," the ump yelled.

I took a deep breath and turned toward the bleachers. Everyone waited for me in the stands, and I ran up. They told me how great I did and congratulated me on the win. Theresa said they needed to drive back, and she hugged me before taking off to her car. I talked to all my friends who gathered after the game. Together we all made our way to the parking lot.

A group gathered by Joaquin's car—about six or seven people with Teo, two of them were Cindy and Lexi. This upset me. Cindy, I understood—but not Lexi. She befriended me. One more chunk chiseled out of my heart, one more lost loved one and one more betrayal.

Teo growled through his teeth, "Soon *hombre lobo*, soon!"

Gabriel said, "*El raton.*"

Teo and his friends got into their cars and left. We all stared at one another. Joaquin leaned his elbows on the top of his car with his keys in his hands.

"More have been turned," I said.
"We'll need help!"

CHAPTER 16

With spring on its way in Texas, the cool weather doesn't last long. It means the heat is on its way—real heat, ninety degrees and higher. We may not have the cooler weather like up north, but we did have our beautiful wildflowers: blue bonnets, Indian paintbrushes, Indian fire wheels, and buttercups... too many to name them all. Since elementary school, we identified them as projects each year, going out to pick them for inclusion in a book of wildflowers.

Friday, we were off school for the long Easter holiday. Even though Mom still lived in the treatment facility, they allowed her a day pass out for Sunday. Since she hadn't worked long enough to accumulate any sick days, she took unpaid medical leave from her job. Other than Dad's savings and social security, no money came in. Theresa took a job to help with bills—she took care of all her own expenses, and she paid the house bills out of Dad's retirement and social security. We received a steady income, but it all needed to be organized, which seemed like a huge responsibility for a nineteen-year-old. We texted every day, and she said she kept things under control. Jose moved in with her after the stalker incident, and I suspected he helped her out with some of the expenses. If I could, I wanted to ask Alberto for some advice on our money situation.

On Easter morning, Joaquin woke me up early. With a brush of my hair, he set a kiss on my lips. He told me I should wake up and shower before we left for church. "And my cousins will arrive from the Valley afterward—Jose's brothers. What about going to the batting cages after the meal?"

I laughed and asked him why.

"I want to show my girlfriend off," he said.

I stretched and got up to shower. I hot rolled my hair and applied some makeup, and texted Theresa to make sure she'd be here to pick me up on time. On the way out to the living room, I picked up a hairband and pulled it onto my wrist on my way out the door. Alberto met us at the church with Mom. When we drove up, Theresa and I stretched our necks to get a glimpse of them. They stood under the covered sidewalk waiting for us. Forgeting about the boys, we ran and gave mom a huge hug. She looked pale and weak, but the bruises from all the IV needles were gone. I hadn't seen her smile like this in almost a year. While we hugged, I closed my eyes and almost forgot about everything. Almost.

Even when we stopped our hug, we wouldn't let go of her arms. Theresa and I held her close as we strolled into the sanctuary. We were perched on either side of her, and Joaquin and Jose sealed the ends of our small family. We were each protector and protected—like a complete family.

As soon as Mass ended, we drove to the De Luna's house for dinner, and to meet even more of the De Lunas' family. The visit held another purpose, too. Theresa and I asked Alberto if he could help us out with our money situation. Before we even changed out of our church clothes, Mom and I went to his office. We found his armchairs more than comfortable. Theresa returned to the car to gather some paperwork. She came back and handed it all to him. She took her place beside me in one of the armchairs. He unloaded the overfilled manila envelope in front of him and flipped through everything.

Something about his expression changed, expressing shock. He set down the papers and frowned at my mother. "*You* are the ones who own the land across the road?" he said.

"Yes, their great-grandmother passed it down to them," Mom said. She pointed at my sister and me. Theresa and I looked at one another.

"What? Why don't you sell?" Theresa said.

"Your great-grandmother left the land for you two girls. The will stipulates it can't be sold. It has to be passed down," she said.

Alberto looked up. His eyes moved back and forth between us. I formed more questions, too—tons of them—but the surprise made it too difficult to formulate a coherent sentence.

"Was our grandmother Native American?" Theresa asked.

I studied the history of our town, but Theresa wouldn't have a reason to research any of it. Maybe she'd discovered more about our world.

"Oh yes," Mom said.

She said it like the information revealed to us was no big deal, and she continued to inform us that her family ancestry was Native American, too. She reached out, all but snatched the deed, and flipped over to the last page. They stapled a black and white photocopied picture of a young woman to the back. Long dark hair waved in the breeze. Her clothes were a fitted leather dress, short and beaded. One slender arm waved and revealed a tattoo on her wrist. I pulled the picture closer, a scripted R.

"For Richards?" I asked Mom.

She laughed and said they changed the name years ago. "It stands for Rios."

I looked down and rubbed my wrist. My mind played tricks on me, I caught a glimpse of the outline of an R beneath the skin, but it vanished when I looked closely at it. It brought back a memory of Teo's wrist—and Joaquin's.

"Our name should be... Rios?" I asked.

"Why did it change?" Theresa asked.

"Your dad told me that several generations back, they changed their name from Rios to Richards. They wanted to hide their ancestry. He never told me any of the details. I always assumed he would tell me or you girls someday." Mom ducked her hand and wrung her handkerchief. "Someday... never came. He did leave me a key to a safety deposit box at the bank. We talked, and he planned to give it to you when Maria turned eighteen. He wanted you to open it together."

"What is it?" Theresa asked.

"I'm not sure. I will give it to you on Maria's birthday."

We didn't beg for information or ask for the key now. Our father's wishes were sacrosanct; if he kept the secret this long, his instincts were best.

Alberto cleared his throat. "Well, the most I can do is to give you some personal advice. With this life insurance policy, I would pay off the house, pay the taxes on the land and put the rest into a high yield savings account."

We agreed and thanked him for his help.

* * *

When Joaquin's relatives made it to the house, all the boys ran outside to greet them. Loud voices and laughter flooded the house. They tumbled inside and traded punches and shoves with one another. A short, frail-looking little girl emerged first. She seemed to be about ten years old. She ducked her head, letting her hair drop over her face. Gabriel put his hands on her shoulders and squeezed, making her flinch and giggle.

He said, "This is Victoria. We call her Tori."

Behind them were four large boys. They were as good-looking as Joaquin and his brothers—Jose stood there, plus Angel, Raul and Roberto. Their parents, Anita and Carlos, came along, too.

Joaquin got our gloves and told me to change then come to the yard.

"We're going to have a practice session," he said and grinned. I pulled my hair back into the band from my wrist, eager to show my mother how good I'd gotten.

Outside, she stayed on the patio and waved to me. I smiled, took my stance, wound my pitch and let it go.

Gabriel yelled "Ooow." Then he said to Jose's brothers in a more serious tone, "I told you." He presented like I was a sideshow act, the main attraction. After a few more pitches, I told Joaquin I needed to stop.

When I got back to the patio, Alyssa whispered, "Showoff," and then she flashed me an insincere smile. I smiled back like I didn't notice. Gabriel leaned forward and whispered into my ear. "She's a little jealous because she isn't the center of attention. She'll get over it."

Mom gave me a huge hug, though, and I forgot Alyssa's insult.

* * *

The backyard glowed with spring. We stayed outside together and enjoyed the De Luna's company and Annette's work on the feast. The harvest table turned into two harvest tables, covered with multicolored tablecloths with four beautiful spring arrangements centered on each cloth. Then the plates were placed on the table with all the pastel colors and silverware. After we were seated, Alberto said grace.

We passed the bowls with salad, vegetables and rolls around the table. There were three kinds of grilled chicken and steak. It all smelled delicious, and the taste put the smell to shame.

My stomach started to stretch after my depression, but I still couldn't eat a full meal. Every piece of clothing I owned still hung off me. I ate more, but with all the softball practice, I hadn't gained back noticeably any weight. If anything, I looked smaller since I built muscle. Joaquin's growth made my size more noticeable. He dwarfed me. He grew more muscular than any of the boys in school—even his brothers.

After the first three courses, I caught a moment alone in the kitchen with Joaquin. He asked, "Are you enjoying our day?"

"It's great to see my mom happy—and Theresa."

"They do have some big smiles. Are you sure your mom didn't want you to herself?"

"No, it has been wonderful for her. She needs to spend time with more people than her seventeen-year-old daughter. She needs to make friends."

"She looks happier these days," he said.

He leaned in and gave me one of the sweetest kisses. My emotions churned, giving my body a lightness. By now, I should be used to rubbery knees from his touch. He caught me around the waist and then kissed me with more passion. I would've never imagined my heart wrapped around one person. Tied to him, and never a need to leave his side, but I stopped the passion for a second. "You want to come to my room tonight?" I looked deep into his eyes.

"I might do that," he said.

"Might?"

"Definitely," he said.

* * *

Sometime after dessert, Gabriel emerged from the house with two cartons of eggs. They all began to laugh. Annette yelled from the kitchen, "Go to the yard. Stay off my patio with those eggs."

"Yes, ma'am."

Some sort of havoc seemed to be close at hand, but by the way Marisol and Alyssa laughed, they must be in on the joke. Gabriel passed off one carton of eggs to Alejandro then they opened the cartons, which were filled with brightly colored eggs.

Gabriel and Alejandro pulled out a couple, set down the cartons and backed away. Then, the other boys grabbed some eggs. The cousins were in on the action, too. I could not believe Annette would allow them to play with eggs outside in their suits. Then, the first boy made his move—Gabriel. He slammed the colored egg on Enrique's head. I gasped as the confetti flew.

"*Cascarones*!" my mother cried in delight. "They're an Easter tradition in Mexican families."

How did we miss out on this growing up? Because we were girls, I guess—Mom liked to keep us tidy. The scene soon sprouted flailing arms and legs with confetti in their beautiful hair, and all the boys laughed. When they were all done, the boys stood up, shook out their hair and straightened their clothes. They trekked back to the patio.

Annette said, "Did y'all have fun?"

They all yelled back, "Yes, ma'am."

I looked back for Theresa. She talked with Jose, she beamed. Her head ducked and she blushed. I've never seen her blush. She picked a few stray pieces of confetti off the shoulder of his coat, a simple but affectionate act.

I elbowed Joaquin. "Isn't it fast?" I asked.

He squeezed me and laughed. "They met a long time ago," he said.

"What?" I asked.

"Jose is the person who brought her to see your father at the hospital," he said.

"They have been together that long?" I asked.

"No. But he hoped to meet her again after the funeral." A sadness fell upon me at the mention of those days. He pushed my hair back. "When I called him about the stalker, he jumped at the chance to keep her safe."

"Does he love her?" I asked.

"We'll see. It's all in the kiss," he said.

I poked his stomach. "What is that supposed to mean?" I asked. He righted himself and took my hand. He played with my fingers and didn't say anything. "What?" I asked.

"It took me a while to kiss you, right?"

"Forever," I said.

"It sounds crazy. You won't believe me." He looked down and didn't want to speak. I pulled on his hand. He looked up.

"Tell me," I said.

"Our love is sealed by a kiss," he said.

"Serious," I said.

"I am a hopeless romantic," he said. He laughed, and I slapped his chest. I cocked my head to the side and gave him a serious look.

"Come on," I said.

In a more serious tone, he began to speak. "When the Tonkawa kiss, the kiss sets our emotions. It's difficult to explain. A deep need ignites within us, and it becomes like a blink of your eye, involuntary. A confirmation, like the sun shines brighter on your life. The person is everything to you, *te amo*. You are my one true love," he said.

I looked for Mom. She was leaning against the counter, deep in conversation with Annette and Anita. She laughed and caught my eye with a wink—the best sight of the day.

* * *

Alberto told us he hated to ruin the party, but he had to take Mom back to the hospital. My throat got tight, but I didn't want to cry in front of her.

We all drove together in the SUV—Joaquin, Jose, Theresa, Mom, Alberto and me. My throat swelled tighter and tighter every mile closer. We talked a little more, and I needed to glean as much conversation as possible. But when we drove up to the hospital, it became hard to breathe.

She said, "Now don't you girls worry. I will be able to come home in a week or two."

My restraint ended. A tear rolled down my cheek. My hand trembled as I wiped it away before she noticed.

Theresa and I led her into the lobby, but we were not allowed to go any farther. We took turns at long hugs. Then she leaned in and kissed both of us on the cheek. "Keep this close to your heart… you are from a long line of strong women. Your grandmother served as the matriarch of her tribe. She wanted a girl, ecstatic when you girls were born. You girls are her legacy."

Before she pushed the door open and disappeared, she mouthed, "I'm sorry." She blew us a kiss. Before we could say or do anything, the door closed, and she disappeared.

* * *

The next day we headed to the batting cages. It doesn't open till eight o'clock, so we hung around the house for a while.

"Let's go," I said.

Joaquin said, "You still want to?"

"I have something to work out with my bat," I said.

Marisol and I took turns for a while. My hands gnashed around the neck of the bat, and then released all my energy in a powerful swing. Even my skin sensed the direction and velocity of the ball. It seemed as if when I woke up today, I woke up different—more. After being in such a fog, now I emerged stronger and more aware than ever. Each pitch reminded me of a different problem; Teo, my father's death, the secrets, the lies and all the questions unanswered. Each slam of my bat vindicated me and increased my strength. There in the moment, my instincts told me what to do—knock the ball into the back net.

My body tingled with newfound strength. I could see every turn of the ball as the lace spun toward me. The blood that pumped through my veins coursed hot, and it burned into my muscles, filling me with more power. My body helped me swing at the exact right time and place. I sensed the distance through my skin.

Swing after swing, the ball went harder into the back net—pounded and pounded. After I hammered the last ball, I sent it clean through the back net. I fell to my knees. The bat clanked to my side, and sweat poured from my body. My lungs filled like a balloon about to pop.

Then a strangeness filled my mind like the eerie sickness would soon arrive. I could smell testosterone. The boys started to growl. I looked over my shoulder and jumped to my feet. Teo, along with Jim, Thomas and two other boys I didn't recognize. Joaquin missed the pitch. He came out of the cage and stood in front of me. Micael slipped in front of Marisol, and I took her hand. The other boys stood shoulder to shoulder.

"I've given you time," Teo said.

"Fair enough," Joaquin growled.

I leaned into Marisol, and she put her arm around me, which helped my heart rate steady, but my mind raced.

She whispered, "Don't worry."

I shook my head and stepped closer to the cage, protected by it but close enough to hear the confrontation. My fingers curled around the cold metal links of the fence, and the tiny points cut into my fingers.

"I'm ready to end this," he said.

"I am, too," Joaquin said.

My mind spun. I understood. This is why he gave us time. Teo recruited from around town and built allies, but these wererats were not what he fought for—they were expendable. He wanted a pack of real werewolves. The Apache werewolf gene was diluted without a Tonkawa female, and even if he bore a son, the gene may or may not be passed on to his offspring. The key to the Tonkawa gene pool. I owned the treasured land on the creek the Apaches fought hard to win but failed. Two birds—one stone.

He didn't want me—he needed me.

This made it all too clear why our father hid us away all these years. We were special, a rarity in our ancestry. He kept us safe from the people out there who plotted against us. People like Teo weren't in search of someone to love, but a prize perfect gene pool to be used and discarded. My answer to the question "why me?" was a question that plagued me for months. He required our land, our history, our common blood. Teo allowed his alpha instincts to pursue me with animalistic aggression—to attack me. Joaquin, on the other hand, fought those impulses and denied his alpha urges. He made a choice to court me in a respectful, loving way.

"Teo, wait!" They all looked in my direction. "After what you tried to do to me in the woods, if I'd gotten pregnant, would you have owned up as the father?"

Marisol gasped, and everyone else stared at me—stunned. Teo chuckled and kicked a rock in my direction.

"You're starting to catch on, sweetheart."

Rage flooded my body. I wanted to inflict pain upon him. My fingers turned purple as they gripped the chain link fence tighter, and a small trickle of blood dripped across my palms. A pulse pounded in my ears, and I began to shiver.

Joaquin put his hand on me. I calmed but shook him off. I wiped my hands on my pants. The dirty hands that moved over me from the night in the woods returned, and I shook Marisol's hand away, too. I didn't want anyone to touch me.

"The regular place?" Teo said to Joaquin.

"Yeah. Midnight next Saturday."

"Can't wait."

Teo blew a kiss in my direction, then he and his minions went back to the car. As they pulled out of the parking lot, they peeled out and threw gravel up in the air.

The mood shifted lower, and clouds appeared overhead. I went to the trunk with Joaquin. When he lifted the lid to load my bag, I asked him if that gang planned a fight to get me on their side, and he said, "Yeah." Then I put my hand on his and looked into his eyes.

I asked, "Are they all wererats?"

He said, "Yes." Then he slammed the trunk lid. "There are more wererats now than there ever were in all our people's history. Teo is the bane to all of this supernatural world."

* * *

Joaquin took time to calm down after the altercation. We drove home and ate dinner. The mood somber; the boys did not joke, and even Gabriel kept quiet. He situated himself and stuffed the food he brought with him in his mouth without looking in any direction. I looked from seat to seat, and every expression revealed the same. Joaquin went into Alberto's office and talked for several minutes.

I went straight to the shower—no amount of water could wash away the memories of Teo's touch. In a way, I was glad the memory of my bad choice didn't swirl away down the drain. The memories made me stronger. I would hold tight to that strength. He would *never* own me.

We got ready for bed then Joaquin snuck over to my room. We laid on the bed and talked about the day, but he tried to avoid anything about Teo, and he held stern and serious. "Tell me what's going to happen," I said. "I'm part of this."

"This day has been coming for a while. We agreed to put off the fight until a few things changed." Teo agreed, and the time arrived. They agreed to fight, a fight between him and Joaquin, "But it looks like he's recruited a few more to help him out. We'll meet out in the field for the last time."

My mind spun on the words *last time*. "Could someone die?"

Joaquin nodded his head, but he wouldn't look at me or say a word. He gave a pat to my bent knee. I ran to the bathroom and threw up. Trembles spread over me as I stood up. I stumbled to the sink, brushed my teeth and washed my face. We were in freakin' high school—this kind of stuff doesn't happen. Over a girlfriend or, I guess in this case—a mate. My hips swayed as I sauntered into the bedroom to lie beside Joaquin.

We kissed; the passion swelled to a different level. I needed to fill up before next Saturday. The magnetism buzzed somewhere deep inside me, some type of primal impulse. Joaquin turned out to be my *alma gemela*, my soul mate. It's dire. Each touch or kiss gave the sensation of being the last, and it sparked fear. I held on tight and let go of my inhibitions. We kissed longer and harder. I tugged at his shirt, and he stood to pull it off. He slipped over to the door and locked it. I clutched the sheets below me. He flipped on the fan and came back to the bed. My eyes never left his body.

He didn't hold back. He kissed my neck and tugged at my shirt; my bare skin revealed for him to kiss around my stomach. My entire body tingled. His scent drew me in—consumed me. I put my hands on his face and pulled him back toward my lips. He moved his way back to my lips and kissed me with strong lips. One of his hands slid behind my head, tangled in my hair. His other hand moved across my stomach, sending sparks of electricity through me. My senses were piqued. My body took over, and this situation thrust me out of control. Then he grabbed my hipbones and fell between my legs. I bent my knees, and then I pulled him closer with both arms. My hands needed to pull him closer to me, but I held his body tighter than I imagined possible. He would pull away, and I would lean forward and pull him back to me.

We moved fast, too fast. My body buzzed. We kissed once more and pulled apart, not wanting to go too far.

He stood at the side of the bed, ready to go to his room, but I pulled him back—I couldn't make it without him for a moment. A deep sigh came from him. Then he lay back down on the bed next to me. We kissed again, and I moved on top of him. He rolled me over to my side and hugged me tight against his chest. He said he would stay until I fell asleep.

* * *

A few hours later, I awoke to howls outside my window. My hands ran across the sheets beside me. The space around me was empty.

I knelt over by the window. Wolves ran off into the wooded area behind the house. I sighed. The moon glowed bright, and the stars shone. The sky was absent of clouds. The Texas night sky will take your breath away, and with our wide-open spaces, you could see stars for miles—nowhere else did the moon shine this silver.

Pushing the window open a little, I took in the fresh night air. The wind caressed my face. I smiled and took in another deep breath. Then I lay my head on the windowsill, listening to the crickets and the water that flowed in the distance. The wind called me. With my hand outstretched, nature seeped into my pores, and a luminescent night moth landed on my hand. I pulled it in close to me and enjoyed the beauty and intricacy of its wings, of its feathered antennae.

I could see my children as they ran through the trees someday, my sister beside me, Joaquin and Jose nearby. I pushed the window open further and stepped outside—I needed the soil on my feet and the fresh air close around me. We were one. I belonged here. Its rhythm beats with my pulse—living inside of me.

CHAPTER 17

At my locker Friday morning, a tiny hand grabbed my shoulder. Becky stood beside me. Tears saturated her eyes as she trembled.

"What's wrong?"

Frantic, she began to explain. "I overheard Teo recruiting people together to fight Joaquin. They talked like they wanted to hurt him. I'm scared."

I hugged her tight and said, "Thank you."

She wiped at her eyes, her face hidden from the people in the hallway, and kept her voice low. "Everyone pointed and stared at Joaquin in first period this morning. Lexi told everyone the boys planned a fight. I don't know what's gotten into her."

"Don't worry, I will tell him tonight. You're a good friend," I said.

"Please, be careful. That guy Teo scares the crap out of me. And I know what he did to you at the party. He's dangerous."

"I will be careful, and I will be safe. I'm not weak."

She wiped at her face and nose, and then she turned and headed back down the hallway to her next class.

Later, Lexi and Jim began to bicker in the hall on the way to the cafeteria. A pang of guilt hit me. Jim, with his newfound abilities, caused him to be more annoying. He endangered everyone around him. Even though Lexi had turned into some kind of a witch, I didn't wish any harm on my former best friend.

Lexi looked off. Her skin gave off a green hue, and her sunken eyes had deep purple circles underneath. I heard her explain her appearance to a friend—she called it "spring fever," from all the allergens in the air. Even at a distance, to my nose, there was a putrid smell of sickness about her and a familiar stench. I took in a deep breath, an attempt to distinguish the scent. She'd been bitten.

The real problem, though, I didn't know how to help her.

I tried to stay focused and moved down the hall, but Lexi called after me in a sappy sweet voice, "Maria, do you have any big plans this weekend?"

"Nope, how about you? Did you want to do something? Hang out, maybe?"

She laughed.

I forced myself through my next class, brooding. I would never hurt Lexi, and I still considered her one of my best friends, but I didn't know how to make this right. The nicer I tried to be, the worse I made it. This could not be made right on my own. As if to match my mood, the sky darkened—we were in for one of Texas's signature spring storms.

At lunch, Ashley called me over to sit by her. Since I made the softball team, we'd spent a tremendous amount of time together. She even met me from time to time on the weekend to practice or go to the batting cages. We talked about the game, our fellow players' skills, the coaches, and the opposing teams, not about my mom, my relationship or rumors in school. But the small talk bored me. There was a more serious question that burned my tongue. The roar of thunder outside and the excitement of the students gave me my chance.

"Who was the girl at the game?" I asked.

Ashley fumbled her fork, dropping it with a clatter. "Huh?"

"Your friend from the game, she doesn't go here, does she?"

"No, she goes to school in Belton."

"Are you embarrassed by me?"

She met my eyes, and hers widen and fixed on my face. "Excuse me?"

"You didn't introduce me. Are you embarrassed by me?" I asked.

Her lips trembled. "Are you kidding? You're basically my best friend."

"Then, what's the problem?"

"It's complicated."

"No, it's not. I am 'basically' your best friend. Right? No complications, no secrets, and I want to know about the important people in your life," I said. My mind reeled a bit, and a twinge of guilt as the "no secrets" comment washed over me. It flew out of my mouth too quick to pull back. I know it made me a hypocrite.

"But..." she said.

"But nothing. Our friendship doesn't stop at school and softball. Or does it?"

"No. You're right, I'm sorry. I didn't know—" Her face turned red.

"Hey," I slid in close to her and threw my arm around her shoulder. "You're *basically* my best friend," I said with a laugh in an attempt to lighten her mood. "I love you! Nothing could ever change that, and I hope it's the same for you."

I noticed a tear well up in her eye, and she looked down to wipe it away. She looked back up and gave me a huge hug. For the first time, she hugged me, other than those so-called half hugs after a win.

"I love you, too." Ashley looked down and nodded. "Her name is Michelle. Yeah, we're kind of seeing each other."

Moisture formed in my own eyes; aware we were in a crowded cafeteria deep into this intimate conversation. At that moment, grateful for the thunder to mask our voices. Everyone around us, absorbed in their conversations, ignored us. Plus, at the word softball from one of us, all the other girls' eyes glassed over, or they scanned the table for a better conversation. This conversation would send some of the girls in our group salivating; a real gossip-worthy secret, it belonged to me, and I wasn't about to share. In this one moment, we were closer than ever, and we crossed the line from teammates to friends. A commonality, we were both in love with someone.

I hated that Ashley needed to be careful about whom she could share such an important part of her life with. I wondered if she'd been judged by others in the past. At least she could trust me to never be someone who wanted her to be anything other than herself—her complete self. We were unconditional friends. After all the trouble with

Lexi, it gave me some relief. Someday, I hoped I would be able to share a touch of my world with Ashley.

* * *

That evening at the De Luna's house, their company arrived. Inside were all the cousins, which included Jose. He said he'd told Theresa he needed to handle a family emergency. He hadn't lied; this constituted as a family emergency. Also, his idea to send her to stay with his mother and father for the weekend pleased me. He didn't want her here in the middle of this mess, but he sure as hell didn't want her in Austin alone. Honesty and passion showed in his eyes as he talked about my sister, and it made me realize that he showed a real interest in her. I made a mental note to call her and ask how things were progressing between the two of them. At the table, they used nonverbal communication. The thunder and rain pounded in my ears. It kicked up again. The emergency tone sounded on the television: The National Weather Service upped the thunderstorm watch to a tornado warning, and the news anchor said a small twister touched down in the counties next to us.

"Guys," I said. "Becky said Teo is bringing at least six friends—but I'm sure it is even worse than I've heard. I need to know what you've planned. Please, don't shut me out."

Joaquin squeezed my hand under the table, and the boys shared a glance. But they said nothing to me.

I got up and went to the kitchen with Annette to try and divert my irritation into dinner tasks. The boys went to Alberto's office to make plans for the battle. I checked the clock obsessively. They talked about Teo's gang without me, and I resented them for it. Joaquin stepped outside—without an invitation to me.

Annette popped her mixed fruit and nuts into her mouth. She didn't say anything to me, either.

Between the darkness and the pouring rain, nothing was intelligible. A deep black hole seemed to swallow up everything in front of me, blinding me. Then a flash of lightning in the distance revealed some movement in the trees. I strained my eyes to see it again. Through the glass patio doors, the lightning lit up the yard, and something sped past the house. I gasped.

"No worries, dear. You caught a flash of Jose and Joaquin. The boys are on patrol," Annette said.

I looked back outside. Soon, they emerged from the trees. They shook their wet hair. Beads of rain flew from side to side, and their dark hair looked silky black. Unsure of what to do with myself, I stepped out onto the patio and met Joaquin. He shook his wet hair at me, and I held my hands up to shield my face. I couldn't help it; the seriousness disappeared for a moment. I smiled, and he hugged me. We went inside. None of them breathless—you wouldn't even know that they left the house except for the wet hair and clothes. Most of them stripped down to jeans or shorts by now, all bare feet and chests. They laughed and joked about how fast Gabriel moved—for a baby.

He gave them a sideways smirk and a sarcastic, "Ha, ha, ha."

Joaquin looked at everyone and said, "We're done for the night. Let's go to sleep." He looked at me, and I shook my head.

"I'm going to stay up for a little while."

Watching everyone scurry like ants, I was trapped in a box, helpless. They talked around me, but no one talked to me. I suddenly realized that I hadn't been told my part or place in all of this.

Alberto and the cousins settled in to watch the weather and acted like nothing of any importance would happen tomorrow night.

Annette said, "Are you still hungry?"

"Yes, ma'am," I said. "A little."

"Well, come on in. I am finished wrapping up the leftovers, and I left a little plate out for you. I noticed you ate only half of your dinner."

A gesture this kind, I couldn't help it. I started to cry. These emotional fits drained the life from me. For months, maybe years, I hid in the shower to shed my tears, but now, they were uncontrollable. My emotions shifted from one intense emotion to the next, an irrepressible mess. In some ways, I hated being vulnerable, but in others, I loved having a motherly figure to share my secret emotions with.

After a few minutes, a soft touch on my back caught my attention. My heightened sense made it easy to identify people without seeing them. This touch belonged to Annette's warm hand. Her scent both wild and sweet—feminine. I wiped my face on a napkin and turned.

"I know things may seem a little bleak, but we're here for you no matter what happens."

Well, the talk didn't give me satisfaction, but I needed the calming effect she cast over me.

"It's me—my body—the fight is over me. And I can't even defend myself," I said.

Annette stood up straighter and put her hands on my shoulders. "Would you like a remedy?"

* * *

Annette and I went through the breezeway out to the garage. With all the cars parked out in the driveway, the garage was a huge empty space. She flipped the switch by the door, and the fluorescent lights buzzed and crackled to life. She told me she needed to show me a few things to help in the battle. I stepped into the middle of the room and turned, my bearings becoming situated in this new space. Annette pulled off her shoes and then dropped her jeans on top of them.

My face flushed, and I turned my back. I feigned interest in Alberto's tool bench.

"Whoa, there," Annette said. "We're all females here. I am going to transform because I want to teach you what to do."

"Wait. What? How to transform? I don't understand." My left-wrist tingled; I gripped it with my right-hand, rubbing.

She lifted an eyebrow. "Or maybe you do, but don't want to. Maybe you're afraid."

Something stirred inside of me. She pulled off her shirt and stood in front of me.

A sound came from her, not a hum or a growl, but like I could hear the rhythm of her heartbeat and the blood as it sped through her veins. It pulsed. A purple and gold aura started to radiate around her—arms out to her sides. The shiver of her body hummed with the sound in my ears. It accelerated. Her fingertips webbed together, forming feathers layered down to her shoulders, and the skin of her back seemed to unfold with feathers. Her face morphed into a pointed beak, and each strand of her hair became a golden feather—she leaped, and her legs pulled up into nothing, vanishing into powerful talons. She turned into the most awesome golden eagle, and she cut a tight circle around the garage. Her wings spread back and lengthened, she landed on her tiptoes. By the time her human heels touched the concrete with grace, she smiled at me.

"You want me to do that?" I asked. My head spun, and I backed up toward the door. The palms of my hands started to sweat, and I clasped at my chest, hoping to restart my heart.

"Sort of. Your transformation will be different, but the process is the same. Clear your mind of doubt. Being attacked can trigger a shift. Use your strongest emotions and let your senses take over."

With a deep breath, I slipped out of my shoes, pants, and shirt, then kicked them to the side. Searching my mind for my strongest emotions brought to mind the fear and rage that the night in the woods with Teo triggered. I visualized him coming after me. My pulse strummed, strong and steady. My temperature rose, and the boil of my blood, as it flowed through my veins, burned throughout every cell of my body. A strange pressure exerted itself on me from within, and every joint in my body popped. My muscles seemed to shift and tighten. I took a deep breath and remembered Teo's weight landing on top of me. The pops and slips became more intense, bordering on painful. My hair grew from every pore all over my body. I could smell the wild scent of nature as it flowed from my pores. My vision sharpened, and I could see a cricket as it moved under the workbench in the far corner of the garage. It chirped.

And then I bordered on transformation, but I could go no further. Fear of my true self lost in this crazy new world.

I fell to my knees and shook my head.

"I can't." I could barely push the words past my lips. My efforts took all my energy.

Annette seemed to realize that I pushed myself to the limit. She told me to be quiet and let the change happen. On the cold concrete, I leaned back on the heels of my feet and watched her. She took a deep breath and closed her eyes. The rhythm in my head, and the smack of each feather as it protruded from each pore of her shin, and the final pop of her shift shook me. I could smell the difference of her phases; her as human and her transformed—shifting from sweet and feminine to earthy and animalistic. Each chemical change within my body aided in the process and took her through each phase. It was crazy weird, like going through puberty again, and nobody wanted that to happen.

"Try."

I stood. My breath slowed, and I started again. The pop and shift of bones and muscle started faster this time—more intense. I seared. Fear gripped me. I fell to the ground again, out of breath and my chest heaved.

When I regained consciousness of myself again, my head laid on her knee, and she stroked my hair.

"It's okay," she said. "Get dressed, and we'll do something to help you through the fight in another way."

We worked on a few defensive moves. She showed me how to be still and wait for the attacker to commit. My senses, even in human form, were lightning quick. She showed me how to use an opponent's weight against him, to flip him over midair. She told me to go for the eyes, throat and groin.

"You're a natural." She embraced me as we moved back to the house.

"I am afraid. I want to help, but I can't," I said.

"You will," she said.

She connected to the boys and communicated with them. In my heart, I wanted her to understand that I tried. I needed her, someone to talk to and learn from—a mother.

I looked at her and said, "And you?"

"Yes, and me. I will protect my boys with everything inside me. That, you can count on."

She assured me Joaquin would be taken care of during the fight. He gained strength from the first altercation, and he built up some kind of new immunity he didn't have prior to Austin. She reminded me Jose would be here, too. Jose's strength exceeded my understanding. "He will take second next to Joaquin, and then Micael would drop to third. Jose is the alpha among his brothers, and we will have two alphas working together. Two—not one. I can't imagine a stronger group of leaders."

"Annette, why are you an eagle? I mean, instead of a wolf?"

She ducked her head. "Because I am Caddo. I'm proud of my heritage. Humankind gleaned many great things from the Caddo—skills like hunting, fishing and building techniques. Few of us transform, but I am lucky." She met my eyes again. "You realize, don't you?"

"Realize what?"

She cupped my face. "Maria, if you can transform, you will be our alpha female."

Holy shit. I didn't have enough time to absorb the fact my father changed our name from Rios. I could transform. Now this. I would be the alpha. What about my sister? Could my father shift? Was this my new life? Every step forward raised more questions than I could answer. The life Dad wanted me to live—this is why I never quite fit in with the kids at my other school; more acquaintances than friends, but no rivals, and I fumbled through life. An existence, yet out of place.

But here I more than fit with true friends, true enemies and a family. A million and one emotions flooded through my body. Visions flashed in my eyes. I grabbed at my throat. My carotid pumped hot, ancient blood through my veins. Inside I tingled, but when I ran my hand over my body, everything was in the same spot. Nothing changed.

This change would turn me into my true self, my birthright. In a way, it thrilled me. My body hungered for this new existence. I wanted to be the alpha.

* * *

A crack of thunder shook the house, and the lights dimmed for a moment. They buzzed and hummed as they came back to life. I clutched the edge of the counter and rubbed my wrist. It burned. We looked up, and I kind of held my breath. Another long electronic tone sounded. It came from the TV. I returned to the living room, and the news anchor reported that we were under a tornado watch. It was two a.m., Saturday, the day of the fight arrived.

The clouds were low and dark as they tumbled across the sky. The temperature dropped, and the humidity dripped thick. All the heaviness in the air made each breath harder to draw than the last. The moisture beaded on my skin. For a moment, my body flashed hot with a fever and then went cold. I grabbed a clip, twisted my hair into a knot and clipped it. My hair would be out of control with this weather.

It sounded like a hundred drummers at practice as the rain pounded on the metal roof. I got up and traveled over to the glass doors. Golf ball-sized hail scattered all over the driveway. The rain canceled our softball game after school on Friday, and it looked like there wouldn't be any practice this weekend, either.

I went to the closet in my borrowed room to change for bed. I put on a T-shirt and some boxers. I went next door and pounced on the bed beside Joaquin, where he rested on the end with the remote in hand. I slid in behind him and started to kiss and blow on his neck; I moved to his ear. He tilted his head, and I did it again. Since the practice with Annette, my body tingled in strange ways—I felt stronger, more alive. Joaquin reached back and pulled me around and across his lap. I looked up at him and smiled. I straddled his lap and lunged forward and gave him a peck on the lips. Then the room shook from the thunder, and lightning flashed. It excited me more.

"Don't be scared," I said. "I'm here."

We started to laugh. He got up and dropped me on the bed.

He pulled my T-shirt off and left my shorts and sports bra on. I pulled him to me. He stopped and locked the door with one hand as he moved toward me. We lay on the bed, kissing, and I pulled his shirt off. He moved to his knees, slipped my shorts down over my thighs, but left my underwear. Before he laid back, I ran both hands down his rock-hard abs. He fell forward but braced himself with his arms as we raced on. My heart thumped. His drummed against my chest as he lay against me. I took a quick breath, but in less than a second, I yearned for more. He pushed his hand up my side, and then he moved it toward my stomach, which made my body quiver. I reached down and popped the button on his jeans and started for the zipper.

My heart raced, and my hands shook. He held my hands and moved them toward his chest. His body temperature rose, and the sweat on his chest cooled my fever. We kissed. My hands moved to the sides of his face and pulled him closer to me. Then, I slid my hand up his back and held tight to his shoulder blades. His hand grazed the side of my chest and moved on. He pulled up. Lightning struck, and I could see the beads of sweat glistening across his shoulders. His torso chiseled like a statue. My hands slid to his hips and tugged on his belt loops. My fingers slid back to the front of his pants. I wouldn't stop the kisses. He grabbed my hands and pinned them against the pillow over my head.

"No," he said.

"When you come back?" I asked as I lunged forward for another kiss.

"No. I don't want this to happen now. Not out of fear," he said.

"It's not. I want to."

"You want to because you're afraid—afraid something might happen or might not happen. Fear should not guide your decision. I don't want any regret for rushing into something."

I leaned up and kissed him on his lips. He kept my hands over my head.

"I'm serious. I won't regret it," I said. I dove forward to kiss him again. He pushed me back.

"Yes, you will, it would be rushed and for all the wrong reasons," he said.

"But I love you. What better reason?" I asked again.

He gave a little and kissed me back. "I love you, too," he said.

"When you come back?" I asked.

"It's not time, not today. Call me a sap, but I want more than a forced moment with my family in the next room. When it's right, we will both know," he said.

I puckered my lips and fell back against the pillow. He hovered over me, laughing. He kissed my nose as thunder sounded and lightning flashed. My head jerked to the side. I could see out of the window. The darkness and rain seemed to reach out to me, as if the storm blackened not only the sky but something inside me, also.

He kissed me on the lips. "What's wrong?" he asked.

"Seriously? Do you even need to ask?"

"You worry more than you need to."

"I can't lose you,"

"We've got this. You don't give us enough credit," he said.

"Don't you remember Austin?"

"Yes, but I'm stronger, and we've upped the odds," he said.

"Will your plan help?"

"We didn't lose last time." He brushed the tears from the corner of my eye. "He caught me off guard and bit. We ran them off into the night and watched them squeal—with their tails between their legs like the mice they are. Now, I'm immune, and he can bite away." He pounded his arm.

"Not funny," I said. Then, I rubbed the scar on his arm.

I lifted myself and pulled my knees tight against my chest. A familiar voice played in my head, the voice of my father, and it said, "Always know who you are and who you are meant to be." My tears stopped. I have always believed my dad protected me, and he prepared me. The talks, the life lessons, the sports, he gave me value in myself. He transferred his strength to me. Joaquin continued with his different love and strength. He gave strength when necessary, but now I bore strength, too. The strength to dig in and move forward, to know what to hold on to and how far to go to protect what I held dear. This time I needed to stand and fight.

I caught Joaquin's hand. "I'm going to fight."

He hugged me close and whispered in my ear, "I know."

* * *

The sun never showed itself once throughout the day, and dark clouds covered every square inch of the dreary sky. The mood in the house hung somber and low. News bulletins posted reports of flash flooding across the county, which left roads impassable and people stranded.

Power lines fell and caused blackouts over sections of town. We lived farther out, away from the major outages.

Joaquin led me to the door. "Do you know any karate?"

"Ha. Funny," I said. "But your mom showed me some moves."

To my surprise, he and his brothers took this seriously. "It's all about defense, right? If you need to protect yourself until we can make it to you, then you can buy us some time," he said.

"Okay," I said.

"Go pick up your raincoat and rain boots and meet me outside," he said as he slipped off his shirt and trotted outside, Gabriel on his heels.

I ran to my room, grabbed my jacket, then pulled my rain boots on and zipped up the jacket. My emotions were mixed, but I was happy he didn't blow off my desire to be in the fight. When I opened the door and moved to the backyard, he wasn't under the patio awning. He stood in the yard with Gabriel. They told me to stand at the end of the yard by Joaquin's room and then back up toward Annette and Alberto's room. Gabriel sneaked behind me in a flash, his arm around my neck.

Joaquin asked, "What do you do?" I used my instincts, stepped back and flipped Gabriel over my shoulder with my hand at his throat.

He looked up at me and laughed, "Mom showed you a few things, huh?"

"Well, I asked her to," I said. "She's a good teacher."

"And I'd say someone's instincts are a little sharper."

He jumped up and grabbed my arm. I twisted around and put him on his knees with my elbow in the middle of his back. He laughed again. Then, Joaquin came at me full speed. As he got within a half step away, I stepped to the side and leaned back. Joaquin rolled. Then, Gabriel grabbed me from behind. I slammed my heel into his foot, elbowed his stomach, grabbed around his head and pulled him over my shoulder and to the ground.

We rested. My muscles moved nimble and excitement pulsed through my veins—I grinned. I stood, stared at my hands, and reveled in my newfound power.

Gabriel looked up and sighed, "She's good."

"Not quite."

Joaquin shifted. The massive wolf crouched. Snarling and growling, he sprang at me—paws aimed at my chest. My heart took off. But my instinct said to run, to defend myself. Something shifted within my body. My joints cracked and popped, my pulse steadied, and my sight cleared. At that moment, my body reacted. Every hair on my body stood on end. It seemed thicker. My fingers twisted, and my nails widened into claws. My senses sharpened; his distance flashed in my mind, and his choices came to me as he made a visual map in my mind of his attack. A realness came over me. This wasn't just any high school altercation; it was life or death.

But as soon as my mind took over, I lost it. Like I feared myself, and the animalistic wave passed. I waited, a girl with bare skin and thin clothes, standing unsteadily on two small feet. The defensive moves seemed harder to remember, but my instincts kicked in at the last moment, and I stepped aside. The massive wolf tumbled across the grass. He stopped himself and rose in his stance. He howled with his nose pointed to the sky. He shook his body, and then my Joaquin moved in front of me.

"Whoa! Did you see that?" Gabriel stared at me, wide-eyed. "I could have sworn... you were about to shift, Maria."

Joaquin frowned. "Good enough. You can buy us enough time to come help, but you're staying way back out of the action. Teo's out for blood. No chances—all right?"

"Okay," I said, still shaken from those massive paws that jumped at me and from the weird sensation in my body. A live wire snapped somewhere in my back and shoulders. I closed my fists then opened them—they were normal.

* * *

Eleven forty-five. We loaded up in the SUV and Jose's suburban. I stroked my palms against my jeans. Beads of sweat formed around my lip and on my forehead, even with the cold outside. My jacket on and the hood up. Everything in my mind bounced around, out of control, going over every single scenario. The rain pounded, and the howl of the wind made it hard to concentrate.

In the backseat, Joaquin let go of my hand and put his arms around me. He pulled me close and held me tight. If I was in his lap, it would not be close enough at this moment.

The windshield wipers didn't help with the hail. They gathered up all the balls and spread slush across the window, and some ice accumulated under the wipers. You could hear the metal dent as the enormous frozen rain hit the hood and roof. We drove fast but took care not to flip the vehicle on the way to the fight.

Lightning struck a tree on the side of the road, and it boomed. I heard the crackle of wood as it split and the rumble as it hit the ground. The radio hissed with static and jumbled words until it landed on the weather channel. Nothing changed. We were still within the path of a thunderstorm and tornado watch. We didn't need to be a meteorologist to make a forecast tonight. We were in the middle of a mighty Texas thunderstorm, and the clouds looked eerily familiar—like the ones from the videos of Jarrell, Texas, the night the tornado destroyed it.

I rubbed my hands to warm them back up. Joaquin took my hands and pulled them against his chest.

The cars came to a stop, and my stomach fell. The time arrived. Joaquin reached across and opened the door for me. I stepped out, and he almost stuck to me. The wind howled. It took all my strength to stand upright. The boys moved in a group. Joaquin kissed me, backed up and then they shifted. Annette took two long strides, jumped, threw her arms out to the side and circled overhead. Joaquin meandered over, snorted and threw his nose over toward the group.

We strolled together. My hand on his side.

I would stand behind Joaquin and in line with Micael and Jose. To my left would be Raul and Alberto. To my right were Enrique and Angel. Behind me would be Alejandro and Roberto. Gabriel brought up the rear while Annette surveyed from the sky. The family surrounded me. They would keep me out of the battle, if possible. I knew all these plans struck me as strange, but I didn't remember any conversation about partners or positions. Somehow, we all moved together with the unspoken plan in our minds, and we fell in perfect formation. Me included.

We made our way down the field to a familiar scene—a clearing, perfect for a fight, with a few sharp dips in the ground and some fallen branches. The grass grew close to the ground as if it were tended.

Thunder crashed, sparks still spraying from the earlier strike. As we got closer to it, I ducked and covered my head. When I looked up, the top of the tree sparkled with fire. It made a strange kind of suction from above, like the breath of a giant pulling us closer to its mouth. My ears popped. I tried to cover them, but it didn't help. The wind blew hard enough that tears fell from my eyes and mixed with the rain. My hair pulled back, but my hood flopped in my face. I pulled it off and threw it to the side. I crouched low to the ground, careful to keep my hands out for balance.

Then movement deep in the trees caught my attention. Jim, Teo and Thomas emerged. They shifted. Teo prowled out in his wolf form—a snarl escaped the jet-black wolf the size of a small car. Jim and Thomas skulked upright in their grotesque wererat form. Four more wererats materialized from behind them—I didn't recognize them.

Then, two more female figures emerged. I squinted.

Cindy and Lexi were between them. At that moment, my heart broke. We would fight against my friends. My friendship with Lexi hadn't ended in my eyes yet. I worked too hard to give it up like this. Worse, Lexi slouched defenseless in her human form; it hadn't been long enough, and she couldn't transform. She was in the middle of this without protection, and I doubted Jim and Teo would offer it.

However, Cindy crouched in her changed form. Her incisors curved past her lower lip, and her chin receded, making fangs that would kill with ease. Her hair tousled, and long hair hung from her arms and hands. She held Lexi. Lexi struggled, but her hands were somehow bound in front of her. She yelled something inaudible from this distance; the swirl of noises around us carried her words away.

We stood atop the highest hill for miles, and I could see the destruction come our way. Annette shrieked, and I looked up in time to dodge debris carried in the wind. Alberto batted it away with his muzzle. He growled, and I sensed the pack's readiness to attack.

Our group made it to the center, but Teo's group approached from the tree line. We took our stances and readied ourselves. I kept my knees bent and my hands out, the way Annette showed me. They trembled. In an attempt to gain equanimity, I opened and closed my fists. No use. Fear clamped down on me.

The wolves hunkered and bristled. Then, Joaquin threw his large snout into the air and howled. The boys matched his pitch in their battle song. My tremors increased to shakes, and my heart thumped. The howl rattled to my core. It called me—urged me to join. I tried to release and let my senses take over, but I started to shiver. I could hear my pulse and my blood heating. But now, I froze, paralyzed by my fear of the transformation and my fear of failure. I could not do it.

Teo threw his head up and let out a cry. The wererat's shrieks could in no way be described as a song, but ugly and crass. The De Lunas snarled and slavered. They pushed back on their haunches, ready to spring. Then, all at once, they slid into a new position. Their paws hammered the earth.

Teo sprang, ready to break through the front line to me. I jumped back. Joaquin knocked him to the ground. Then, Jim and Thomas sprang. Jose threw Jim down with ease and took a snap. Micael slapped Thomas away with his head, but Thomas flew back. With a leap, Micael sank his teeth into Thomas. Thomas dropped, bleeding and twitching. The four transformed boys behind them fanned out to the sides, but they were a little less eager to spring. They crouched and skulked around in a circle. I looked back and forth as the other wolves kept their protective stance around me. I could anticipate each step and which way to move in response—a choreographed dance of death.

Lightning struck again. The tree, already engulfed in flames, swayed sideways. With a loud crack, the trunk broke. Flaming branches slammed down to the ground, breaking our careful formation. Teo dove in again, now with his jaws open and white teeth glistening in the firelight, reminding me of my dream. Fight or flight urgency coursed over me. Rage burned through my veins. My instincts decided for me. He would not hurt me. I began to shake, and a growl rumbled from deep inside of me—the wolf inside me snarled, and I let it go.

With a hard, graceful motion, my entire body shifted. I stood on four feet and bristled. The clearing rang sharper, brighter. I took a deep breath of the sooty, ozone-scented air; it came out as a snort. But most of all, time slowed down. Teo hung in the air, still mid-leap. I lunged forward, a sinuous line of muscle like I was born to this body. With no effort, I knocked him out of the air. He landed on his side and rolled from the unexpected force.

Reveling in the fear in his eyes, I stood in front of him. Payback time. My wolf form was covered in auburn fur with hints of silver. Though less massive than Joaquin, my whole body stretched taut and strong and was meant for battle—or protection from monsters like Teo. Below me were my tattered clothes crumpled in a pile.

In a quick bound, Joaquin crouched in front of me before Teo could steady his legs. He tried to run, but Jose knocked him to the ground. The others jumped on the wererats, who shrieked and squawked. I heard a screech, and Annette swooped down—Cindy stumbled backward and went down in a three-point stance with a hiss.

This distraction gave Lexi enough time to run toward us, stumbling and off balance. She made her way straight for me. With one paw, I pushed her behind me. At the same time, Cindy attacked. With a quick snap of my head, I knocked her to the ground.

Lexi collapsed, either too injured or too sick to struggle, and she curled up in the mud, on the edge of consciousness. Gabriel rushed over to us and took a protective stance over her. Now, I was free to deal with Cindy once and for all. She got up, and I tackled her back to the ground, pinning her there with my front paws. She thrashed her head about and snapped at my legs. Instinct took hold of my physical body, and I bit her. Her flesh gave way, and a metallic flavor of blood flooded my mouth. It tasted good and adrenaline coursed through me. She went still, and I gave a triumphant howl. Wow. I mean, who didn't want to take a bite out of Cindy?

I ran over to check on Lexi. She lolled lifelessly, but Gabriel hovered with his best attempt as a guard. I fell back in line with the others.

Off in the distance, a funnel cloud formed a tail, and it reached down lower and lower to the ground. Around the area, several more of the attackers fell limp on the ground. The boys stood in protective stances over the wererats as they transformed back into their former selves. Another wererat moved in, and Micael took him down to the ground in one fell swoop and bit his throat. The weather kicked up, and the tornado alarms sounded in the distance. We needed to finish this and move out of here, fast.

Teo crouched before Joaquin. Joaquin rocked back on his hind legs, his nose close to the ground and snarled. For the first time, Joaquin scared me.

Joaquin and Teo circled. Teo backed up, and then Joaquin snarled and stomped toward him. My new body intercepted Joaquin's plan an instant before it happened. Wolf telepathy made me officially part of the pack. Then Joaquin dove into him, teeth exposed. A violent growl ripped loose from his muzzle, and it quaked in my chest. I howled. The thunder rumbled, and the field blazed with lightning bolts. He and Teo tumbled over each other on the ground. Joaquin thrashed about, and something flew past. He snapped again and flung his head. Something flew out to the other side—some part of Teo's body. I heard a painful cry, and then Teo lay silent.

Gabriel looked at Joaquin, and I sensed the agreement transmitted between them. Gabriel hesitated, his eyes locked on Lexi. The storm hollered like a train, and Joaquin barked for his brother to hurry up. Gabriel's head dipped, and in an instant, he'd sunk his teeth into Lexi's shoulder right above her original bite. She screamed and then fell silent.

I closed my eyes and steadied my breaths. I looked at my hands—I shifted back. Like that, I was back to myself. Even though my clothes were torn, I pulled them on to cover my nakedness. On my way over to Lexi, I found my jacket and shoved it against her bloody wound. Gabriel ducked his head and backed away. I hugged her close, and her eyes fluttered open. Her hand touched my face before she went limp.

The boys were back in their human forms, too. They stood, eyes on the carnage sprawled across the ground. In unison, they picked up the wilted, pink bodies of Teo's friends and carried them across the field to their cars. They set them down. Then they went about staging a car accident.

They fumbled with keys and braced their shoulders against doorframes and pushed the vehicles into each other. The storm hissed, and I couldn't hear the glass break, but the force of the impact left massive dents. The boys tore off a limb from the fallen tree and smashed out the headlights. They grabbed the driver's side chassis and tipped Jim's truck into the ditch. When they completed the wreckage, they dragged the wounded wererats to the vehicles and shoved them into and around the scene of the "accident." Angel picked up one of the kid's cell phones and reported a bogus incident to 911. He said some kids raced, and it looked like one of the vehicles rolled. He tossed the phone next to the owner and shrugged.

"We better hit the road."

Behind him, the funnel cloud touched the earth and turned black.

"Let's go," I yelled.

CHAPTER 18

I stepped out of the shower and cataloged my bruises in the mirror. I'd come through the fight all right, but one thing puzzled me. I wrapped myself in a robe and went out to show it to Joaquin, who rested in bed.

I pulled my sleeve up and held it out. Joaquin looked at my wrist and peered at a purple bloodstain that peeked through my skin. A clear letter R branded on my wrist, an outward symbol of my transformation—the mystical mark that identified me as a shapeshifter. He pulled it to his lips, kissed it and rubbed it with his fingers. He smiled.

"*Te amo*," Joaquin said.

"*Te amo*," I replied.

"See, nothing to worry about," he said.

"Because of your family. They risked everything for me. How do I thank them?" I ask.

"You keep me happy."

I got on my knees and straddled his lap. I put my arms around his neck.

"And how do I do that?" I asked.

"You should do whatever I want," he said with a playful bite to my bottom lip. He put his arms around my waist.

I gave him an *I don't think so* look. "Watch out. I bite now."

He laughed and held up his hand in surrender. "Total joke. You've already done it. Being yourself."

I hugged him extra tight, and then I cuddled up beside him and fell asleep.

* * *

We got up Sunday morning and gathered in the living room. The newscaster broke the regular broadcast and said, "Last night, a storm rocked our town. We have two unconfirmed tornados. Also, a two-car accident on highway 2310 with eight injuries and one missing person. When police arrived, they found one car with substantial damage to the front end. The second car rolled over in the ditch. The owner of the first car is missing. The other eight people were unconscious when police arrived. Some of them had been thrown from their vehicles. They were taken to the hospital, but they were all in stable condition. They were unable to give a statement concerning the accident."

Alberto picked up the remote and flipped to a baseball game. We took it in for a minute. Then the silence broke.

"Anyone else famished?" Gabriel asked.

* * *

On Monday morning, the school buzzed with rumors of this weekend's accident. People who didn't like Joaquin and his brothers tried to connect them to the disaster, but their theories seemed far-fetched. People laughed at the conspiracy theorists.

Becky met us at lunch. She said they hospitalized Lexi, and she asked us if we would like to go with her to visit her.

"I don't know if she wants to see me yet," I said.

My hands fidgeted with a napkin. I didn't know if I could face her. She'd been herself during the whole night. She watched me shift. And my face was the last distinguishable sight to her before she passed out for the night—after the bite. It couldn't be denied.

Becky said the school planned a vigil for Teo tonight in the school parking lot. They set up a search of the fields near the wreckage. Trying to see if he may have gone for help. The police believed he could've passed out somewhere in the fields.

"Well, it's at eight if you want to come."

"I'll try." I gave her a little smile, one that I'd tried to hold back all morning, and confessed, "The hospital called me. I'm going to pick up my mom after school. She's coming home today."

"Seriously? That's great. I'm happy for you."

"I know. It's been too long. She seems to have it together. I can't wait for things to go back to normal."

Normal. Would my life ever be normal? Maybe I'd etch a new kind of normal, a new life with my mom, my sister, my boyfriend and my new self.

* * *

Theresa waited beside me in silent anticipation. I wiped my hands on my pants, and each beat of my heart came closer to the last. My eyes scanned the room, and I peered out the hallway windows. I couldn't wait a second longer. We heard the buzz, clank and the release of the automatic door, then a whoosh of air hit me in the face. Theresa and I ran to give mom a hug. There were no tears, only happiness. Joaquin took the suitcase from the nurse behind mom. Then the nurse gave Alberto a few instructions. I didn't hear all of it, but I picked up on the key points: no stress, back to work part-time and a big bag of prescriptions. Mom would come to the hospital three days a week for group sessions. As things progressed, that would drop off. Theresa and I would need to talk with the psychiatrist for a time as well. They also suggested that we, Theresa and I, come to group at least once every two weeks. We said we would, and we were out the door. Theresa asked if we could take mom home in her car and meet the boys later. She wanted some time alone with mom.

Mom and I would have plenty of time together once Theresa left for college, and I kissed Joaquin goodbye.

"I'll call you later about the vigil," I said.

Annette put a bouquet in Mom's hands, "We will see you at church."

In the car, I teased Theresa about her new boyfriend.

"Who?" Mom asked. She smiled. Her face appeared gaunt from the rapid weight loss, but the brightness to her green eyes had been absent for too long. She had applied lipstick and some eye shadow, and her hair was blow-dried straight. Her natural dark brown color showed at the roots. I made a mental note to make her an appointment at her favorite salon.

"It's Jose. He is Joaquin's cousin, remember from Easter?" she said.

Mom seemed shaky still, but she smiled. "I hope he's a nice boy."

"Oh yeah, and he attends The University of Texas," Theresa said.

"And he's hot," I added. I fanned myself, rolled my eyes and fell over on the backseat. Theresa smacked me. I lifted myself back up, covered my mouth and giggled.

"If I remember, he *was* a good-looking boy," Mom said.

Theresa said, "Oh yeah!"

We all laughed and talked more about boys. Jose took her out several times on real dates; we left out the part about him living at her apartment to fend off stalkers. By our conversation and the look on Theresa's face, I could tell they liked each other. She said it exhilarated her, and she didn't want to be without him even for a day. I couldn't wait a second longer, but I bit my tongue until we'd reached the house. I helped Mom inside, then hurried back out to help Theresa with the suitcase from the truck.

I pushed up beside her and asked, "Did you *kiss* him?"

The need for a verbal confirmation flew right out the window when her cheeks exploded with scarlet. I've never seen her at a loss for words. She nodded. And with the simplest of motions, my answer. Thousands of things flooded my mind. I threw my arms around her. Her life would be forever drawn into my new life filled with all its delicious flavor of love, loss and legends. Or did she already know? Too soon for me to know, but we held each other tight, happy to be a family again.

* * *

We arrived at the vigil after dark. Becky dragged me up to the front. Joaquin and Gabriel came with us, but the others stayed back, leaning against the cars.

Alyssa said, "I feel like a hypocrite at this thing. I'm glad he's gone," she muttered.

Up front, we picked up a candle from a large box. Becky started. She lit her candle and passed the flame to the people closest to her. Then they moved outward and passed the candles until the parking lot filled with light. Pictures of Teo were tied to the fence and almost all the victims who'd survived the fight spoke. They wanted everyone to pray for Teo and the victims recovering in the hospital. They came through this with their lives, and they still had hope that Teo was alive.

What liars. I looked up at Joaquin. I hoped, too. A different kind of hope, though—that Teo would never come back. Joaquin stood behind me with his arms wrapped in front of me at the waist. A pastor from one of the local churches said a prayer. Then, all the victims started the school song. Everyone linked elbows and sang. We blew our candles out.

Joaquin hugged me close on the way to the car.

I asked, "Teo's father was killed in an accident?"

"Yes," he said.

"When was he killed?"

"Last year."

The connections were clicking together. My mind reeling at the thoughts running through my head. Forming the words and questions I wanted to ask came harder than climbing a mountain.

"Teo Valdez. His father is James Valdez?"

"Yes, that's his father," Joaquin said.

"His father murdered my Dad."

He looked at me and then at the floor. Fidgeting with his keys and without looking up at me, he answered, "Yes."

"Is Teo alive?" I asked.

"I'm not sure. When we ran back across the field to our car, his body disappeared. Maybe," he said.

"Why hasn't he come back to school?" I asked.

"He may be stuck in his wolf form trying to heal."

"Will he come back?"

"If he does, we'll be ready," he said.

At the heavy brush and wooded area, something ran past us. Gabriel and Joaquin used their instincts to make a protective move toward me.

Then, that quick, it disappeared.

* * *

Joaquin needed to complete his homework, and I told him I wanted to spend some time at my house. I jumped back into my jeep and drove to the hospital instead. In spite of my reluctance, I needed to see Lexi. I needed her to tell me what she remembered.

With the late hour, I barely made visiting time. The door opened a crack, and I could see the glow of the TV. I knocked.

Lexi said, "C'mon in." The TV tuned to the news footage from the vigil.

"Hey," I said.

Lexi shifted in her bed to make room next to her and patted the open space. "If I would have known guests would come, I would have cleaned the place up."

I laughed, "I see you haven't lost your sense of humor."

"Nope. Still intact. What are you doing here?"

I took my place next to her and squeezed her hand. "I was worried about you."

"Even after me being such a crappy friend?"

"A little hiccup, are we fine?"

"I would love that."

"Great, let's hug it out, and get me out of here before the visitor police kicks me out. I'll visit tomorrow."

We embraced, laughed and a weight lifted. Friends were people who forgave each other—who could find their way back to whatever effortless love drew them together in the first place.

* * *

The next day, I went back to the hospital with everyone else. The building seemed large but less menacing than all my other visits. A nice modern building with lots of windows and landscaped grounds with ornate iron benches. The parking lot filled with cars, and it seemed like miles to travel to the front door.

Becky knocked on the door. We heard someone say, "Come in." Lexi rested in the room alone with the TV. An IV stuck in her arm and one long bandage on her shoulder. Becky ran over and gave her a hug. I did, too. Gabriel strolled in and placed the flowers on the table next to her bed. Joaquin slipped over and hugged her. Gabriel followed and held her a little longer than a normal hug.

Lexi said, "Gosh, Gabriel, I'm not dead."

This made him smile, and he said, "That should be my line. I'm the funny one." We all laughed together.

"How are you?" Becky asked.

"OK, I guess. It's crazy," she said.

"How's that?" Becky asked.

"I don't remember even getting into the car."

I looked up at Joaquin and smiled. He mouthed, "I told you so." A big deep breath and I turned my attention back to Lexi.

"Seriously?" I said.

"Yeah, it seems like I'm not the only one. We must have totally smashed our heads."

"Sorry, Lexi, I need to go home, but I wanted to come check on you," Becky said.

I noticed Gabriel leaned against the windowsill. He stared at Lexi. His regular quick wit still absent, which gave me an urge to chatter.

"Gabriel and I should go, too," Joaquin said. "Are you sure you're good? Do you need anything?"

"No, I am good. My mom will be by later. Come back if you can, even you, Gabriel," she looked at him, and he smiled. "But bring your sense of humor next time. I'm totally bored."

Joaquin caught my eye again and said he'd wait for me in the car. They hugged her again before they left. As we traveled toward the door, Lexi said, "Gabriel, thank you."

His shoulders tensed, and he turned to look at her. "What?" he asked. "Why?"

"For the flowers, silly," she pointed at the bouquet. He let his shoulders drop and sighed.

"It's from all of us."

"Thank you, *all*," she said.

When we were alone, Lexi leaned in close to me, gave me a weird look, and then she whispered, "Why does Gabriel look at me like he wants to take a bite out of me?"

I took a drink of Coke, and the comment made me choke and sputter. It took me a minute to catch my breath and to stop the spell her comment caused. Then I wiped my tears. Lexi laughed.

"You know, I'm sorry for the way my cousin treated you guys. And me. A touch of jealousy, I guess. What can I say? I'm spoiled, used to all the attention. Jim, too. Then you made the softball team, and you were all the rage. Not an excuse. An explanation."

"I already told you we're good," I said.

"I know. Needed to be said."

"We watched Cindy at Teo's thing. She seemed different—humble. Almost."

"Yeah. I would say that is different," Lexi laughed.

"I brought you a candle from the vigil. Thought you might want it. They held the vigil for you, too, after all," I said.

Lexi tossed it in the garbage can beside her bed and shrugged. "Not anything I want to remember or think about."

We smiled and nodded. Lexi was back.

* * *

When I got home, Theresa said Mom went upstairs to take her first good bath in over a month. We rested on the couch and caught an old episode of *Friends*. But when Mom didn't make it downstairs after another fifteen minutes, we went and knocked on her door.

I didn't hear a response.

My stomach sank. We peeked in the door and called out to her. My legs were shaky, and my heart raced. We pushed the door open. We heard her say to come to the bathroom. Theresa and I looked at each other and made our way into the bathroom.

Mom's weak body perched on the edge of the bathtub with her hand balled up in a fist, and her stare locked on it. As we hugged, her ribs and even the bony knobs of her pelvis poked me. The sight of her intensity and her withered body terrified me, and I scanned the counter for pill bottles. When I looked back at her, her hand opened, containing two rings nestled in her palm. She said she couldn't put them on.

"I miss him. Every time I look at these, I can't catch my breath. But it's wrong not to wear them. I need to wear them," she said.

Theresa stepped over to a stand-up jewelry box, and I heard the crunch and tink of metal as it bumped together. Her fingers stirred around.

"I've got it."

She held up a long gold chain and slipped over and took the rings. She slid them onto the chain and slipped it around Mom's neck.

"This way, they're near your heart, and you can touch them, even though you can't see them," she said.

Mom smiled and held them up for a moment, then she dropped them into her shirt. We both gave her a huge hug. She grabbed us tight, and we almost knocked her into the tub. It made us laugh, and we cried a little.

"This is what Dad would want for us," I said.

Mom sighed, the tears out of her voice, and got up and wrapped herself in a bathrobe, tying the sash tight around her waist. She motioned for us to follow her to her room. We looked at each other and shrugged. Our feet shuffled into her room. She opened the large chest at the end of her bed. The hinges creaked, and the scent of cedar wafted across my nose. I'd respected her wishes to stay away from it all this time, and in truth, I'd forgotten about it by now. Pulling a few things out and positioning them on the floor. Her hands meticulously rummaged through the items and pulled out two old books. With a gentle stroke of her palm across the leather, she admired them for a moment. The books were bound in soft deer hide and closed with an old buckle. She stood and held one out for each of us.

We stood there, waiting for some kind of explanation. We looked at each other. A need to draw the book up to my chest and breathe in the scent overwhelmed me.

"They are journals from your Dad's family. He planned to give them to you when you were mature enough and were in a serious relationship. It is obvious with everything that's happened this year; you two girls are women now. You deserve these."

We hugged her together, "Thank you," we said in unison.

"These will answer some questions. They were handed down from your grandmother, and they will tell you about your ancestry. They are important."

As I flipped the pages, I read the rules for the land we now owned, some hand-drawn maps, and some rules about love. Theresa and I laughed. Mom did not—she shut us down.

"This is not any kind of joke. Your family took its heritage seriously, and these books will help you understand some of the things your dad worked hard to instill in you. He continues to teach you—he's still with you."

At that moment, I swore I could smell my father's cologne in the air, and a gentle feather's touch brushed my cheek. It gave me a chill. Theresa and Mom shivered at the same time. They must have sensed it, too. We hugged, and then Mom stood.

"Come on," she said. "It's been a long day. We all deserve to sleep in our own beds, no?"

CHAPTER 19

Before long, Sunday came, and it was time for Mass. The one-year anniversary of the murder of my father. Joaquin and Jose were at our door at nine-fifteen on the dot, like they said. Theresa introduced Mom to Jose—again. Her face glowed with delight. A brightness filled her eyes. She made everyone around her happy with this funny habit of giggling when her mood fell on the good side. She'd been in a funk for too long. I'd forgotten about my mother's true personality and why I loved her at home with me. The sparkle in her eye returned, and it elated me.

In the car, the mood changed. I rode in the backseat with Mom. She seemed to rub her hands together a lot and bite her fingernails. She'd always had manicured nails. Mom went to church on Easter, but this time the entire fog had been lifted. The doctor lowered the dosage of her medication a few days ago, allowing her to see things through unclouded eyes. She'd mentioned something about guilt, a sense of responsibility for what she'd put us girls through, and it bothered her now.

In the church parking lot, Jose opened the door for her, but she didn't seem to want to leave the car. I leaned in and whispered, "What's wrong?"

Dread flooded over her face, and her chin began to tremble. "I don't know if I can be forgiven for what I've done."

"We all understand," I said. "God must."

"I almost took my life..." She shook her head, and I hugged her tight.

I caught Theresa's eye. A good sign. Mom wanted to be alive, and the shame accompanied by it almost squandered her life—as stupid as it might sound, her shame made me hope she wouldn't try that ever again.

"Let's go in and light a candle and pray."

She brushed the tears from her face and took a deep breath.

After Mass, we waited out in the foyer, and then out under the pavilion, where Mom received even more hugs and well wishes. No one gave the slightest hint of judgment or disapproval, and each hug seemed to remove a little more weight from her stooped shoulders. Joaquin and Jose pulled the car to the curb for us. When some of the crowd dissipated, Mom looked at me and said, "I'm ready."

* * *

The wildflowers lined the sides of the road. The dew hadn't evaporated from the blades of grass; it made them sparkle in the sun as we headed out of town. I reached back and put my hand on Mom's hand, already on Theresa's. Jose's arms wrapped around Theresa. On his other arm, I could still see the scratch from the battle. I wondered what he told my sister about his injury.

Even now, I could smell Dad's cologne. I turned to stare out of the window, and I went back in time. My mind was busy with memories of all the great things from life with him—the small things, like when he pushed me on the swing at the park, the warm sun on my face, and the wind blowing my hair back. As we passed the Cove Theater, a memory rushed back. One of me tiptoeing at the counter to see the tickets, and he took my hand and Theresa's as he led us inside. I could almost smell the popcorn puffing through the air.

The car came to a stop. I turned around. Joaquin got out and opened the door for my mom. Jose opened the door for Theresa and me, and then we all moved out in front of the car. Theresa and I moved up and took Mom's hands. The boys stayed one step behind us. It sprawled out before us: our land.

There was a gravel pathway shaded by pecan trees. The road cleared, aside from a few fallen branches from the latest storm. Dad must have kept it up—before. We stepped over the downed limbs and kept at a steady pace until the way opened. The fields to the right and left were sprinkled with wildflowers, bluebonnets and firewheels. At the end of the road, there was a long ranch style house built of white native stone with a green tin roof and a porch all the way around. I stopped and stared. Mom reached into her pocket and pulled out two keys—for Theresa and me.

"Your father hoped you would live here. Together. It has two separate wings with a common kitchen and living area. We didn't get around to furniture. We planned it to be a surprise when Maria graduated," Mom said.

"Wow," I said.

"Ditto," Theresa said.

"You could be happy here?" Mom asked.

"Uh. Yeah," I said. We hugged her and jumped up and down like little kids.

Theresa pulled back and looked at Mom. "But what about you?"

"I have the house in town. I like it there. Being close to people."

We stepped out to the field and knelt together. My hand reached for a flower, and something in me stirred. My body shook with my ancestral blood as it came to the surface. I controlled my breaths—not here, not right now. As I pulled some flowers, careful to pull the root and all, my senses were on overload. The wet, cool scent of the earth wafted in the air. Theresa brought a small brown box and filled it with dirt, then closed the lid. The smell of the dirt, as she lifted it to the box, sang to me. This may have appeared to be normal dirt, but it was soaked with the spilled blood of our people—the people of the wolf—blood I shared. Their sacrifice hammered as every grain fell into the box. I stood and held my sister's arm as we returned to our mom.

Together, we moved back to the car with the boys. We made a short drive to the cemetery.

This was my first visit to Dad's grave since the funeral. We headed up to the grass, and we moved toward the middle under a young pecan tree. The wind blew my hair back, and the sun started to shine in earnest. We stepped up to the four-foot marble monument. Engraved on the stone was *Loving Husband and Father*. I dug a shallow hole and placed the flowers on Dad's grave, and Theresa mounded the dirt from our ancestral land at the foot of the headstone. Together, we patted the dirt down around the flowers.

We stepped back and leaned on Mom's shoulder. She stood there for a long moment before she smiled and kissed us both. In many ways, the past year seemed like an eternity. Over my shoulder, I caught a glance of Joaquin and Jose. Extreme loss held a vice grip on our family, but it didn't destroy us. On my own, I built a full life. This is what Dad would have wanted for us.

"I love you, Dad," I whispered. "Now wish me luck at our quarterfinals game next week."

* * *

Inside, several girls were already dressed. I slipped in front of my locker and dropped my bag. I flopped down on the bench and propped my head against my locker. The nametag I made had started to curl at the edges, and the locker room smelled a bit like ammonia. The showers were musty from the constant drip—all things I hadn't noticed before. I stood up and went to the bathroom area and splashed the cool water on my face. Brown paper towels to pat my face dry. Then, I went back to my locker and pulled on my shirt and shorts. Ashley plopped down on the bench next to me.

"Ready to go?" she asked. We jogged out to the field together.

"Yeah. Ready to ice your hand?"

She laughed. "Did you know there will be some scouts at the game?" Ashley asked.

"No way," I said.

"Yeah, and if we do well this year, they will be back next year to make some real offers. Word might even travel to bigger schools."

"That would be great!" I said. "But way to make me nervous."

"Shake it off. Just think about throwing strikes." Ashley swung her hand for me to follow her and jogged toward the fence. "I want you to meet somebody before the game." She led me over to the end of the dugout, where a fair-skinned brunette beamed at the sight of Ashley.

The girl stood about five-ten with some serious curves. But her most distinct attribute was the purple tattooed *F* on her left wrist.

"This is Michelle. Michelle, this is my best friend Maria."

Michelle stuck her hand out, and I went right past it and hugged her hard with the chain link fence clanking between us. I pulled back and smiled. She looked taken aback.

"Nice to meet you. You'd better be good to my friend here," I said.

"You know it," she said, and she smiled and grabbed Ashley's hand.

Ashley and I jogged back over to the center of the field. I looked down to conceal the smile on my face as I followed behind her onto the field. My back turned to face the home plate; we threw balls back and forth until the coaches called for us. We made our way over to the locker room. The coaches told us how proud they were of us. A great year. They asked us to try our best, and we would come out on top. This could be our last game, but they hoped not. We ran out to the field. The stands were full by now, and people parked in the outfield and along the side fences.

I scanned the bleachers, and my heart jumped; Joaquin's family and mine, all together. Theresa came with Jose, too. Becky, Lexi and Cindy watched together. Lexi didn't remember that Cindy had literally thrown her to the wolves, so they were still friends. They stood and clapped. I could smell popcorn and nacho cheese. The sun shined, and the temperature rose to a scorching level.

We were the home team, and that meant I would be pitching first. I hit the mound with newfound confidence. I stood on the mound in my zone. The balls blasted past the batters. From time to time, I would glance into the stands for a little bit of a boost. My energy level exponentially increased with my new body, and after seven innings, I still held strong. Energy would be needed with the game being super close and no runs.

By the top of the ninth, we were still tied zero to zero. No scores, not even a hit. We were in the outfield first. My arm seemed a little shaky during the inning warm-up. Ashley dropped her helmet and jogged out. A serious look on her face.

"Look at me," she said.

"Okay," I said.

"Remember all the times we've practiced. I give you a target. You give me the ball. Hit this," she said. She smacked her fist inside her mitt.

"Okay," I said.

"Put the ball into my glove," she said.

"Got it."

She jogged back and got set. She pounded her fist into her glove and shouted, "Here you go."

I looked around the field and took a long deep breath. I turned toward the field and looked at my teammates. They'd back me up, and when I turned back, I spotted all my family cheering me on.

Soon, I went back into my zone, Ashley and me. I fired in the first one, strike. I did a fist pump. I caught the ball and looked at Ashley. She wanted me to send it inside. It fell on the inside corner, but the batter missed, strike two. The third she told me to zing it. I did, and the batter struck out. On the way back to the mound, I bounced a little.

The next batter proved to be less easy. I threw two strikes and then two balls. I stretched my arm, swinging it over my head. The pitch went out and *crack*. She hit a line drive right to third base. With a hard pop, the third baseman's glove flew back. Out.

The third batter moseyed up, and I fired it in over the plate. *Thwack*. It went higher and higher, then right back down into Ashley's glove.

"Out," the umpire yelled.

The crowd started to yell and clap. We ran to the dugout, and I batted first. I took my spot in the box and milled my feet into the dirt. Pulling my bat back, I waited. A ball followed by three more. The pitcher lost her arm.

Ball four. I took my base and stood on first. I led off, but coach would not send me.

The next girl struck out. My stomach tightened, and my mouth dried like they filled it with cotton. Ashley came up, and excitement sparked inside of me. The first pitch, a ball. I looked at the coach. The second pitch—ball. I sighed, readying myself to run like mad for second. The third pitch touched the outside corner, and Ashley reached for it and caught a solid piece. She hit it, and it sailed over the infield, the outfield and then over the fence. The ump threw his arms in the air.

He yelled, "Home run!"

I jumped up and clapped. Jogging around the bases, cautious to touch each one. Ashley trotted one base behind me. After I touched home, I turned to congratulate her. We hugged and found ourselves swarmed with cheering teammates.

"Ball game!" the umpire yelled.

The crowd stood excited. They were yelling. We shook hands and then went to the dressing room. My mind spun, and the coach wanted to talk to us. She reminded us we would practice tomorrow.

Changing out of my uniform, I went out. I didn't even put my glove into my bag. Hugging it against my chest and my bag slung over my shoulder. In the stands, I spotted my family, and I headed straight for them, but Becky, Lexi and Cindy stepped out and stopped me before I could make it to them. Becky hugged me and gushed about how great I did. Cindy rolled her eyes, but she did tell me I did a good job. Lexi grabbed my hand and pulled me close for a hug.

She said, "Good game."

I told them I needed to go and pointed to my family. They smiled and waved. Lexi and Becky gave me another big hug. Cindy leaned in and gave me a side hug. The most she could muster, but I would take it—I'd won that fight, fair and square.

I went over to my family. They all hugged me and told me we played a great game.

"Looks like that won't be the last game," Alberto said.

We laughed, and they started to talk about specific plays and Ashley's game-winning home run. "I see you still love that old glove," Mom said.

I hugged my glove and smiled.

Mom said, "We'll see how far it takes you." She handed me a card, a burnt orange card with a black longhorn logo and some writing. I looked up at her with my mouth gaping open.

"UT wants you to come for a visit this summer," she said.

I jumped up and down and threw my arms around her frail neck, almost knocking her off the bleachers. Then, I hugged Joaquin and showed him the card. He said we should celebrate.

"What a day, huh?"

"Yeah, pretty amazing," I replied.

He stooped down and whispered in my ear, "Can I steal you for an hour?"

* * *

A beautiful drive, but totally hot. The grasses faded a bit from the heat, and the greens varied even more in the fields and pastures, giving it a patchwork effect with trees and shrubs lining the different colors like the stitches. Yucca plants grew along the highway and started to bloom. The wildflowers were sparse, but a welcome treat when you did see a patch.

I couldn't believe all the things that occurred over the past school year. My life started bleak and upside down. My grief pushed through many phases, but today my emotions healed. Joaquin, my sister, my mom and all these new friends helped me along my journey. I listed everything that happened this year in my mind. I transitioned into my new school, my first date happened, Joaquin was my first boyfriend, and we were in love. Annette and Alberto welcomed me into their family, Joaquin's soccer team won the state championship, my mother's sickness, I regained my relationship with my sister, I made the softball team and had a winning season. We hadn't won the championship yet, and maybe it wouldn't happen. Next year would be our year, too.

Best of all, I found that the legends in our town were more than mere myths and that the history of this place ran in my blood. My family belonged to that history. We were part of the legends, and with our sacred ancestry. My father gave his life for that secret, and he continued teaching us from beyond the grave. And through it all, my true self, the one on the inside, the person my father wanted me to be and my destiny would emerge in the future. My life gained purpose, and I fell in love.

Now, with one more day of school, I would have Joaquin all to myself for three months.

We took a ride to our special place. What better way could we end the year? As we drove, the billboard by the railroad tracks leading out of town held a picture of Teo and the word MISSING. I looked down, a little sad—not for him, of course, but for his mother and the sadness it must be causing her. The loss of my father devastated me, and I didn't wish it on anyone, ever.

As we drove a little farther, I noticed the cows in the pastures along the roadway.

"Hey, look, it's going to rain," I said.

"What?" Joaquin said.

"The cows are lying down. That means it is going to rain," I said.

"Only half of them," he said.

"Fifty percent chance," I said. I slapped my leg and gave an exaggerated laugh. "I crack myself up..."

He grabbed my leg, shook it and laughed.

"No, I'm serious. It's some kind of old wives' tale. It has something to do with the barometric pressure." We talked and laughed the rest of the way to the park.

We made it to the park and unloaded. Joaquin held out his hand to lead me to a spot under the pecan tree. You could tell we'd gotten plenty of rain this spring because some of the grass remained green and a few blue bonnets were still in bloom. We spread out the blanket and made ourselves comfortable. The cottonwood trees were shedding, and we watched as the pollen swirled into a kind of summer snowstorm.

I leaned on my side and faced Joaquin. He pulled me closer to him. Safe in his arms. He pulled my hair back out of my face and started kissing me on the forehead, then the temple, then the cheek—and our lips met. Aware of his strong hands on my hip, I liked it. No, I loved it. The minutes turned to hours.

I leaned up on my elbows, and he followed. He pulled at my left-hand and looked at the mark. With his finger, he traced the bloodstained symbol on my arm. The R formed, and after my transformation, it remained permanent. Marked.

"Your grandmother led a Tonkawa tribe?" he said.

"I guess that's right. My dad never mentioned it. I'm glad mom gave us the books to teach us more about our family." I said.

"Us?" he said.

"Theresa got one, too." I said.

We laid back down, and I opened my backpack. My hands shook as I unbuckled the book—one of the last pieces of my father, an important one. The first page held our family name, and then I opened to the double page that bore an ornate family tree. The last names entered were Theresa's and mine written in purple calligraphy pen. I rubbed my wrist, purple everywhere. I skimmed my hand over the pages gritty and yellowed with age. I caught one of the tattered edges and pulled it across to expose the next one.

A page caught my attention, a script with some sketches. One of the sketches turned out to be a wolf: a sleek, auburn wolf with beautiful lines around her eyes and at the tips of her ears. I touched my face as I looked at each feature, me. The wolf looked like me when I shifted. The journal started with the fact that we were descendants of the Tonkawa tribe. Its first rule, "Once love is found, it should be cherished, celebrated and kept close. Betrayal is not in your nature. After a choice is made, you will be solid in that decision. Do not waver from your heart's decision, and your partner will not waver from his. Trust in him. Hold your loved ones near: They are a blessing."

I closed the book. Joaquin leaned over me, took the book, and laid it on my backpack. He leaned across me to put the book away. He stayed there and began to kiss me. All the fear inside me, the part that made me hold back portions of my love, was set free. I found my partner. I slid my hand behind his head and held tight to his hair, pulling him in for a kiss.

A noise in the distance caught our attention. We looked into the trees and made out the outline of a person. When I strained my eyes to see it, a black blur slid into the trees. We looked back at each other. Joaquin stood and took both my hands in his, pulling me up to him. He picked up the blanket, folded it and put it under his arm. I put my arms around his neck and gave him one more long loving kiss.

"*Te amo*," I whispered to him.

"*Te amo.*"

He held out his hand, and I took it.

ABOUT THE AUTHOR

GINA CASTILLO was born while her father was in the military. The family moved back to Texas a few months after her birth and Texas is her home. She loves the small-town feel. Gina went into the medical field as her first career. In 2000, she changed paths and entered the teaching profession and her passion is in Language Arts. She met David, a lawyer, in 2004. They had a magical wedding in a castle in 2007. One year after their marriage their family of three grew to a family of six. Now, they work together to raise their seven boys, who inspired the stories she tells.

CPSIA information can be obtained
at www.ICGtesting.com
Printed in the USA
BVHW081744130123
656258BV00002B/225

9 781959 770558